BEAUTY RESTORED

A WINTER SOLSTICE CHRONICLE

ASHLEY BEACH

LifeRich
PUBLISHING

LifeRich Publishing is a registered trademark of
The Reader's Digest Association, Inc.

LifeRich Publishing books may be ordered through booksellers or by contacting:

LifeRich Publishing
1663 Liberty Drive
Bloomington, IN 47403
www.liferichpublishing.com
1 (888) 238-8637

ISBN: 978-1-4897-3010-7 (sc)
ISBN: 978-1-4897-3009-1 (e)

Library of Congress Control Number: 2020913987

Print information available on the last page.

LifeRich Publishing rev. date: 07/30/2020

Dedication

To my mom, Alisa, who has always been the biggest supporter of my dreams and a listening ear when I've needed it.

To Bobbie, my mentor and professor, who showed me the power of story and taught me to make each day a story worth telling.

And, to the ultimate Author and Storyteller who gave me these stories and continues to write a beautiful story with my life despite my faults and failures.

"Until the beauty in your heart is reborn,
you shall bear no rose, but only thorn."

Contents

Prologue

"Beautiful rose, glow clear and bright. Rest your head in the cold winter's light. Let the power of love be born deep within your quiet heart. Wintery sky and silvery moon, fill you with their lyrical tune. Let your heart be born again, and may you seek the power within."

"Still crooning your lovesick lullabies to these formless little orbs, Archimedes?"

The silvery blue orb Archimedes had been holding slipped from his small hands. The tall dark man who had startled Archimedes reached out his staff and scooped up the glowing orb before it reached the ground.

"Luscian. You are not allowed to be in here. As a matter of fact, I seem to recall some sort of law that prevents you from entering this realm at all unless you have business with the Mage," Archimedes growled out as he crossed his small arms across his chest.

"I do have business with the Mage. Unfortunately, He wasn't here when I came in, so I decided to have a look around the place. See if he has done anything with it since I left." Luscian sighed as his eyes roved around the room. "Still the same blaringly bright gaudiness he was so fond of all those years ago. What a disheartening disappointment."

"At least it has some character, unlike you."

"Now, now, Archimedes. No need for cheekiness. I would feel no remorse in letting this orb meet an ill-timed fate for remarks like that."

Archimedes' small frame stiffened as he watched Luscian swing his staff upwards with the globe. "Ye best be careful with that orb, Luscian. It won't be my head the Mage will want on a silver platter if anything happens to it."

Luscian scoffed, "Not the gracious Mage. Would he really want my head on a platter? That would be so unlike him."

"You know more than I the wrath of our Mage when his anger is aroused."

"Hmm. Yes. His so-called *righteous* anger. I have been the unfortunate mark of that anger a few too many times." Luscian swung the orb from his staff into his hand. As he twirled the glowing orb between his dark fingers, the light accented a dark scar that ran across his filmy eye.

Archimedes watched with trepidation as the silvery light played off the fingers of the scar that rose out of Luscian's left eyebrow like tangled roots from an uprooted tree. Beneath the blackened scars, the man's filmy eye looked unseeing at Archimedes, while the dark line of the scar continued below onto his ashy cheek.

Luscian stopped twirling the orb and drew it close to his seeing eye. "Tell me, what is so special about this particular orb that has you so worried about me destroying it?"

"Every orb is special in the Great Mage's eyes."

Luscian glared at Archimedes over the orb. "That soppy old sort. You know as well as I that the Mage cares more for some over others. Why would he let me have my fun with some of them if they were all so precious to him?"

"Only the strongest and most precious jewels undergo the greatest trials."

"Enough with your cryptic riddling, you codgering old man," Luscian hissed at him. As the hissing sound left his lips, a pink and yellow orb glowed peculiarly bright behind him. Luscian sensed the powerful glow and turned to look at the golden orb.

"Magnificent," Luscian let out in an eerie, wanting whisper.

"Luscian. Stay away from that globe." Archimedes marched towards the ominous man.

"And you stay away from me, little man. Don't think for one instant that because I am in your Great Mage's realm that I will play nice with any of these dancing little firefly balls."

"If you touch any of these orbs without permission from the King, you will answer to a higher law than either of us care to discuss, Young Dark Lord."

Luscian's seeing eye glowed hot as he stared at Archimedes. The entrancing orb's light shrunk away from the outer casing of the globe. Luscian hissed and threw out his staff towards Archimedes.

Archimedes smirked, "You know you can't hurt me as long you are standing in the Mage's realm."

A small growl escaped Luscian's lips as he glared menacingly at the little hobgoblin. "No. I cannot hurt you, but I know all too well how angry the Mage will become if he finds out what dark magic his little apprentice has been dabbling in while he is supposed to be watching out for his precious little orbs." Luscian waved his staff towards a glowing orange orb and caused it to fly from the shelf.

"Imagine how angry the Mage would be if he discovered your dirty little secret *and* your lack of responsibility regarding these orbs." Luscian let the orb drop.

Archimedes dove toward the orange orb but wasn't quick enough to catch it before it hit the ground. Miniscule cracks formed in the core of the globe.

"What a shame, such a precious stone, and to think, it cracked because it slipped through your pudgy little fingers. Let's see what the Mage's grand apprentice can do with this one." Luscian held up the silvery orb he still held in his hand. As he was about to toss the orb away from Archimedes, he noticed a large, deep fissure in the middle of the orb.

"My, my. It looks like this one is already damaged goods," a wry, eerie smile pulled at his thin lips. "I suppose someone is already a worse globe handler than I thought. Makes it much easier to finish the job." Luscian's demonic smile widened as he let go of the silvery orb.

"Luscian."

The orb stopped inches from the ground as a booming, majestic voice filled the room.

A look of irritation fluttered across Luscian's face as he turned to face the Great Mage. "Ah, your mageliness. I was beginning to wonder if you had forgotten our little appointment."

"I was preparing a gift for one of the young queens in the winter realm."

"A gift? How generous of you."

"What have you come here for, Luscian? Surely you know better than to mess with my orbs or my apprentice." The Mage looked at Archimedes cowering on the ground, a fiery orange orb glowing in his small hands.

Luscian's lip curled into a snarl as he watched the Mage bend down to help the goblin up. "Of course, your majesty. I would never dream of hurting such precious oddities. I merely came to ask if I may bestow my own gift upon the young queen."

The Mage eyed Luscian, "You may bestow on her one thing. But, her unborn child must remain untouched."

Luscian remembered the silver orb that still hovered above the ground. He smiled as he whisked the lighted orb from its impending doom and held it up. "You mean this? In truth I would have loved to grant this snow babe a gift as well, but it seems her globe already has a sizable crack in it. I have no need to deepen this poor child's hurt."

"You have overstayed your welcome, Luscian. Return to your realm before I send you there," the Mage said in a commanding voice.

"Of course, your *majesty*," Luscian hissed out. As he bowed and turned to go, he caught a glimpse of the glowing pink and yellow orb again. He smiled as he leaned toward it.

"Luscian," the Mage's voice sounded behind him. "Leave. And don't touch another orb in this room."

"Of course. Let me just return this one to its place," Luscian continued smiling. He turned to place the silvery orb on the shelf next to the glowing pink and yellow one. The silvery orb slipped from his hand. As he bent to pick it up, he breathed his dark breath into the pink and yellow orb. As he stood and replaced the silver orb, a small black spot filled the sunrise colored globe. A wiry smile spread across his lips.

"Your Majesty," he bowed toward the Great Mage and backed out of the room.

Chapter 1

The sterile sun rose high in the winter sky. Erianna's eyes slowly blinked open only to close again at the throbbing ache that began to fill her head. A thousand pins and needles poked her skin as she began to stretch her tender muscles. She could not remember a time she had been in this much pain. If she laid here a bit longer she might be able to convince herself that the pain wasn't as bad as she believed it to be. Once she convinced herself of that, she could move herself back to her bed and sleep for the rest of the day. Or, the rest of winter.

A shattering noise caused Erianna to shoot up from where she had been laying--a reaction she immediately regretted as the throbbing in her head increased ten-fold.

"I am so sorry. I did not mean to startle you."

Where had that voice come from? Erianna looked around but couldn't see anything through the darkness that threatened to settle in around her eyes. She blinked several times and forced herself to focus on the person who had spoken. After several minutes, her eyes finally cooperated enough to allow her to see the figure of a young girl crouched on the ground picking up the pieces of what had shattered.

As Erianna's eyes came more into focus, she quickly scanned the area. The bare branches of a tree hung over her head and a long line of what appeared to be bushes of some kind ran as far as she could see to her left with a tall hedge shape to her right. The young girl appeared to be the only other person with her. That was a relief. She would have to remain on her guard until she figured out exactly who the girl was and where she had ended up after last night's incident.

Erianna turned her head back to the girl and was about to ask her a question when a wave of dizziness sloshed through her head causing her to lean back. The young girl dropped the shards of broken porcelain in her hands and ran to help her.

"Easy," the girl soothed as she helped Erianna lay back on the bench. Erianna closed her eyes and took in a deep breath, forcing the dizziness to recede back into the bench beneath her head.

"I am so sorry for startling you like that." The young girl touched Erianna's forehead as she spoke, "You don't seem to have a fever which is good."

Erianna heard the swish of the girl's skirts as she stood and started to walk away. The tension of not knowing where she was or how she had gotten here made Erianna want to open her eyes and surreptitiously question the girl but the pounding in her head made it difficult to keep her eyes open and her muscles were still too tender to try and defend herself if she needed to. She hated feeling this vulnerable and defenseless. Her body tensed unexpectedly as something cold and wet touched her brow. Adrenaline coursed through her veins, causing her to rise quickly off the bench. Electricity sparked in her eyes and before she knew what she was doing, she grabbed the girl's wrist and wrenched her to the ground, her other hand poised and ready to strike.

Fear cracked the icy blue eyes that stared back at Erianna causing something to stir within her. As she stared into the depths of the girl's eyes, something like a dream played across Erianna's mind. A dream of two little girls playing in the woods together. One of them made little dolls and a house out of snow and the other one giggled as she watched and played with the enchanting objects. "Brinn," Erianna let out in a breathless whisper.

"What did you say?" the young girl asked as she stared up at the strange woman.

"What?" Erianna asked. She blinked and took in a sharp breath as she realized she still held the girl's wrist in her hand. She let go of the girl's wrist like it had suddenly become a hot iron and took a step back, landing on the bench with a thud.

The young girl rubbed her wrist and began to stand as she asked, "Are you all right?"

Erianna rubbed her head with her hand and looked back at the girl. "I'm fine."

The girl stared at her for a moment and walked over to a small table that sat near the tree. She poured water from a crystal pitcher into a glass and brought it over to Erianna.

"Here. Drink this. It might help."

Erianna reached out a shaky hand and accepted the offered drink. As she took a sip, she watched as the girl cautiously knelt beside her and dipped a cloth into the bowl of water that sat at Erianna's feet.

"I'm just going to clean some of the scratches on your face if that's alright with you," the girl said as she wrung out the excess water.

Erianna nodded and set the glass of water down on the bench beside her. She watched as the girl began to dab at a cut above her brow.

She took in a shaky breath before she spoke, "I'm sorry for how I reacted a moment ago. I'm not usually around people when I've been--" she stopped and looked at the girl before continuing-- "I'm just used to being on my own," she finished in a stilted manner, unsure of what to say.

The girl looked up at her and smiled, causing the icy blue of her eyes to sparkle, "I'm sorry for startling you not once but twice this morning. I guess I'm not used to being around people either.

And apparently I'm better at making messes than cleaning them up." She crinkled up her nose as she smiled again and indicated the broken pieces of porcelain that still sat in a shattered pile on the ground behind her.

Erianna smiled as she looked past the girl to what had woken her up this morning. Now that her eyes were more focused, she could see that the girl looked to be about 17 or 18. The paleness of her skin looked almost white against the winter snow but the silvery flecks made her skin sparkle and prevented her skin from being washed out. Her hair hung in a long braid down her back with other braids of various sizes woven into it and it was so blonde it looked almost white in the dull sunlight. Her gown was a deep azure blue that splayed out around her like an ocean as she sat on the ground and capped at her waist in an elegant silver belt. Very elegant indeed. Erianna guessed this girl was not a common townsperson in whatever village or town they happened to be in.

"There. That should be clean enough for now." The girl put the cloth in the bowl and stood to walk over to the table. "Would you like some bread or fruit? I think there's a little something I didn't ruin when I dropped your breakfast this morning," she said, an impish look crossing her face as she set the bowl on the table.

Erianna smiled, "Bread would be fine."

"Good," the girl smiled as she picked out a piece that looked less damaged and brought it over to Erianna.

Erianna took it and held it in her hands as the girl sat down next to her on the bench.

"You look like you were in quite a brawl or something last night. What happened to you?" the girl asked as she tucked a piece of hair behind Erianna's ear.

Erianna stiffened at the question and unknowingly crumpled part of the bread in her hand.

"Oh, I'm sorry. I shouldn't have asked such an impertinent question. I told you I'm not used to talking to people or being around them much.

"No. It's fine. I just--I'd rather not talk about it." Erianna subconsciously scratched at a patch of scaly white skin on her arm.

"Of course," the girl looked down at her hands as they fidgeted with a thread in her skirt.

Erianna looked at her and smiled. Laying a hand on the girls she said, "Why don't you tell me about you and this place.

The girl's hands stilled at Erianna's unexpected touch. She glanced at Erianna and a shy but winsome smile formed on her face.

"Well," the girl leaned in closer to Erianna. "This is my secret garden and you are the very first visitor I've ever had here."

Erianna glanced around at the endless bare branches and snowy ground, "I see why you would want to keep it a secret."

"Oh, but this isn't how it's supposed to look. It really is quite beautiful. At least, I imagine it would be quite beautiful if this garden were somewhere not so cold and desolate. Somewhere like the spring or summer realm maybe."

She sat up straighter and pointed to the tree beside the table, "See that tree? I imagine it has the prettiest blossoms that rain down, covering the green grass in a blanket of pink in the spring."

She turned Erianna to look at the rows of scraggly bushes beside them, "And those are the most magnificent rose bushes with blossoms of every color. Yellow and pink and red and another color I'm not quite sure how to pronounce. Or-ang. Or-on--"

"Orange?" Erianna prompted.

"Orange," the girl repeated. She sat and thought for a moment. "Hmm. I never could figure that one out but that sounds so perfect just the way you said it. Orange"

Erianna bit back a smile as the girl tried out the word a few more times. "Your mother never taught you how to say the different colors?"

A shadow covered the girl's enthusiastic face. "No. She didn't want anything to do with the other realms. She said their vibrant colors were glaringly brassy and unnecessary. She felt the beauty from the other realms detracted from the purity and impeccability of the winter realm and viewed them as a threat to her kingdom so she banished everything having to do with the other realms years ago."

"Banished." A hollowness echoed in Erianna's mind as she repeated the word. "It sounds like your mother has a lot of power if she had everything banished from the other realms."

"Oh she does. She's the queen."

Erianna's head began to spin. "Your mother is the qu-queen?"

"Yes. Everyone calls her the snow queen because they say her heart is filled with snow and ice and that's why our land is in such desolation."

Erianna's breathing was beginning to come out in short, shallow gasps. The girl subconsciously picked up a sun shaped charm that hung off a chain that sat around her neck as she continued, "I suppose they might be right. I don't know much about how the other realms are run or what their rulers or people are like. I guess that's why I like to read so much. My books take me to places I've never been and let me see things I can only imagine in my head."

A sharp, piercing pain cut through Erianna's head as she caught sight of the golden necklace with an amber stone set in the middle of the sun charm.

"Where did you get that?" Erianna asked through raspy breaths as she touched her hand to her own necklace.

The girl looked at Erianna, surprised to see her looking so unwell. "What?"

Erianna tried to push past the haziness that was clouding her eyes to focus on the amber charm. "The necklace," she pointed a shaky hand at the girl's necklace.

The girl looked down, uncertain of the necklace's importance, "My mother gave it to me when I was very young. It's the only connection I have to the other realms but, why do you ask?"

"Your mother. The queen." Erianna's body began convulsing despite her efforts to keep her tensing muscles under control.

"What's wrong?" the girl asked.

Erianna had trouble responding as her body continued to shake. "N-n-othi-ng. I'm fine"

The girl stared at her with wide eyes, "You need help." The girl stood and started to go but Erianna reached out and grabbed her arm.

The girl looked down and was surprised at the unnatural strength with which Erianna held onto her. "Please, let me find someone to help you," the girl reasoned as she tried to pull away.

"No." Erianna rasped out as she tightened her grip. "You must tell no one of this." It was getting harder for Erianna to see anything let alone hold onto this girl but she couldn't let her get away and tell anyone she had seen her. Another pain gripped Erianna's head causing her to slide off the bench and fall to her knees on the ground.

Erianna still held tightly to the girl's arm so the girl knelt down beside her to relieve the pressure from her arm. She touched Erianna's face and tried to look her in the eyes. "I promise you that nobody is going to hurt you. Just let me go and I promise everything is going to be alright."

Erianna looked into the girls crystalline blue eyes. As she looked into them, something calmed within her. She slowly released the grip she had on the girl's arm and let herself sit more fully on the ground as her body became more contained. Her breathing became more normal and she felt a strange calmness come over her as she stared into the girls endless blue eyes.

Suddenly, the sound of bells started ringing in the distance. The girl looked behind her and looked just as shocked to hear them as Erianna was. She pulled her arm away from Erianna and stood up to go.

Erianna began to grow agitated again at the sudden movement and she reached out to grab the girl's skirts. The girl stepped quickly backwards and she apologized as she continued to look back toward the sound of the bells. "I'm sorry. I really have to go. I didn't realize I had been here that long."

"Brinn no. Please, don't go." Erianna tried to stand to her feet but her muscles were too exhausted to support her.

The girl had fully turned to go but came to a dead stop when she heard her name. She slowly turned back around to face Erianna. "How do you know my name?"

Erianna looked at her with surprise, not realizing she had let the name slip. "No. I-I don't know your name. I don't know who you are." Erianna started breathing in shallow gasps as she pulled herself back onto the bench.

"No. You called me Brinn. You know my name. Why are you denying it? Who are you?" she asked as ice began to etch her words.

"It must have been a mistake. I didn't say your name."

"Yes you did. You said it earlier too, didn't you? That's what you said when you were looking at me earlier."

"No." Erianna had scooted to the other end of the bench and had pulled herself up to a standing position. "Look, I need to get away from here as soon as possible. If the queen finds out I'm here, it will not end well for anyone so please, promise me you won't say a word to her about finding me here and I will let you go."

Brinn's eyes took on a steely coldness as she studied Erianna. "Why can't the queen know you're here?"

"I can't explain. Just please, promise me." Erianna's head began to spin again and she clutched the edge of the bench to prevent herself from melting into the snow where she stood. She blinked several times trying to focus on the girl in front of her. She couldn't let this girl tell anyone she was here. She took a step towards her and teetered. She balanced herself and tried to take another step but as she did, the impending darkness clouded around her eyes and closed in around her pulling her softly to the wintry ground.

Chapter 2

Erianna's eyes flickered open as a cerulean glow filled the air around her. Brinn was sitting next to her on one of the garden chairs reading a book by the cool fire she had started when she had returned to check on Erianna. Erianna squeezed her eyes shut again trying to make the dull ache in her head go away. What time was it? She wearily lifted a hand to her head. Brinn's eyes were drawn away from the pages of her novel by the movement. She put her novel down and came to kneel down beside Erianna.

"How are you feeling?" Brinn asked as she brushed her hand against Erianna's forehead to see if it was hot.

Erianna groaned, "Fine, I think." She glanced around her. "What happened?" she asked groggily.

"You passed out before you answered any of my questions," Brinn said as she grabbed the damp cloth she had been keeping beside the bench and placed it on Erianna's forehead.

"I'm sorry." Erianna said as she closed her eyes again and placed her hand over the cloth.

Brinn stood and walked over to the table. "I brought back some more food and a fresh container of water. Although I'm not sure why. My mother keeps enough secrets from me. I don't know why total strangers feel they can keep secrets from me too."

Erianna moved the cloth enough to see Brinn's back turned to her, her shoulders slightly slumped as she put some pieces of food on a plate she had brought with her. Erianna removed the cloth and sat up slowly as Brinn walked back over to the bench.

She took the plate of cheeses and cold meat and invited Brinn to sit next to her. "Thank you for the food and for taking care of me today. You have shown me more kindness in one day than I've experienced in nearly an entire lifetime. I'm sorry I couldn't answer more of your questions. The queen and I parted on bad terms many years ago and I didn't expect to be this close to her kingdom after all this time. I know that leaves many unanswered questions but that's the best I can do for now."

Brinn chewed her lip as if trying to decide whether to believe her or how much of what she said could be accepted. She finally looked at Erianna and asked, "Can I at least know your name?"

A twinge of hope mixed with pain crossed Erianna's eyes as she looked back at Brinn. "I suppose I owe you that much," she said with a half-smile. "My name is Erianna.

Erianna sat and watched Brinn's reaction, hoping, waiting.

"Erianna." Brinn studied her for a long moment before continuing. "That is a very pretty name. It suits you." She smiled causing her blue eyes to sparkle again.

Erianna quickly looked down at the food on her plate to hide the disappointment that filled her eyes--and her heart. "Thank you," she replied quickly as she shoved a piece of cheese into her mouth.

The sound of bells tolling in the distance drifted over the high hedge wall into the garden. Erianna stood quickly and dropped her plate to the ground sending pieces of meat and cheese everywhere.

"What is it? What's wrong?" Brinn asked as she stood to steady Erianna.

"What time is it?" Erianna asked as she bent to pick up the food she'd scattered in her haste.

Brinn bent to help pick up the food as she answered, "The bells tolled curfew which is about an hour after sunset. Why?"

"I have to go." Erianna tried to stand again, but bumped heads with Brinn as she was still bent over picking up the remaining food.

"Ow," Brinn exclaimed as she rubbed her head and stood up the rest of the way. "Go where? You are in no condition to go anywhere."

Erianna rushed to put the food she had picked up on the table and turned to go but as she did, she tripped on the chair leg and sent herself hurtling face first into the snow. Brinn deposited her food and reached down to help Erianna up. As she did, she slipped in the wet snow and fell down beside Erianna.

"I have to get out of here before it's too late," Erianna let out an exasperated gasp as she untangled herself from Brinn and pulled herself up.

Brinn took Erianna's offered hand and stood up, trying to straighten her skirts that had become a tangled mess. "Where could you possibly have to go this time of night? You are still recovering from whatever mysterious thing happened last night and you won't let me help you from that."

Erianna looked at her with rising panic in her eyes. "Look, Brinn. You have been very kind and you took excellent care of me but I have to go. Please, be content in knowing that you helped more than you realize and go home to your palace." A sharp pain lanced Erianna's head causing her to grasp her head.

Brinn reached out to pull Erianna back to the bench, "See. You are in no condition to go anywhere. Rest her for the night and you can start your journey in the morning."

Erianna shook the pain from her head and looked up at the darkening sky. "How far are we from the edge of the town?"

Brinn looked at her with growing concern as a strange glow began to emanate from her eyes. "This garden is on the edge of town."

"Which side of town are we on? Are we near the forest?" Erianna asked as she began to grow more agitated. She scratched at a patch of skin on her right arm.

"Quite near," Brinn responded as she took a small step towards the table and picked up a teacup to use as a defense against the crazed girl if needed while keeping her eyes on Erianna.

"How near? How do I get there once I leave the garden?" Erianna asked, the panic growing in her voice as she scratched at a piece of scaly skin on her neck.

Brinn stared in disbelief as a puff of smoke appeared beneath Erianna's nostrils.

"Tell me," Erianna commanded in a gruff, low voice.

As if shocked into a response, Brinn suddenly answered, "Follow the path to the garden entrance and go east for about two miles. You'll see the forest past some of the fields."

"Thank you." Erianna's hand went to her head and she shook it as if trying to ignore a pain or dizziness.

Brinn looked at her, moving the cup behind her back, ready to throw it at Erianna, or something, if she had to. "Are you sure you're alright?"

The strange glow had left Erianna's eyes as she looked back at Brinn. "I'll be fine. Now, please. Go straight home and promise me you won't stop for anything on the way."

"Erianna, I--"

"Go."

Brinn let the teacup drop as she stared at the strange woman before her. Slowly, little slivers of moonlight began to fill the garden, causing Erianna to look up and cringe. A shudder shook her body. When she looked back at Brinn, her eyes were filled with the strange glow again.

"Get out of here now."

Brinn grabbed her book from the table and sprinted down the path, afraid to turn back and see Erianna further altered.

Chapter 3

Frost crawled across the ground and climbed up the trees like vines of ivy that had grown wild and untamed. Gabriel had heard stories of how cold it became in the Northlands, but he never imagined it would be this cold. He had found very little in the way of making a fire to keep warm as everything was frozen solid and covered in snow. He was grateful for the enchanted cloak Mauriden, the wizard in the Springlands, had given him as a parting gift.

"Wrap this cloak around you when the cold becomes too much for you to bear on your own. Drops of the golden spring sun have been woven into it and will surround you with its warmth when you become cold. And think warm thoughts."

Gabriel could still remember the twinkle in Mauriden's eyes as he said the last part. Mauriden was such a dear old man and had served his father as chief advisor to the land of Genesia for as long as Gabriel could remember. In fact, it seemed reasonable to believe that Mauriden had served his father's father as well. Mauriden was an amazing wizard who wore his age well. Images of his long, flowing white beard blowing in the gentle spring breeze filled his mind. Gabriel could see him as he stood with his father on the balcony overlooking the kingdom. A smile crossed his face as he remembered the stern looks him and his sister received from Mauriden when they acted out during lessons. But no look could compete with the one he had given them the day Gabriel had turned his beard purple on accident when he misfired a spell intended for a hydrangea bush. Followed by a small frog hopping out from under his robe when Julianna misfired her animal spell on a butterfly that had been flitting by. Gabriel let out a rapturous laugh as he remembered how furious Mauriden had been and how flustered he became when he tried to explain the mishap to their parents. Mauriden was right, warm thoughts did help. Gabriel was beginning to feel warmer already.

He had to be careful how much he used his cloak. The winter sun was not as close as the fiery orb that warmed their kingdom and its light wouldn't stretch far enough to recharge the golden strands and fill them with its warmth. And who knew when he would see that beautiful sun again.

Gabriel shivered and pulled the cloak tighter around him as he remembered another warning Mauriden had given him before he left. "A son of spring touched by ice can rarely be returned to his former self." Those last words from Mauriden echoed in his ears. Gabriel shook the haunting words from his mind and tried to focus on the bright-colored marigolds and hyacinth and peonies that grew in his garden at home. The sweet scent of baby's breath mixed with soft lilac. And the perfume of the roses. How he missed his beautiful roses. His mind settled on the roses he had nurtured last spring as he slowly drifted off into a warm, peaceful sleep.

Moments after Gabriel drifted off, a horrifying, piercing screech cracked the silence of the chilled night air. The sound was so sharp. It sounded like a huge whip had been cracked across the entire forest, snapping the icy trees. Gabriel woke with a terrifying start, his mind trying to sort through the fog between sleep and alertness. Had he dreamed that sound or had it really happened? Another howl pierced the air causing the icy phalanges of the trees around him to shake from the intensity and closeness of the sound. That sound had not come from his dreams, and it sounded uncomfortably close to him. Gabriel had no idea what creature had formed such an earthshaking noise but he didn't want to be the one to find out.

Gabriel gathered up his cloak and shoved it into the satchel he carried, figuring it would be easier to run without tripping over his cloak in his haste. As he began to make his way through the frostbitten forest, he began to realize just how sorely his sun touched skin stood out against the wintery landscape. "Why couldn't that cloak Mauriden gave me make me invisible as well?" he huffed as he picked up his pace. Hopefully that creature was blind or had a horrible sense of direction so he could get a head start and make it through the night.

The soul wrenching screech filled the air just as Brinn reached the back entrance to the palace. She stopped short at the woeful sound and looked toward the direction where it came from. The east, toward the forest. That was the direction Erianna had wanted to go. Another ice shattering sound cracked the placid night sky, and all around the kingdom Brinn heard what sounded like a million mirrors cracking and falling to pieces on the frozen ground. Brinn ducked into the doorway as several icicles fell from the palace walls around her. What kind of creature could be so powerful that it could shatter that many icicles with a mere screech? Whatever it was, if it found Erianna, she would not have the strength to fight it off and save herself. Brinn had to get to Erianna before the creature did.

She turned to go into the palace. If she hurried, she could hopefully sneak back in and grab her bow and arrows, a thicker cloak, and maybe slip into a pair of pants she kept hidden from her mother, before anyone noticed she was gone. She raced up the winding steps through the pantries and storage rooms and was about to make it past the kitchen to the next staircase that led to her floor from the servants quarters when the castle sprung to life in a flurry of activity. A stampede of footsteps could be heard descending the staircase that led up to her room from the kitchen. She couldn't go that way. Brinn sprinted to the other side of the kitchen and peeked out around the door to see if she could navigate the hallways without getting caught. The hallway right outside the kitchen was still bare, for now. She had to make it through to the front hallways before they were flooded with servants---and before her mother discovered her out and about. Brinn quickly made her way to the front hall with the towering staircase that led to the living suites, ducking in and out of shadows like a lynx weaving through the wintery night.

Brinn reached the top of the last staircase, breathless and ready to collapse. Just a few more steps and she would be in the clear. She took the last few steps to the tall, thick ice door that led into her large bedroom. Her hand reached for the handle to her door. As she pushed down on the cold snowflake engraved handle, a hand reached around her face and covered her mouth, causing her to jump and scream out. Before Brinn could pull away, another arm encompassed her waist and she felt herself being dragged backwards into the room she was about to enter.

"You better be glad I was the one who saw you sneaking into the palace and not your mother," a smooth, baritone voice whispered against her ear.

"Tharynn!" Brinn gasped as his muscular hand fell away from her slender face. "How dare you sneak up on me like that!" She wriggled out of his strong arms and turned to smack him for his impudence. He was too quick for her and caught her small wrist in his hand, twirling her back into him.

"If the princess were in her room where she is supposed to be, she wouldn't invite sneaking upon," he playfully reprimanded. The nearness of his breath to her ear caused shivers to run down her spine and a small shudder shook her shoulders. He smiled as she tried to diminish the effect he had on her. Tharynn had grown up in the palace and had always made a sport of torturing the princess with his charming sense of humor and sweet, playful demeanor. As she had no siblings, he had always been the first person she could call on as a companion and the knight in the adventures they had as children running around the palace grounds. Though he had a way of getting under her skin in a way no one else could, he was still the dearest friend Brinn had and she couldn't imagine ever being apart from him.

As Brinn pulled away from her captor, she caught a glimpse of the roguish smile that played upon his lips in the moonlight. "You are a horrid beast." She crossed the room to the table near her bed to light a candle.

"And you are a minx, sneaking out of the palace after nightfall," he crossed his arms and leaned against the armoire that stood by the door.

"Sneaking out? Me? Why, you are crazier than a loon, my good sir." The candle flickered to life casting a cerulean glow on her playful smile. She continued to light the other candles, the flames flickering playfully against the wall as if reflecting the lilting, mischievous tone in her voice.

His eyes followed her as she crossed to the armoire and she began to untie the ribbons of her cloak. "Aye, and I suppose you would call your mother a loon as well if she saw you walking about in your day dress and cloak at this hour of the night." His smile widened as she turned, annoyance clearly etching her beautiful face.

"Of course I would not call my mother a loon," she replied as she finished untying the knot at the base of her neck. "I would simply tell her that a horrifying noise woke me up and I dressed myself to see what it was. It would be highly improper of me to be seen in my dressing gown by the palace guards after all." She caught the gleam in his eye as she turned to finish removing her cloak and hung it in the armoire. The gleam that said he knew exactly what she had been up to and she was crazy if she thought she could hide it from him. She hated that smile. And the fact that he always had to be right.

"If you don't believe me, you are free to remove yourself from my quarters at any time." she crossed to her icy mirror. She was surprised to see that it hadn't cracked based on what she heard when she had entered the palace.

"Oh, I believe you," he said as he stood up straight, "but, that horrifying noise that woke you up is exactly why I happened upon you in the hall outside your room. I came to check on you and make sure you were all right when this hooded figure came racing up the steps and was about to dart into your room." His tall figure appeared behind her in the looking glass. "Brinn," his royal blue eyes stared at her from her reflection. "You know I want you to have your freedom and find your escape wherever it is you go. But, I wish you wouldn't go off by yourself at night." He placed a hand on her shoulder and their eyes met in a glassy stare. "Especially now that there is some unknown creature out there."

Another screeching howl resonated throughout the kingdom followed by a chilling silence. Brinn and Tharynn stood unable to move for a few moments. Tharynn crossed to the window to see if he could see anything outside that would give a clue as to what was out there. Brinn followed, thoughts of Erianna being out there on her own, or passed out somewhere in the cold, crept back into her mind.

"The soldiers will be ready to go soon," he turned to see the look of terror creeping into Brinn's face. "Brinn." She startled at his touch as his hands grasped her shoulders and turned her to face him. His sapphire blue eyes met her glassy, almost transparent blue ones. "Brinn," his hand came up to touch her face. "Promise me you will not leave this palace until I return."

Brinn's thoughts were swimming. How could she promise him something she knew she couldn't keep? His thumb traced the shape of her cheek and came to rest near her ear. No. She had to go save Erianna. She couldn't stay here, locked away like a bird in a cage.

"I--" she closed her eyes and tried to think of any way she could convince him to let her go. Her eyes opened and caught his full gaze in the moonlight as it streamed through her window. There was something in his gaze she had never seen before. Something that caused her heart to flutter. Something so powerful she couldn't possibly deny him his request. "I promise."

"Thank you." He stared at her, taking in every feature in that beautiful face one last time. The horn sounded below alerting all the soldiers to mount up and head out. Tharynn looked at Brinn one last time and turned to go.

Brinn was filled with an icy coldness as the reality of the situation slowly set in. Her gaze drifted to the window as she watched the soldiers mount their horses and ride past the palace gate.

Her heart whispered a silent prayer into the frosty air, "Please, let him come home to me."

Chapter 4

A dim light reached into the small hole of the cave opening and tickled Gabriel's nose. Though the light was weak and distant compared to the light at home, he sensed the small energy from the sun just the same. His father came from the long royal line of sun guardians that brought warmth and rebirth to the earth with their golden glow and their ability to use the sun as a guiding light. Memories of his family filled him with a warm glow.

His mother was the most beautiful of the flower fairies and had captured the heart of his father the moment he spotted her in the palace gardens one day. He had been practicing his sun magic when a wisp of chestnut hair caught his eye. The wisp of hair became a waterfall of long ringlets that fell delicately around an angelic face. The roses and ivy that wove their way through her hair offset the gentle pink glow that graced her soft cheeks. The green eyes that met his golden ones were like the deep emerald green of the grass that reflected the warmth of a perfect summer day. She had been trying to bring a few roses back to life that had an unfortunate run in with a bout of frost when his father ran into her. She looked into his father's eyes that glowed like a perfect sunrise and asked him if he could use his sun magic to help her. The use of their magic together brought the withered plant to life, creating the most beautiful rose either of them had ever seen. Bits of sunlight shone through the velvety petals and emitted a stronger magic from within. And that magic did more than bring the delicate flower back to life, it intertwined their hearts in a way two hearts had never been united before. From that moment, they knew they would forever be more powerful together than they would ever be apart. Shortly after, they were wed and ruled the kingdom with so much love and light that the kingdom prospered and became more and more beautiful with each passing year. And they raised him and his sister in the same nurturing and guiding light.

In recent years, the king and queen's ability to bring warmth and rebirth to the world began to wane as the sun began to lose its power over their realm. The kingdom blossomed under the power of a magic crystal that was supposed to absorb the power of the sun on the solstice morning and store it in the caverns below the kingdom to be used throughout the year to bring the power of spring to the realms and allow the rebirth after winter's cold to take place. Rumors reached their kingdom that the queen of the north had been absorbing the power into the crystal of the winter realm to keep the power to herself and prevent the beauty of the other realms from exceeding her own. The council of the seasons met together to discuss what could be done with the queen's greed. Many had journeyed to the north to reason with her but few had returned, and even fewer had made an impact on swaying the cold heart of the queen.

Mauriden told them of the legend of how the seasons began and how each of the first kings and queens had come together and laid down a stone specially designed for each realm at the place where the sun and moon met the earth. On the eve of what would become the solstice, the moon's rays touched the stones for winter and fall and filled them with its light. As the sun rose, the sun's light filled the stones for spring and summer. Each year on the solstice eves, the stones would be returned to this spot to signify the changing of seasons. Winter's light would give way to spring. All that was dead or hidden beneath the snow would come back to life and all would be renewed. The same would occur at the end of summer as its hot rays gave way to the chill of fall when everything would be put to sleep again for another winter to come. The harmony of the seasons brought harmony to the world until the northern queen's greed began to set things off balance and caused things in the other realms to change.

Gabriel asked Mauriden to educate him on everything he had known about the beginning of the realms and the special stones needed to reflect the sun's power and where the place where the sun met the earth was located. Who knew if the sun's ancient powers worked the same as they did at the beginning, but Gabriel had to try to find out for the sake of his kingdom.

The little bits of light began to dance upon his eyelids and Gabriel knew he had to start making his way to the wintery mountains. Mauriden had told him that the mountain in the north would be where the stones would be located, if they still existed. He started to move and felt a twinge in his back where a rock had lodged itself during his restless night of sleep. At least this cave had provided cover from the creature and what little warmth and protection from the cold that it could during the night. Gabriel crawled his way over the rocky ground, staying low to avoid the close ceiling above, and was relieved to stand up fully once he reached the outside of the cave. He pulled a small pouch from his satchel that contained some summer berries and greens. Food that wasn't completely frozen solid seemed hard to find in this realm of frigid ice and snow. After he ate a handful of berries, Gabriel put the small pouch of food away and pulled out the enchanted map Mauriden had given him. He glanced around the clearing and tried to decipher the direction he should be heading. After getting a pretty good idea of where he was at, he packed up the rest of his satchel and was about to set out when a flash of color caught his eye.

A patch of royal blue fabric waved at him in the chilly winter wind. Gabriel approached carefully, unsure of what he might be stumbling upon. As he came closer, he could see what appeared to be a body lying under the bright blue stitching of a once beautiful dress. The dress was torn and tattered but he could tell it was very elegantly made with the threads of silver forming delicate snowflakes in striking contrasts to the brilliant blue against which they fell. Dark marks of purple and tinges of red stood out in a stark, painful contrast to the pale white skin of the maiden. The prince knelt beside her motionless body to see if she was still breathing. As he brushed the mess of tangled curls from her delicate face, his heart stopped and the world around him stood frozen in time. Never before had he seen such beauty. The delicate beads of ice that laced her long eyelashes. The shimmering glimmer of her frosted cheeks. The pale blush of her frozen lips.

The prince's gaze was interrupted by the slight groan that escaped her frosted lips. She was alive. Relief spread across the prince's body as he watched the soft flutter of the maiden's eyelashes. The beads of ice on her delicate lashes reflected the sun and looked like an iridescent butterfly taking flight. The fluttering stopped long enough to reveal a pool of deep crystal irises staring up at him. The endless clarity of the eyes staring back at him held his gaze until another moan from the maiden shook him from the trance.

"Are you alright?" he asked, gently brushing another wayward curl from her face. The warm touch of his finger against her icy skin felt like the heat of a blazing fire. The strange sensation sent snakes of heat slithering down her cheek and neck and down to the tips of her left hand. Erianna's pupils narrowed in her crystal blue eyes and she swiftly rolled to her side and pushed herself up in an attempt to escape her captor. Her sudden movement caused the prince to fall backwards, which was just the effect she hoped for.

The prince, who had become a sprawled mess of legs and arms in the snow, called out to her, "Please. Calm down. I am not trying to hurt you. I want to help." He scrambled to his knees and reached out to grab her. Erianna tripped on her gown in her haste to get away and lurched forward, giving the prince an opportunity to close the small gap between them.

She quickly gathered as much of the full gown in her hands as she could so she could get to higher ground over her pursuer and defend herself. Gabriel launched himself at her before she could pull herself up and pinned her to the ground. Erianna began thrashing about in an attempt to free herself. He was so much stronger than she was and her only defense would be to outsmart him. When he grabbed her wrists, he was ill prepared for the sharp pain that pricked the skin of his arm like a small thorn and then blossomed into a full flower of pain. His grip immediately loosened and Erianna looked up, stunned by the sudden cease in struggle. The eyes of her captor glazed over with pale shock and his right hand left her wrist completely to grasp his left arm. Erianna scrambled out from underneath him and crawled breathlessly backwards until her back came into contact with a tree not too far from where they were. As she focused on the man she had just freed herself from, a sea of emerald green eyes met her crystal blue eyes. Something in his vibrant eyes caused her to be lost to the world around her for a moment. A tempest of pain clouded his eyes and broke their gaze as a drop of crimson red fell slowly and silently to the pure, snow white ground.

Chapter 5

Erianna stared in disbelief as the crimson drop made contact with the snow and splayed out in a splattering of red against the white of the ground. Her eyes followed the path of the drop to the source where her eyes were met with an agonizing sight. An arrow sat lodged in the upper arm of her assailant, piercing the very thing that had been holding her captive a few moments before. Fear and a sudden awareness of another presence with them in the wooded area filled her with an unsettled feeling. If she made any sudden movements she could very easily become the next target for the mysterious archer in their midst. Erianna tried to bring her patchy breathing to a more normal pace but the silence that filled the glen made it difficult to keep the growing tremors in her muscles at bay. Her eyes darted around the band of trees that stood around her as she tried to pick out anything that might give her an idea as to what was out there.

A moan from the injured man averted her attention back to him. As she stared at him, her eyes caught sight of a dim shadow that stood out just enough amongst some trees beyond the injured man. Erianna had to draw the shadow out or do something to distract it long enough for her to take cover. She drew in a deep breath and settled the growing anxiety within by keeping her eyes focused on the figure ahead of her. As she began to calm, she gracefully arched the palms of her hands slightly over the ground where they rested and allowed a small patch of ice to form beneath them. The small patch of ice began to make its way to the cluster of trees protecting the shadow. As it reached the area where the shadow stood, a twirl of her finger caused a small swirl of snow and ice to form around the figure's feet and begin to slowly wind its way around the shadow's legs. As her swirl of snow ascended the shadow, a growing air of confidence began to settle on her. Her entrancing swirl made its way to the shadow's head and she was about to snap her slender vortex into its full force, blasting its victim with a blinding snow burst, when a small gasp escaped from beneath her winding spell.

Erianna's hand froze in place, stopping her snowy powers in midair. The gasp carried an air of innocence and made Erianna rescind her icy attack. No longer feeling in danger, she slowly brought herself up to a standing position and began to make her way to the darkened figure. As she approached the figure, a long blue gray cloak trimmed in white fur came into focus. The figure's face was covered by a large hood and not much else could be seen aside from the outline of a bow in one hand and the silhouette of feathers from the arrows on the figure's back. Erianna stepped up to the figure and reached up to remove the hood. She paused and drew her hand back as a small sob escaped from beneath the hood. Another sob compelled her to reach out for the hood again and see who was hidden underneath.

As she gently pushed the hood away from the shadow's face, she was surprised to see the same face of the young girl who had rescued her the day before.

"Brinn?" she asked as she looked at the girl's shimmering cheeks. The girl's long blonde hair had been pulled into a simple braid that rested over her thin shoulder. Her slate blue tunic covered the long gray sleeves that extended from the large cloak. The silver gray pants she wore gave her a much different appearance than when Erianna had met her a day ago.

The girl looked up at Erianna and Erianna's breath caught again at the sight of those endless blue eyes staring back at her.

"Erianna?" she asked as recognition filled her teary eyes.

"Yes. It's me." She smiled as her pale hands came to rest on the silvery cheeks of the young girl. "What are you doing out here in the middle of woods by yourself?"

"I--I came to find you and make sure you were all right."

Erianna's face clouded, "Brinn, Did you follow me last night?"

"No. I went home shortly after I left you. But, when I got home, I heard a horrible screeching noise from the direction you were headed. I was worried that whatever terrifying creature was out there would find you or kill you or--" Brinn's voice trailed off as her eyes drifted to the growing stain of red that painted the wintery ground behind Erianna.

Erianna glanced back and remembered the man with the arrow in his arm lying on the ground.

Brinn's eyes filled with pain as she realized what she had done. "I shot him. I shot him and he is bleeding because of me."

Erianna looked back at Brinn. As she saw the terror that laced the young girl's eyes, an impulsive urge to protect the young girl filled her. Erianna's hands came to rest on the girl's shoulders as she spoke. "Brinn, look at me. You did what you thought was the right thing to do."

"No," she pulled away, "He is hurt because of me. I did this to him."

"Brinn." Erianna reached out for Brinn's trembling shoulders. "Look at me."

Brinn's crackled eyes met Erianna's strong, cool ones. "You were extraordinarily brave in thinking and acting so quickly the way you did. You may have saved my life because of it."

A shuddery breath filled Brinn's lungs as her crying slowed. Erianna brushed away a tear as it made its way down Brinn's shimmery cheek. "His injury may not even be that bad. We can check on him together and make sure he is alright."

Brinn looked past Erianna at the man lying in the snow.

"You were an excellent nurse to me yesterday and I am sure he would heal quickly under your gentle touch."

Brinn looked back to Erianna and sniffed in as she replied, "Do you really think I could help him?"

Erianna smiled as she replied, "I do."

Brinn smiled and allowed Erianna to lead her over to Gabriel's body.

The two girls knelt on either side of the injured man, ready to inspect the damage left by Brinn's arrow. He had fallen face first into the snow and his breathing had slowed considerably since he had been hit.

Brinn's eyes went immediately to the place where her arrow had lodged. Her already pale skin lightened another shade giving her a ghostly pallor as her eyes widened with terror at the sight before her.

Concerned she may soon have a second patient on her hands, Erianna asked, "Do you need a moment before we proceed?"

Brinn's eyes opened and closed quickly as she shook the shock from her eyes. Taking a deep breath, she replied, "No. I will be fine." With a stronger reserve, she continued, "We need to break the shaft before we move him to prevent the arrow from lodging itself further into his arm."

Erianna nodded, relieved to see Brinn's features returning to a more normal hue.

Brinn grasped the arrow in her left hand as close to the point of insertion as she could while her right hand made contact a couple inches further up the shaft of the arrow. Holding her left hand firmly in place, she took a deep breath and brought her right hand down forcefully, snapping the arrow in two pieces.

An anguishing groan came from where the man's face lay in the snow. Brinn froze, her features blanching again. Erianna looked to Brinn. She could tell half the battle of caring for this man lied in keeping Brinn from falling apart every time he groaned.

Erianna gave Brinn an encouraging smile as she said, "Excellent work. Can you help me turn him over so I can take a better look at his injury?"

"Yes, of course." Brinn replied as she took in a shaky breath.

"Since the arrow is in the side facing you, it would probably prove best to keep that side up, don't you think?"

Brinn looked at Erianna, seeing a small glimmer of laughter in her eyes. Brinn appreciated Erianna's attempts to lighten the situation and allowed herself to relax a bit. "Yes, I suppose that would be best," she replied, a small, tense smile curling the edge of her lips.

Erianna joined her on the injured side of the body and together they heaved the body over to where he was facing up. While rolling him over, Erianna made sure to hold his arm close to his body to keep it from flailing about or causing further injury in the move.

Erianna knew the remaining stub of the arrow still needed to be removed and she was unsure of how the man would react. Or how Brinn would react for that matter.

"Brinn, why don't you gather some wood and see about getting a fire going?"

Brinn brushed the last traces of wet snow from the man's face and stood to go. She undid the white leather strap that held the cloak in place under her chin and laid it beside Erianna. "In case he gets cold." She laid a cold hand on Erianna's shoulder and turned to go into the woods to gather supplies.

"Thank you," Erianna said as her hand squeezed Brinn's, "for everything."

Brinn gave Erianna's shoulder a tight squeeze and headed into the wintery wilderness. Erianna watched her go, praying nothing would harm her while she was on her own.

"She seems like a very brave, kind girl."

Startled by the masculine voice, Erianna returned her attention to the man lying before her. "Yes, she is."

The man's emerald eyes caught Erianna off guard as he stared up at her. A strange feeling of warmth washed over her as he held her gaze.

"It seems our roles have been reversed from a few moments ago," he said with a glib smile before a fountain of pain seized his arm.

Erianna blinked away the strange feeling he invoked in her as his stare was broken by the pain. "You are fortunate she hit your arm rather than anything serious. If she hadn't, I might have done far worse." Erianna moved to the other side of his body to look at his injury.

Gabriel scoffed, "Far worse? I can't imagine what you would consider to be far worse than being shot in the arm with an arrow."

Erianna looked at him and replied with a hard coolness in her voice, "You are alive. If you can't imagine far worse, the people of your realm must be quite simple and addle brained."

He studied her for a moment before he replied, "Do you treat all visitors to the North with such generous hospitality?"

"There are few visitors to the North. Those who are ignorant enough to come quickly discover how cold and uninviting our realm truly is. You would be wise to leave as soon as you are able to travel."

"Forgive me for attempting to help you. If you will help me up, I will no longer be a burden to you or your realm." Gabriel tried to sit up but his injured arm buckled beneath him, causing him to cry out in agonizing pain.

A small twinge of concern passed through Erianna as she watched the man's face contort with pain. "Careful. There is still a small piece of the arrow in your arm."

"That explains why there is still a poignant bud of pain in my arm," Gabriel replied with a sardonic edge to his voice.

Her eyes narrowed at him, "Perhaps you should have thought of that before you attacked me."

"Attacked you? I was trying to help you," he replied through clenched teeth as the pain continued to blossom throughout his entire arm.

"I didn't realize pinning a maiden to the ground was considered helpful in your realm." Erianna grunted as she pulled the man back to a tree behind them and helped him sit up against it.

"I hope I was more helpful than you are being right now," Gabriel grunted as his head knocked back against the tree.

"And how is pinning me to the ground more helpful than trying to get you to a better position so I can remove the rest of the arrow?" she asked as she brushed a loose strand of hair from her face. She huffed as she knelt beside him and tried to catch her breath.

Gabriel's breathing was also labored as he replied, "I thought you were injured. I didn't realize I was playing into your sorry trap."

Erianna looked at him as her breathing returned to normal. She sighed. "I'm sorry. I should have realized what you were doing."

Gabriel's gaze softened as he watched her. "I'm sure it must be very startling to see a strange man leaning over you in the middle of the woods. I'm sorry if I caused you any unnecessary fear or harm."

His warming eyes bored into her. She felt very safe in his presence all of sudden and another twinge of compassion pricked her heart. Perhaps if she hadn't been so hasty to defend herself, he wouldn't have been prompted to stop her and make sure she was well. And Brinn wouldn't have shot him.

"I'm afraid my actions caused you more harm than anything you did, or didn't do, to me." Erianna looked down at her hands as they messed with the embroidery on her dress.

"We all reacted within our views of the situation. But, if you are willing to remove the remaining cause of my present pain, I might forgive you."

31

Erianna's eyes darted to his as a playful smile danced across his lips. The cool anger that had flashed through her at his remark quickly dissipated under his warm smile. "I suppose removing the rest of the arrow is the least I can do." She returned his smile with a playful grin of her own.

Chapter 6

Tharynn and his men rode through the palace gates and headed to the stables after a long night of searching. The creature left no trace of being within the kingdom limits and it had become too dark to search the deeper parts of the woods. He wasn't sure whether no signs of the creature was cause for relief or more cause to worry but he wanted to check on Brinn once more before setting out again.

Some of the squires who had been left behind the night before to watch over the young pages, stood waiting to assist the soldiers with their horses upon their return. Tharynn looked up to see Terrence, the young boy who had served as his page and now as an eager and dedicated squire. He was growing up so quickly, Tharynn could hardly believe the young man he was becoming.

"Ah, Terrence. Always a welcome face to greet me upon my return."

Terrence smiled up at Tharynn as he helped him down off his horse, "My face may be welcoming but I am afraid the news I have for you may not be."

Tharynn looked at the young boy, "News?" he asked, uncertain of what his squire had in store.

"Yes, sire. The queen has requested that you join her in the throne room as soon as you return."

Tharynn grimaced, "The queen. Just the person I want to see after a long night of searching her dark, frigid kingdom for something we know nothing about."

"Careful sire, the queen might sense your disdain from here and send a permanent chill into your armor before you ride out again." Terence's eyes sparkled as he began to remove the saddle from the large cream colored charger.

"Quite the vibrant tongue for such a desolate hour of morning." Tharynn responded.

"Only as sharp as the smith who crafted it, my liege," Terrence replied as he gave an elaborate bow towards his tutor.

As annoyed as he wanted to be at the boy's manners this early in the morning, Tharynn couldn't help but laugh at the fruits of his tutelage. "I suppose manners and decorum are to be addressed in our next lesson, young squire. But first," Tharynn grabbed the young boy and wrapped his arm around his neck, rubbing his knuckles through the boy's straw blonde locks.

Terrence quickly positioned his right foot in front of the inner leg of the captain and behind the outer leg. He then thrust his hip back into Tharynn's stomach and slipped his head through the arm around his neck as the captain was launched over him and into the horses watering trough.

Tharynn pulled himself up from below the water's surface and stared at Terrence, a look of shock mixed with pride filling his face. "The teacher has just been taken to school. Well done young squire. If your swordsmanship has improved as much, you may not need my tutelage much longer."

Terrence beamed as he reached out to help Tharynn out of the trough. Before he knew what was happening, Terrence found himself sitting in the trough next to Tharynn. They both started to laugh.

"Sir Tharynn," the daughter of the queen's lady in waiting came running across the courtyard.

"We are in for it now," Terrence whispered as they began extracting themselves from the trough.

"Yes. Perhaps I should pray for a frost to hit me before I reach the queen in this state." Tharynn replied, heaving Terrence from the water.

"It would be more agreeable I am sure."

"Sir Tharynn. The queen would like to see you right away." The girl stopped before them, breathless from running across the courtyard.

"I am on my way, milady." Tharynn gave a slight bow to the young girl, causing her to blush and giggle amidst catching her breath.

"Terrence, you and the other squires brush down the horses and make sure they are well fed. Have them ready to ride again in a few hours."

"Yes, sire," Terrence nodded as he began to squeeze the excess water out of his tunic.

"And Terrence."

"Yes, sire?"

"Ready five additional horses."

"Five, sire? You need that many for supplies?"

"No. We will need a few more riders to join us."

"Riders? Who will be joining you?" Terrence asked, his eyes scrunched in confusion.

"A few young, well trained, men riding out into the great unknown, protecting the kingdom. Unless you would rather stay here and watch after the younger lads." Tharynn smiled as he turned toward the palace, allowing the reality of his words to sink in.

Terrence let out a breath and a smile spread across his face, "Yes sire, I mean no sire, I mean, I will have the horses ready and will inform the other squires to ready themselves, sire."

Tharynn turned back and looked at Terrence, "Thank you Terrence. I knew I could depend on you." He smiled and continued on his way to the palace entrance. A slight squish in his boots reminded him of his soggy state. Unfortunately, he didn't have time to stop and change into a better ensemble to please the queen. Her patience was already thin enough. He would have to risk looking like a drowned dog rather than make the queen wait any longer.

He raced up the grand staircase that led up to the front entrance of the palace as it was closer to the throne room than the labyrinth of stairs that wound through the servants quarters in the rear of the palace. The grand hall reflected frigid hues of blue as the dull winter sun shone through the immaculate windows and reflected off the massive ice chandeliers that hung in the middle of the expanse. Columns of ice spanned the halls of the palace topped with sculptures of dragons and griffins and other mystical snow creatures that emitted a terrifying presence to ward away any visitors who dared to cross their paths. Large rooms designed to house balls and grand celebrations sat vacant and cold, some no longer able to open their doors due to the bonds of ice that had grown over their bolts and hinges after years of no use. The one room of the palace that was used most often remained coldest of them all due to the constant presence of the queen.

Tharynn stopped at the entrance to the throne room, his large frame engulfed by the voluminous doors that stood before him. He had defeated many evils in his short life and brought many of the kingdom's enemies to their knees, but he had yet to figure out how to vanquish the icy fear that stalled his heart every time he entered the presence of his queen. He reached out his strong hand to touch the handle but pulled back when the cold emanating from the room reached out to greet him. He closed his eyes willing away the wisps of fear that pulled at his mind and exhaled, releasing a small white cloud of air. His hand made contact with the icy handle and he pushed open the door before allowing himself the chance to retreat. Tharynn stepped cautiously into the cavernous cathedral of a room with its floor to ceiling windows that ran the entire expanse of the room. He hated how small this room made him feel.

"Sir Tharynn. How kind of you to *finally* make an appearance to your queen."

A tall, luminescent throne stood at the other end of the long hall, silhouetting a tall, slender figure of white. The queen was indeed one of the most beautiful creatures ever beheld by the eyes of men. Her hair was plaited in intricate weaves that were wound in tight spirals around her head. Drapes of jeweled snowflakes hung throughout her frosty white weaves and came to a point beneath a delicately crafted crystal crown. Shimmering flecks sparkled on her stark white skin like the shimmer of a freshly fallen snow blanketing a barren field in winter. A one shoulder gown with long, airy sleeves wrapped around her strong, graceful frame accented by a silvery embroidered bodice. Her completely white, statuesque features were contrasted only by the electrifying blue of her eyes. Jagged irises that held the power to reflect the greatest fears of those who looked into them.

She spoke again, etching each word into the air with an icy chisel for a tongue, "Haven't you anything to say to your queen?"

"Your Majesty. My humblest apologies for my delay in coming to see you upon our return. I had to see to the preparations for our continued search." Tharynn gave a deep bow, avoiding the eyes of the queen.

"Continued search. You mean to tell me you returned before you found the beast that disturbed my kingdom last night." Queen Anwyne's words were smooth and cold and ran down Tharynn's back like beads of ice, sending a chill down his spine.

"Your Majesty," he continued, eyes still cast down to avoid being caught in her glassy stare, "We found no traces of a beast in the kingdom and found nothing of concern in the wooded area in the immediate vicinity. It became too dark to venture further into the woods in the wee hours and we hadn't enough supplies to make a longer journey of it last night."

"Has the wood run out of game for you to hunt?" she asked, never taking her eyes from him.

"Not to my knowledge, Your Majesty," Tharynn replied, trying his hardest to keep his nerves at bay.

"And did you not bring weapons with which to hunt the game as well as the beast?" the queen asked with a monotonous coolness.

"We were armed and prepared to face the beast as well as anything else we may have come upon, Your Majesty. As the kingdom was not in immediate danger I felt it best to return and gather supplies. Our hasty departure last night left us little time to prepare for a longer journey," he replied.

"Underprepared. Ill equipped. Unable to locate a threat upon the kingdom. My, my, Captain. This is painting a distasteful portrait of the man I appointed as the leader of my army." She rose and crossed to one of the large windows that overlooked the valley where her kingdom sat, her iridescent cape trailing behind her.

"Your Majesty. This army is one of the greatest armies in the lands and has always provided great defense and protection to the kingdom and its inhabitants. I would not be so quick to discredit them."

"Discredit them? I believe you are doing a fine job of that on your own, Captain," she hissed. "Leading them out on a fruitless search only to return after a few hours because you didn't feel you had enough supplies."

"Your Majesty. I swear we will find the beast or creature or whatever it was and will do everything in our power to ensure the safety of the kingdom before our return."

"And what assurance do I have that you will complete your task without returning once more like a forlorn pup coming home with its tail between its legs?" She turned to face him, icy sparks electrifying her eyes.

"I swear upon my life, Your Majesty." Tharynn shouted, anger starting to stir in his cold blood.

Anwyne scoffed, "Your life. What is your life to me, Captain? Surely the life of one man cannot mean that much to a powerful queen who can have anything in the world if she wanted." She walked slowly towards him, daring him to answer her with something she felt worthy.

Uneasiness settled on Tharynn as she began to walk around him. A shutter filled his voice when he felt the icy touch of her fingers upon his shoulders as he replied, "You have my word that I will not return until we have searched every inch of the realm for the creature and make sure it can never harm anyone or anything."

As the queen circled the captive soldier, a vein of ice began to weave its way around his ankles and make its way up his legs. "My brave Sir Tharynn," her whispers landed like ice picks in his ears, "I am afraid that is not enough for me to be convinced of the safety of my kingdom."

The trail of ice worked its way further up his body. Tharynn could feel his muscles tightening in defense against the cold intrusion of the queen's magic. He swallowed and braced himself against her wiles, unsure of where her powers would end.

Her hand reached over his shoulder and he cringed as he felt her long spindly fingers reach towards his heart as she continued, "You see, Sir Tharynn. Nothing can quite fill the void a parent feels when their child goes missing. So even if I were to take your life as well as the lives of the rest of your army, it would never replace the fact that my daughter went missing the very eve a monster absconded upon my kingdom. Not to mention my dimwitted army didn't have the brains or nerve enough to go after it and destroy it and bring my precious snowflake back to me."

Anwyne had come to stand face to face with Tharynn, her eyes meeting his as her hand began to close over his heart. Despite the debilitating pain in his chest, his thoughts focused on only one thing.

"Brinn is missing?" he asked through clenched teeth as she closed her hand further.

She stopped as a glimmer of the boy's deeper feelings for her daughter came to the surface for a brief moment. A sickeningly serene smile crossed her icy features as she loosened her grip. She looked into his eyes and said, "You care a great deal for my daughter."

Unwavering, Tharynn replied, "I would die for her."

"That won't be necessary," she smiled as she released him. "At least, not yet." Anwyne crossed to a table near her throne where she kept a mix of potions and spells and different things to aid her in her magic.

Tharynn fell to the ground, gripping his heart as he replied. "Your Majesty. I will go with my men to find your daughter and the creature and promise I will not return until she is safe."

"I know you will." The queen smiled, pulling out the silver box she had been searching for. She turned back to the gasping soldier and knelt before him, blowing a handful of mirror dust into his eyes. Tharynn yelled in pain as the miniscule shards embedded themselves into his eyes. After a few moments the queen pulled his hands from his eyes to check her handiwork. The dust had indeed landed its mark, giving his eyes the glassy pallor she desired.

His eyes blinked, adjusting to the new sight he now possessed. Anwyne asked, "What are you going to do, Sir Tharynn?"

His eyes opened wide and he answered, "Kill the beast."

Chapter 7

"Ah," Gabriel pulled his injured arm into himself as Erianna gripped the remaining end of the arrow.

Erianna tightened her grasp, "You realize you only make this more difficult by pulling away."

"My apologies. The next time you have half an arrow hanging out of your arm, I will remember to observe how well you handle the pain," Gabriel replied through clenched teeth while trying to diminish the pain as much as he could.

"Indulging my pain is a luxury I rarely can afford. But if you wish to carry on with your pity campaign, then I will leave you to remove the arrow yourself and be on my way." Erianna stood to go.

Gabriel reached for her arm, "No. Please." He gasped through the wave of pain that swept over him. "I'm sorry."

Erianna's icy pride prompted her to leave the pathetic being to his own vices. But, as she turned to go, a small prick of guilt at being the cause of his pain stopped her. She turned back to the injured man and knelt beside him preparing once more to extract the remains of the foreign object.

"What is your favorite childhood memory?" she asked.

"What?" he replied.

"Tell me about your favorite childhood memory." Erianna placed her left hand under the arrow on his arm to provide the leverage she needed to pull it out.

"How is that going to aid in extracting an arrow from my arm?" he asked as confusion mixed with pain in his emerald green eyes.

Erianna tightened her grip on the arrow sending a shooting pain up his arm. "I would just like to know more about you."

"And me telling you a favorite childhood memory will tell you what you nee--" Gabriel let out an anguished scream as Erianna pulled the arrow from his arm.

"Not what I need. Asking for a childhood memory was more for your sake than mine." Erianna ripped a strip of cloth from her tattered dress to use as a bandage.

"Distraction from the pain. How thoughtful of you." Gabriel held his arm. Though the prominent, piercing pain was no longer there, his arm was now filled with a deeper aching pain in its place.

"Distracting the patient usually gives the healer the freedom to work without much of a struggle. It also helps relax the muscles enough to pull out what is in there without causing further harm or damage." Erianna put a handful of snow on his shoulder. If she figured right, the warmth of his skin would melt the snow so she could clean his wound.

The sudden cold on his shoulder caused Gabriel to jerk back as water dripped into his open wound. "Are you mad?"

"If trying to help you is madness then yes, I am. If you haven't noticed, water isn't exactly gushing from the forest floor. I am trying to clean your wound. Unless you would prefer to bleed out on the forest floor or die from infection or both."

"I will die either way if any of the ice of your realm reaches my heart and now that I have a gaping hole in my arm, you don't need to help it along by packing my arm in snow and allowing it to freeze in my veins." He rubbed his aching arm wishing he had some of Mauriden's sweet elixir he received as a child when he had injured himself to take the edge off the pain.

Erianna's jaw tightened as she replied, "Believe me, if I wanted to stop your heart by freezing it, I wouldn't have to pack your arm in snow and allow the water to slowly drip into your veins. Now, if you will allow me to continue, I promise, I will only melt enough snow to clean the wound and bandage it up to prevent ice or snow from entering your *gaping* hole."

Gabriel sat silent for a moment, contemplating what kind of bewildering female he had gotten himself tangled up with. He knew he wouldn't make it far in this land with an injury and she seemed quite capable of taking or saving his life without a second thought.

"It seems I am at your mercy either way," he replied.

"How unfortunate for you," she replied. An unusual softness entered her voice that hadn't been there before as she stared back at him. Breaking his gaze, she tore some more cloth from her gown to use as bandages.

Gabriel winced as she began to wipe away the blood from his arm. She paused, afraid to cause the man further injury. "Please. Continue. This is nothing compared to the pain you caused moments ago."

Erianna shot him an icy glare and was about to lash back at him but retracted her words when she saw the small smile that curled the edge of his lips. He shouldn't antagonize her but couldn't help himself. There was something enchanting about the way her pale cheeks hinted ever so slightly at a pale pink hue to display her anger.

"Why a memory from childhood?" he asked, studying her as she tended to him.

"What?" she paused and looked up at him.

"You told me to think of my favorite childhood memory. I figured there must be some importance in asking for a memory of that specific nature."

Erianna finished off the bandage by tying a knot around the front to keep it in place as she replied, "I suppose a more recent memory might be too easy to retrieve. It would be thought of and gone before anything could be done for the injury."

"A childhood memory on the other hand is from a distant past," she said as she crossed to where Brinn had left her cloak for Gabriel. She picked it up and ran her fingers over the soft embroidered edge. "It forces you to focus harder and farther away from the present pain. It reminds you of a time when all was right with the world."

"Do you have many fond memories from childhood?" Gabriel asked.

"Not many, but the few I have are very dear and precious to me," she replied as she followed the pattern of snowflakes along the white fur edge of the cape. She shook her head and turned to walk back to where Gabriel sat, "And you. Do you have fond memories of your childhood?" Erianna helped him lean forward enough to drape the cloak around him, making sure his injured arm was completely covered.

Gabriel grunted from the pain as he settled back against the tree, "Aye, I do. My sister and I had many adventures growing up. Running through the gardens, splashing in the streams, playing hide and seek in the fields until dark." A sweet, broad smile spread across his face as his thoughts drifted to home and his sister and the fun times they had together.

"One of my favorite memories was going up on top of our favorite hill with our parents just as the sun was about to set. The sun would drop below the horizon and as dusk settled in we would wait for the first light of the night to appear."

"You would watch the stars come out as a family?" Erianna asked, intrigued by the closeness of his family.

"No. Not the stars. The fireflies," he said with a whimsical smile.

Erianna raised a quizzical brow, "Fireflies?"

"Yes, fireflies. You know, little bugs that fly around and light up at night." She looked at him with a questioning stare trying to imagine little flying fireballs.

He sighed, "You have not lived until you have seen an endless void filled with the twinkling lights of the little creatures."

"It sounds intriguing to say the least." Erianna smiled.

"I didn't realize you people of the North were capable of such magic."

"What magic?" she asked.

"Smiling," he replied.

"Believe it or not, we do smile on occasion. Our faces are not frozen in a downward frown," she replied with a small laugh.

"Well, you should do it more often. It really is beautiful." He smiled as a pale pink graced her silvery cheeks.

Erianna cleared her throat and stood up, "I should check on Brinn. See how she's coming with the firewood."

"You won't have to go far. I have returned without scathe or scar." Brinn smiled. "I am sorry it took so long." She stood at the edge of the clearing with a pile of wood wrapped in her scarf.

"Brinn. Thank you. Why don't you see about getting the fire going and I will see what I can find for food." Erianna crossed to Brinn and grabbed a few pieces of the wood to lighten the load a bit.

"Thank you Erianna," she said as they laid the wood down. She whispered to Erianna, "How is he?"

Despite her cheerier demeanor, Erianna could tell Brinn was still a bit shaken by the morning's events. She responded confidently, hoping to ease Brinn's fear, "He is better. I have cleaned and bandaged the wound and with some rest and nourishment he will likely recover."

A look of relief spread across Brinn's face, "Thank goodness. How shall I tend to him while you are gone?"

"Check his bandaging to make sure the blood isn't soaking through. Try to keep him as comfortable as possible. You were an excellent nurse for me yesterday, I have confidence you will do the same for him." Erianna smiled and continued, "I will be back shortly."

As Erianna turned to go, Gabriel called out to her, "Erianna."

Surprised to hear her name, she turned back to him. "Thank you."

"You're welcome, ---" she struggled trying to remember if he had mentioned his name or not.

"Gabriel." He smiled.

"Gabriel. It was the least I could do." Erianna curtseyed and turned to go.

Gabriel nodded and watched the vision of blue and white disappear into the trees. A smile spread across his warm cheeks as he rubbed his injured arm. What an enchanting journey this would be indeed.

Chapter 8

B rinn sat beside the prince, continuing to wipe the drops of perspiration from his brow. Gabriel had drifted into a feverish sleep a few hours ago but his skin continued to grow hotter as he slept. A jerk in his arm startled Brinn. His head moved side to side and stifled moans escaped his burning lips as he began to thrash about in the snow. He was clutched in what seemed to be a nightmare of sorts, induced by the fever. Brinn tried to calm him as best she could but her touch seemed to only increase his thrashing. Panic began to set in as it became more difficult to subdue him.

"What is going on?" Erianna asked as she entered the clearing.

"Erianna. Help. Please. I don't know what to do. He started moving and I can't calm him down." Brinn's speech was broken up by short, rapid breaths as panic filled the young girl's voice.

Erianna rushed to kneel beside him. Brinn's eyes began to fill with tears as she continued, "I did this to him. This is all my fault."

Erianna reached out to touch the prince's forehead but pulled back at the amount of heat radiating off his sun scorched skin. It felt as if the fiery orb itself was within him. She was afraid of this. The combination of the open wound and his exposure to their cold climate was sure to bring on an infection of some kind. She had hoped it would have stayed off a bit longer, at least until morning.

"Brinn, look at me." Erianna grasped the shoulders of the girl that were now beginning to shake from her tears. "I need you to look for a wintergreen root. Do you know what the wintergreen plant looks like?"

Brinn nodded, calming a bit as Erianna brushed a strand of hair from her face. "Good. Now, go quickly. The root should help to calm him. And perhaps it will help all of us to sleep through the night." Erianna smiled as she wiped a few tears from Brinn's face.

Brinn smiled back and gave Erianna a hug before she ran into the forest to begin her search for the soothing plant.

Erianna turned her attention back to the writhing man before her. The rate his fever was increasing she was worried if he would even make it through the night. She needed help but she couldn't risk moving him in the state he was in. Her only hope was to pray for the kindness of the Great Mage himself to be with him and to keep him until morning when she could get him to a better physician. First things first, she had to do whatever she could to calm him down and bring him back to a more restful sleep.

She took a deep breath and closed her eyes as she pressed two fingertips to his burning forehead. His fiery skin seared her icy fingers but she forced herself to focus on the ancient language that had become her lasting companion over the years. She was accustomed to using this gesture to calm her food, inducing a cooling coma before ending its life but this time she had to induce just enough to return him to a peaceful state and not hasten his death. Just as she was about to utter the familiar words, his entire being instantly calmed.

Erianna's eyes flashed open at the sudden stillness beneath her touch. Her hand dropped to the side of his neck hoping to find even the slightest pulse of blood still pumping through his veins. A small thump thump against her finger reassured her that he was not completely lost but the drastic change in his demeanor still worried her. As she looked at his placid face, Erianna felt a small twinge of remorse run through her at the thought of losing him. Why did she suddenly feel bad about the possibility of him dying? He was a stranger to her. He was no different from anyone else in the world. So why should she care so much if he lived?

Erianna held her breath as her eyes searched his face, almost as if she were willing him to breathe by withholding her own. She watched for what seemed like an eternity until at last she saw a small rise in his chest followed by a small cloud of breath. He was alive. A trembling hand reached up to his face and brushed a damp curl from his forehead as relief spread over Erianna. Thank goodness he was alive. She wasn't sure how she had calmed him so quickly without the aid of her magic, but she was glad he had not left her completely.

The crunch of snow behind her diverted Erianna's attention from the prince. Brinn stopped short as she saw how still the prince lay in the snow.

Eyes wide with fear, Brinn asked, "Is he--?"

Realizing how awful the scene must appear Erianna responded, "No. No. He is resting."

Brinn's features relaxed as she walked closer to them, "Thank goodness." She knelt beside Erianna and pulled some green leaves from her side pouch. "I found some nearby, though he doesn't appear to be in need of it anymore."

Erianna looked at the sprigs of wintergreen Brinn handed her, "Thank you, Brinn. He may not need it now but we still have a long night ahead of us." A wave of dizziness swept over Erianna as she went to stand up.

"Are you alright?" Brinn asked, concern lacing her voice and eyes.

"Yes. I'm fine. I'm probably just tired from today's events." She brushed her hand across her forehead to wipe away the dizziness as she continued, "Why don't you crush up the leaves and put it in some water for him? Hopefully it will prevent his fever from returning so quickly and ease his pain a little. I'm going to take a walk to clear my head."

Erianna was showing symptoms from the night before when Brinn had cared for her and Brinn was beginning to worry that something deeper was going on with her new friend. She watched as Erianna wavered as she walked toward the trees.

"Erianna, let me come with you." Brinn started to get up and go after her.

"No." Erianna held out her hand, her breathing becoming ragged like it had the night before. "You have to stay with him. I will take the first watch."

"Eri--"

"Drink some of the tea and get some rest. We've all had a long day." Erianna stumbled into the wintery night. Brinn was tempted to follow her but a groan from the prince redirected her attention. She knew she had to remain with him, she only hoped Erianna knew what she was doing.

Brinn awoke from her sleep to a scratching sound nearby. She looked to where she expected Erianna to be lying but saw no one in the wooded area but herself and the prince. It seemed odd that Erianna had never returned to the camp. Brinn crawled over to the prince to check on him. His breathing was steady and he was resting peacefully. She heard another noise, one that sounded like something clawing the earth to itch something that was deep within. Though it sounded close, Brinn could see nothing in the immediate vicinity of the camp. The sound grew louder in her ears, almost as if the sound were resonating in her mind. She closed her eyes trying to rid herself of the scratching sound in her head.

Upon opening them, her eyes were immediately drawn to a shadow in the distance.

"Erianna?" Brinn called out into the silent night. No response. Brinn grabbed her quiver and slung the leather strap over her shoulder. Before leaving the camp, she pulled a small dagger from her boot and placed it beside Gabriel. In the event that something should happen while she was gone, she didn't want to leave him defenseless. She checked his forehead for any trace of the fever and put a small bit of the wintergreen plant beneath his tongue to try keep the fever at bay for a while longer. Assured he was stable and sleeping soundly, Brinn grabbed her bow and entered the dark woods.

The thick trees made it nearly impossible to see where she was going but she could sense something was there with her. She paused for a moment allowing her eyes to adjust to the dim light of the forest. In the stillness, a small thumping sound began to resonate at the back of her head. She closed her eyes and slowed her breathing, allowing herself to focus completely on the faint sound. The distinct rhythm of a heartbeat began to break through her silence followed by the heavy breathing of someone out of breath from running.

Brinn opened her eyes with a sharp inhale at the realness of the sound in her head. As she did, silvery rays of moonlight began to cut through the trees, casting an ethereal glow around her. A movement in the shadows a few feet in front of her caught her eye.

"Erianna, is that you?" This time Brinn was met by a cry of pain through the silence. "Erianna?"

Brinn took a few steps towards the direction she had seen the movement. She pulled an arrow from her quiver and cocked it in her bow. As she stepped forward, the thumping sound began to resonate once again in her head. The sound grew louder and more intense causing Brinn to drop her bow and grasp the sides of her head to make it stop. Screams of anguish joined the pounding chorus driving her almost mad until they were suddenly silenced by a bright flash of light that knocked Brinn to the ground. A screech similar to the one she had heard the night before filled the air.

Brinn lay there trembling for a few moments, afraid to open her eyes to the eerie silence that now filled the wintery wood. She willed her eyelids open just enough so she could see through a small slit in her eyes. She then allowed her eyelids to open more fully and began to sit up, ensuring she had no injury from her fall. As she sat up, a cool breath at the back of her neck caused her to freeze where she was. The hairs on the back of her neck stood on end as she felt another puff of breath, as if whatever stood behind her was sniffing her to find out what she was.

An arrow that must have fallen out of her quiver when she fell caught her eye. If she moved quickly she might be able to catch the creature off guard and distract it with her arrow. At least long enough to let her find a better hiding place. She took a deep breath and prepared herself to attack. Just as she was about to make her move, she felt the creature turn from her and begin to walk away. Unsure if the creature was leaving her for good or simply toying with her, she leaned forward ever so slightly to reach for the arrow. As she reached for it, a long silvery tail landed in her path and slithered past her.

Curiosity outweighed her fear in that moment as Brinn's eyes followed the tail to its place of origin. There in the moonlight stood a magnificent beast of majestic proportions. The body of the creature was covered in shimmering specks of silver that reflected the luminescent beauty of the winter moon. Thousands of tiny ice crystals lined its skin, woven together to look like the links of chainmail in a knight's armor. It sat with its hind legs underneath itself and its front legs fully extended, wrapping its pointed tail around them. Opalescent wings protruded from the beast's strong shoulders and flickers of light revealed intricate crystalline patterns of snowflakes throughout the webbing. A long, slender neck led up to the daintiest and most graceful head of a dragon Brinn had ever seen with silver cheeks and icy horns that stood out in the back of its head. The creature was absolutely breathtaking.

Brinn knew she should be terrified, but something about the creature made her feel safe and completely unafraid. In return, the dragon seemed at ease with her there and gave no signs of becoming aggressive with her. She stood slowly to take in the beautiful beast.

Holding out her hand as she did when she made friends with a new horse or one of the palace cats, she softly clucked at the beast, encouraging it to trust her. Intrigued by her quiet actions, the dragon slowly lowered its pointed head to meet her hand. Brinn's eyes widened with surprise as the giant muzzle made contact with her tiny hand. She stood breathless as her eyes met the brilliant cerulean blue eyes of the dragon. Something familiar within the eyes of the dragon pulled at Brinn as she stared back into the clear, scaly eyes. Brinn was about to open her mouth and speak to the dragon when a twig snapped behind her, causing the dragon to pull away.

Brinn's attempts to calm the dragon were ineffective as it became defensive very quickly. A burst of cold wind following a flash of light were all she remembered before falling into a world of darkness.

Chapter 9

Brinn awoke with a start and looked around her. She wasn't falling. She was on the ground where she had been the night before. She exhaled, relieved that it had only been a dream.

"Were you being attacked in your dream?"

She looked around the wooded area and saw Gabriel crouching beside a small pile of wood, trying to light it with one hand. Brinn smiled. At least he was feeling better. She stretched her achy muscles as she sat up, "No, not attacked. Just falling." Brinn stood up and walked over to help him.

"That is a horrible way to wake up," he said, holding a flat rock in his injured hand and a steel dagger in the other.

"What are you doing?" she asked, crouching beside him.

"I'm trying to start a fire," he said, struggling with the two pieces.

"I have never seen one started that way," she laughed.

"I don't mean to offend, but your fires provide little warmth. Especially to those with warmer dispositions." He smiled, revealing a beautiful row of perfectly white teeth.

Brinn smiled back, "We have little need of warmth in this country. Our fires are more practical and provide sources of light rather than heat. You are from the warmer kingdoms then?" she asked.

"Yes. I come from Genesia in the spring realm. My father is the king there," he replied.

"The spring realm? What is it like?" Brinn asked, her curiosity peaked.

The prince laughed, surprised at her eager interest in his country more than his status as a prince. "It is wonderful. Quite different from here," he said as he looked at the barren wood around them.

"I would hope so. Tell me about it," she said, excitement gleaming in her ice blue eyes.

He smiled. "I dropped my satchel somewhere in that direction yesterday when I came upon your sister. If you find it, I can show you some relics from my realm," he pointed towards the other side of the clearing.

Brinn's eyes clouded over. Concerned, he asked, "Have I said something wrong?"

She looked at him and replied, "No. Of course not. I mean, you did, but it wasn't offensive or cause for apology."

"What did I say that was amiss?" he asked.

"Erianna and I aren't sisters," she replied. Sadness diminished her bright demeanor.

"I am sorry. I thought--Well, it doesn't matter what I thought. I have caused you sadness and I do apologize for that."

"It is fine, you didn't know. We probably all look alike to you up here," she said with a half laugh.

"No. Though you are both beautiful, you are both unique and different in your own rights. I shouldn't have assumed. It's just," he paused, afraid to continue and make things worse.

"Go on. There must be something that caused you to think we were sisters."

She smiled and encouraged him to continue.

"In truth, it is your eyes that carry the strongest similarities," he said as he stared into her glassy blue eyes.

The faintest hue of pink colored her pale cheeks as she smiled and looked away.

He smiled, "And you both make it nearly impossible to tell when you are blushing because of your pale color, but perhaps that is a trait of all Northern people."

She looked back at him and saw the playful gleam in his eyes making her smile even more as she replied, "I imagine you always look like you are blushing."

He laughed, a cherry, warm laugh like none Brinn had ever heard before as he replied, "Yes. In fact, the moment we start to lose color in our cheeks, we send for a physician to make sure we haven't contracted some deadly disease."

Brinn's laugh tinkled like crystals in the wind which caused him to laugh even more. When their laughter subsided, he looked at her and said, "Thank you."

"For what?" she asked.

"For making me laugh. I dare say it is the best medicine in the world and I feel much warmer already. So much so, I don't believe I will be needing a fire after all."

A disappointed look crossed Brinn's face.

"Now what have I done. Do you not wish me to recover?" he asked.

"Oh, no. I mean. Yes, I want more than anything for you to recover," she replied. "I was just hoping to see how you make fire in your realm," she continued as a sheepish smile crossed her impish face.

"Well, I wouldn't want to disappoint a fair maiden this early in the day," he replied with a smile. "I will need a bit of help though."

Brinn's smile grew wide with excitement, exactly the way Julianna's did when she discovered something new. He smiled, "Are you ready?"

Brinn nodded. "Hold the stone in your hand like this," he put the flint stone in her right hand and held it out over the tinder. "And take the dagger in your other hand and strike down the rock as quickly as you can to create a spark."

Brinn swiped the dagger with the rock a few times with no success. "It certainly takes effort to start a fire in your realm."

"Patience. It will come. Hold the dagger closer to the tinder pile and strike it with the rock as hard and as fast as you can."

Brinn did as he instructed and focused all her energy on creating the spark he described. As she struck the steel blade with the rock, a small fiery star jumped off the end and disappeared into the cold air.

"That's it," Gabriel said with growing excitement, "Now, continue doing that until a spark takes to the dried wood."

A bright smile and a look of determination fueled Brinn to strike the rock a few more times until a small flame could be seen in the pile of dried plants and leaves. The sparkle in her eye was just like Julianna's too.

"Excellent work," he said as he moved a few of the loose twigs around to catch the flame and allow it to grow.

"I've never seen such color before," Brinn said as she sat completely entranced by the small flame. "What do you call it?"

"Orange, with bits of yellow and red mixed in."

"Orange." Brinn smiled. "I've always wanted to see that color in person. I've only read about it in books on the spring and summer realms. I suppose Fall would have that color too, wouldn't it?"

"I have never visited the Fall realms, but I am certain they must. And we have plenty of it in our realms as well." He smiled as he looked at her bewildered face, "You remind me a lot of a sister I left behind in Genesia."

Brinn took her eyes from the dancing flame for the first time since it started, "You have a sister? What is she like?"

"Beautiful. Smart. Witty. Curious. Always looking for adventure and new places to explore. Much like you, I would gather."

"If only I could. I am always reading about the other realms and the brilliant and wonderful things there. I have always dreamed of visiting them someday," she replied, a whimsical, far off look filling her eyes.

"Why don't you?" he asked.

"Much of my life has been spent trapped in the palace walls of Silvania," she said with a touch of sadness in her voice. She sighed as she continued, "My mother destroyed anything and everything connected with the other realms many years ago when I was a small child. She said any connection to the other realms would only bring us destruction and weakness. Luckily, I was born with a curious nature and after years of seeing the same palace walls, I eventually found all the secret passages and hidden doorways and found one that led to a library filled with books on all the realms. So, I read about them and cling to the hope that one day I will see them with my own eyes."

"I am sure you will," he said, compassion filling his heart for this sweet, trapped girl. "I know for a fact my sister would be delighted to meet someone with the same amount of tenacity and sense for adventure as she."

"I would like that equally as much," she smiled. "And you, what is your tragic tale?"

"Tragic? What makes you think mine is so tragic?"

"People generally don't leave their loved ones behind to set out for a God-forsaken land without some greater purpose in mind."

"You are right. I am not here for the freezing weather or intriguing landscape," he responded as he looked around at the barren scenery so different from the bright warmth of home. "In truth, I have been sent here to bring the sunlight back to the spring and summer realms."

"I didn't realize the warmest realms were losing sunlight. It must be difficult for you all."

"Indeed, it is," he sighed. "Our realms have been losing their magic over the last few years and we can't figure out what is causing the sun's power to grow weaker in the realms where it should be the strongest."

"That is strange. Do you know where or what you must seek in the winter lands?" she asked.

"No. All I know is what I seek lies somewhere in or near the Shaelyn Mountains."

"Shaelyn Mountain? I've never been there but Erianna seems quite familiar with the woods. Perhaps she can help guide you there."

"That would be wonderful. I admit, I feel quite lost in your woods. Everything looks the same to me." Gabriel rambled on as Brinn's eyes snapped wide open, realizing she hadn't seen Erianna this morning.

Flashes of her dream began to play in her mind along with events from the past few days. She had found Erianna torn and tattered a couple mornings ago and Gabriel had found her in the same state the morning before. Both nights Erianna disappeared in much the same manner, making sure she was out of sight by the time the moon rose. And her dream. She had gone searching for Erianna around midnight but couldn't find her. The only thing she found was a---.

"Good morning. You both look well rested." Erianna stepped into the clearing carrying a white furred rabbit with her.

Brinn's eyes sparked with surprise at seeing Erianna. "Where have you been?" she asked.

Erianna looked at Brinn, "I was out catching some breakfast for us. I hope that is alright?"

"You were unwell when you left the camp last night and you didn't come back until morning. Where were you?" Brinn asked pointedly, an edginess creeping into her voice.

"What do you mean I wasn't here? Of course I was here. I needed a few moments to clear my head and when I returned you were already asleep," Erianna responded, confused by the icy tone that laced Brinn's voice.

"No. You weren't. I remember waking up and when I did not see you here, I went searching for you." Brinn's uneasiness urged her to stand and pace.

"Brinn, you are mistaken. I was here all night and got up before either of you to find us some breakfast."

"No." Brinn spun around, growing frantic as she continued, "No. I checked on Gabriel and put my dagger beside him in case something happened while I was gone. I went looking for you. I started to hear this pounding in my head that sounded like a beating heart." She closed her eyes and clutched her temples as the memory began to replay in her mind.

Gabriel looked from Brinn's tormented face to Erianna's, concerned for the fragile state of the girl's emotions. Expecting to see a look fraught with concern for a dear friend, he was surprised to see her icy blue eyes wide open and drawn far away. Her breathing was short and shallow as if she too were reliving the terror of the girl's nightmare.

Brinn continued to describe her harrowing experience with such vividity. The heavy breathing, the painful screams, the bright flash of light. With each description, Erianna's beautiful face contorted in painful submission to the evocative tale. An unsettled feeling washed over Gabriel as he watched the two feed off each other like a reaper or death spirit sucking on the life force of the other. The strong, otherworldly connection between them filled the placid air around them.

He pulled himself up and was about to reach out to Brinn, hoping to break them of their shared pain, but Erianna sensed the intrusion and shot him a furtive glance.

"Brinn." Erianna reached out to her and pulled her away from him. "Brinn, calm down." She wrapped the girl in her arms and began to stroke her long, flowing hair. "It was a nightmare. A terrible nightmare that is over now. I'm here. You don't have to worry about it anymore."

The girl began to sob. She pulled away from Erianna, "But the dragon. It was so real. I could reach out and touch it."

Brief alarm crossed Erianna's eyes, but was quickly replaced by an icy coolness as she pulled Brinn back into her. "Dragon? My dear, it was a dream. There are no dragons to be worried about in this land. Besides, a dragon would never allow a human close enough to touch it."

Erianna began to gently rock Brinn back and forth as she continued to calm her. She placed an icy kiss on her forehead, hoping to wash away the terrible memories the girl's sleep had induced the night before. She looked up and saw Gabriel staring at them. Something in his sunlit eyes gave her the feeling he suspected something wasn't quite right.

Pulling away from Brinn, she looked at her and said, "Tell you what. Why don't you think of one of your favorite stories from all those books you've read to share with me and I will make some tea."

Brinn returned her gaze, tears still streaming down her face. "Tell you a story?" she asked.

"Yes. I'm sure there must be at least one story that you return to when you are sad or distressed. One that makes you happy to think about no matter the circumstances."

Brinn thought for a moment and allowed a bright smile to cross her face as she replied, "Yes. There is."

"Excellent." Erianna smiled and wiped the tears from Brinn's shimmery cheeks as she continued, "Give me a moment to ready breakfast and prepare some peppermint tea and then you can share your special story with us."

Brinn smiled and gave Erianna a big hug, "I am so glad we found each other."

Surprised by the girl's sudden gesture, Erianna stood frozen for a moment, unsure of how to respond. Slowly her arms relaxed and began to wrap around the sweet girl she had only met a few days before.

Aware Gabriel was still watching, Erianna abruptly pulled away from Brinn. "Well, I suppose I should see to breakfast. Would you be a dear and find some peppermint leaves for the tea? And some winter berries would be a wonderful addition if you can find any."

"Of course," Brinn replied, a little startled by Erianna's change in demeanor.

"Thank you. There should be some not too far from here."

Brinn nodded and tightened her cloak as she began to make her way once again into the woods.

Gabriel watched her go and made sure she was beyond earshot before he turned his tentative gaze toward Erianna.

"What did you do to her?" he asked as he watched her build up the fire to cook their breakfast.

"What do you mean?" Erianna took the dagger that was lying by the small fire and began to skin the rabbit she had caught.

"The arrow injured my arm, not my eyesight," he replied. "She was terrified by the visions she saw and you appeared to be somehow living her nightmare with her. Perhaps you were the cause, putting dark images in her head."

"I would never put those images in her head. How dare you accuse me of such a heinous crime," Erianna snapped.

Gabriel's hands shot up to defend himself as he stared at the bloody steel blade Erianna held at his throat.

Erianna's steely gaze faltered. She blinked several times and shook her head. The crystal blue eyes he had seen the day before widened as she looked at the dagger in her hand. She flinched and dropped the dagger into the snow as if the handle had just turned into lava in her hands. Her icy, terrorized eyes met his questioning ones, but quickly looked away.

Erianna stood and began to walk away. A subtle tremor filled her voice as she spoke, "I need to go."

Though she tried to appear strong, Gabriel could see the way she clutched her hands, as if trying to subdue something inside.

"I will leave you in Brinn's care. If your fever returns, have her take you to a healer in the southern part of the realm. His name is Archimedes."

"Erianna, wait. You can't just leave her in these woods. Whatever happened earlier, I can tell that she needs you."

Erianna stopped, her head tipped down and back as if listening, but unwilling to look back at him. "No. She will be better off without me. Both of you will."

"Erianna, stop. Maybe it's not about how much she needs you. Maybe you need her just as much. Maybe that's why you found each other."

"And yet just moments ago, you were concerned about my honesty and intentions towards Brinn," she replied, an icy coolness replacing the uncertain tremor in her voice.

Unwavering, Gabriel pushed a little farther, "I admit. I've never seen closer strangers."

Erianna paused before she turned to look at Gabriel. "You don't hold back, do you?"

"Honesty is a trait my mother insisted on implanting in me and my sister," he replied as his softened gaze held hers.

"You carry a good and noble heart within you. Be careful how you use it in this realm. It may be your undoing." She placed her slender hand over his heart. A cloud of pain filled her eyes as she stared at his chest. Something fluttered within Gabriel as she drew near to him. He reached up to grab her hand but she quickly pulled away as Brinn entered the clearing.

He watched as her icy facade reemerged and formed a fortress around her. After seeing the last remnant of her inner beauty disappear within her, Gabriel felt a strong urge to be the one to uncover it. No matter the cost.

Chapter 10

Gabriel could not get over how short the days were in this realm. It seemed the sun had only just come up a few hours before and it was already starting to disappear through the frosted trees. How people could live with so little sunlight he would never know.

He shivered. "Here." He looked up to see Brinn standing next to him with her suede cloak.

"You are too kind, princess, but I couldn't take your only barrier from the cold."

"You forget. I grew up here. I am far more used to the cold than you are." She smiled as she began to wrap the cloak around him.

"I pr-pr-omise, I am not th-tha-that cold," Gabriel replied through chattering teeth.

"Oh, right. I suppose it's just a hidden stutter that only makes an appearance after the sun goes down," she replied, her smile widening at his attempts to hide how cold he really was.

Gabriel warmed at the twinkle in her eye. "Yet another secret you have dis-covered, Princ-ce-cess."

"And not the last I am sure." She tied the ribbon in a bow around his neck to secure it in place, though she wasn't sure how effective it would be on his larger frame.

"A b-bow. J-just the touch it needed." His smile faded as his arm jerked from his shivering and sent pain shooting through his shoulder.

Brinn's face clouded, "Are you alright? Your fever isn't back, I hope?" She touched his burning forehead with her slender fingers but pulled back quickly as the foreign feeling of heat touched her skin.

"N-no. I don't think so. Just my arm reminding me it is still there."

"You should rest. I will gather some more wintergreen leaves to make you some tea to soothe the pain."

"It will be dark soon. You shouldn't trouble yourself."

Brinn was glad to see his speech was becoming normal again. His shivering was beginning to subside. "I will be fine. Just rest for a while."

"You are so much like my Julianna." He smiled, as she helped him settle back against the tree.

"Then you would be wise to listen." She smiled, happy to be compared once again to someone he clearly loved and admired.

"I will return shortly. Erianna should be back soon as well." She stood and disappeared into the forest.

Gabriel nestled back against the tree and allowed his thoughts to run free in the cold dusk air. After what seemed like mere minutes, his thoughts returned to him, colliding in a violent shiver that shook his entire body. The small cloak the princess had given him was not much to keep out the deep cold he was starting to feel. He needed his cloak to restore some of the heat he had lost over the last day. Gabriel opened his eyes and glanced around the clearing.

Which direction had he come from the day before? As Gabriel's eyes roamed the small clearing, a large shadow caught his eye. He blinked to make sure his eyes weren't playing tricks on him in the dimming glow of the wintery sunset. Gabriel focused on the spot again. The shadow was still there. It was too large to be Erianna or Brinn. Gabriel glanced quickly around him trying to find the small dagger Brinn had given him earlier. He caught a glimpse of the handle sitting not too far from him. Perhaps if he allowed himself to fall over towards it, the shadow might think he had passed out and he could reach the dagger before the shadow had a chance to make itself known.

Gabriel watched the shadow through half closed eyes as he slowly tipped himself over into the snowy earth.

Erianna entered the clearing carrying more game but stopped when she saw the prince lying on his side. "Gabriel." Panic etched Erianna's voice as she ran to him.

Erianna knelt beside the prince and began to roll him over onto his back.

"Easy. We're being watched."

Erianna stared at him. His eyes remained closed as if he really had passed out but she could have sworn she heard him say something.

"What did you say?" she whispered.

Gabriel remained still except for the movement of his lips, "There is something in the trees across from us. I was hoping to get the dagger without being noticed before you returned."

Erianna's muscles tensed as she became aware of the unfamiliar presence in the forest.

"Don't move," she whispered. Erianna moved to the other side of Gabriel to check his wound and pull Brinn's cloak up around his injured arm.

As she knelt close to him, her piercing gaze scanned the trees around them. Nothing looked out of the ordinary but the hairs on the back of her neck pricked her skin and warned her that something was off.

"I'm going to pour you some tea and retrieve the dagger," she whispered as she tucked the cloak further into the crook of his arm.

Erianna walked over to the small fire and placed a small handful of snow into the small glass she had made earlier for Gabriel to drink out of. The snow in the glass began to melt as she held it over the fire. Erianna watched the woods around her, waiting for whatever was out there to make itself known. When the snow finished melting, Erianna slipped the small dagger into the folds of her gown.

Erianna knelt beside Gabriel and lifted his head so he could drink the water she brought him. As she laid his head back down he said, "Thank you," followed by a whispered, "What are we going to do?"

She brushed his forehead and forced a smile, "Just rest now." As she leaned over him to adjust the cloak one more time, she slipped the dagger beneath his arm and made sure he touched it with his other hand so he knew it was there.

"Stay on the ground until I can draw them out. And don't fight if you can avoid it."

Gabriel opened his eyes to look up at her. "What are you going to do?" he whispered.

She looked down at him with her piercing blue eyes, "The less you know the better."

He grabbed her hand as she was about to stand, "Be careful."

She looked down at him, surprised to see concern in his eyes. She gave him a quick nod and stood.

Erianna ducked into the trees right behind them just as Brinn re-entered the clearing.

"Gabriel, I found some winter berries I thought you might like--" she stopped when she saw Gabriel lying on his back. "What happened? Are you alright?"

Brinn ran to kneel beside him. "Don't move," Gabriel whispered as she knelt over him.

"Why? What's wrong?"

"Just be quiet," Gabriel whispered.

Brinn looked at him, puzzled by the harshness of his tone. Brinn scanned his features and found the dagger lying just under his injured arm.

"What-?" she whispered, looking around her to see if she could figure out what was putting him on edge.

His emerald eyes caught hers. The look he gave her was intense and commanding. A look he often gave his sister she imagined.

Brinn headed his warning glance and looked around the clearing again. When she didn't see anything out of the ordinary, Brinn closed her eyes and allowed her breathing to slow enough to focus her other senses. As she focused her other senses on the woods around her, she was drawn to a large figure not too far off. Something familiar about the figure caused Brinn to open her eyes and gaze right at the looming shadow.

Just as Brinn was about to stand and approach the figure, she sensed another presence in front of her. This one was different. Smaller, a deeper strength within than with the other larger form behind her. But something familiar stood out with this other presence as well. Something that pulled at her like a memory from beyond her earliest recollections.

Brinn sat in the silence for a moment, trying to read the deeper presence in front of her. A sound behind her drew her back to the present. She focused as she sensed a darker tension, like a predator zeroing in on its prey and about to pounce. Just as she was about to narrow in on the dark presence, an arrow launched past her sailing into the trees in front of her.

"Erianna," Brinn screamed as she shot up and spun around, ready to defend the girl and the prince.

Another arrow whizzed by Brinn's ear and in the split second it would have taken to warn Erianna to move, she turned to see the arrow suspended in midair between her and Erianna.

Erianna's hands were raised in front of her face, protecting her from the arrow. She lowered her hands, dropping the arrow to the ground. Brinn's eyes widened with amazement. She had only ever seen her mother use such magic.

Brinn's eyes met Erianna's. Erianna looked like she wanted to explain but her gaze was drawn by another arrow following the same path as the first.

"Brinn, Look out." Erianna put up her hands once more, sending Brinn to the other side of the clearing and stopping the arrow with one swoop of her arms.

Erianna rushed to Brinn, afraid she had harmed her in her attempt to protect her. Gabriel untied the cloak and grabbed the dagger before standing to fight off whatever had come to destroy them in the woods.

Another arrow sailed through the clearing headed straight for Gabriel, but it was just as quickly thrown off its path by Erianna's magic. She knelt to check on Brinn. She lifted the girl's head, careful not to move her too much to prevent further injury.

"Brinn?" She gently patted the girl's cheeks to bring her around.

Brinn stirred and opened her eyes, "I'm fine," she smiled but her eyes were quickly drawn to Gabriel, who was about to be met by a blade three times the length of the small dagger, "but you may want to help him."

Erianna turned in time to see a large man charging Gabriel with what appeared to be a sword of the royal guard. "Gabriel," she cried out. With another flick of her hands the man was sent flying backwards. As he landed, the hood that covered his face fell back revealing a head of long blonde hair.

Brinn gasped, "Tharynn."

Erianna grabbed a long stick and began chanting cryptic words over it as she laid it in the snow and waved her hands over it. The stick was transformed into a long blade of ice. She picked up the enchanted sword and rushed to give it to Gabriel before the man was up and able to fight again.

"A blade of ice? Will this hold up against a steel weapon?" Gabriel asked, looking at the intricate, fragile looking weapon he now possesses.

"Would you prefer a stick?" Erianna asked as the man came to. The man got up and ran at Gabriel again with his blade poised and ready to make contact.

Gabriel swung his blade to block the man's blow and was surprised at the strength which the dainty sword held up under the force of the soldier's steel blade.

"My apologies," he glanced at Erianna and then pushed back against the soldier and threw him off of his sword.

Erianna raised up her hands again, ready to assist where she needed as Gabriel's blade met Tharynn's a few more times.

Brinn got up off the ground and ran to Erianna, "Please stop." She grabbed Erianna's arms and tried to pull her away.

"Brinn, stay out of this."

"No. Please. He is a friend from the palace. He is probably here to rescue me. My mother didn't know I left and I'm sure she thought I had been kidnapped or something. Let me speak to him and explain."

Tharynn continued to swing his sword at Gabriel. Erianna could tell he was struggling to keep up with his injured arm. She raised her hands to release another icy blast but Brinn stopped her.

"No. Erianna. You will hurt him."

Erianna looked back to Gabriel. Tharynn had struck a blow that sent Gabriel to the ground and was getting ready to attack again.

"Brinn, I have to stop him. He is going to kill Gabriel if I don't."

Brinn's anxious eyes filled with tears as she looked towards Gabriel and Tharynn.

Erianna didn't have time to wait. She threw out her hand and stopped Tharynn's sword from striking Gabriel just as it was about to make contact and whipped it from his hand, tossing it across the forest floor. Tharynn looked at Erianna, surprised that he was no longer holding his sword in his hands. His hand clenched in a fist and made contact with Gabriel's face before he had a chance to strike. As Gabriel's head hit the ground, Tharynn's anger turned toward Erianna.

"Brinn. Run." Erianna held out her hands and began to circle Tharynn.

Brinn's feet wouldn't move. She stood frozen in place, terrified to see her dearest and oldest friend so enraged. Something wasn't right.

Tharynn ran towards Erianna and dodged her icy blast as he advanced. Erianna tripped over the sword she had thrown from his hands earlier and fell backwards. Tharynn picked up the sword and swung it viciously toward Erianna. Erianna tried to protect herself but before she could put her hands up, Tharynn was suddenly thrown back across the clearing. His large frame collided with a tree, causing a large amount of snow to fall on top of him. Erianna quickly transformed the snow into icy chains that wound themselves around him. When she looked back, she saw the terrified look in Brinn's eyes.

Brinn slowly lowered her hands and stared at them as if they were diseased.

"Brinn," Erianna whispered as she stood and stepped towards her.

Brinn's tear filled eyes met Erianna's, "My mother said I wasn't born with magic."

"It appears she was hoping you hadn't been." Erianna reached out to her and pulled her into herself, "But it's ok to have magic. It can be a very beautiful thing if it is used for good."

As she spoke, Erianna suddenly felt faint. She looked up at the sky and saw how dark it was getting. "We can't stay here and discuss the morals of magic though. If your mother sent him, he won't be alone, and I'm afraid we can't fight them all." Erianna gasped as a sharp pain shot through her.

Brinn looked at Erianna. She looked up and saw how dark it was getting as well. The moon would be rising soon and it seemed to have the same effect on Erianna every night.

"Erianna? Are you alright?"

Brinn's endless eyes bore into Erianna's. The concern Erianna saw behind Brinn's icy pools made Erianna wish just for a moment that she could tell her everything. But she couldn't. It was far too dangerous. And she didn't have time to divulge everything tonight.

Putting on her best smile, Erianna replied, "Yes. I'm fine. Check on Gabriel and see how he is doing," she stopped for a breath before she continued, "I will check on your soldier and make sure we have a chance to get away before he comes to." Erianna wiped small beads of sweat from her brow and walked over to Tharynn.

Her breathing was becoming thread again and Brinn was becoming very concerned for her.

"Let her go."

Brinn turned towards Gabriel, who had pulled himself to a sitting position.

"Something isn't right with her but she won't let me help her." Brinn came to kneel by him and reached out to wipe the blood that was dripping from his lip.

Gabriel grimaced. "Sorry," she replied as she pulled her hand away.

"No, my apologies for being a child and wincing at my pain," he smiled.

She returned his smile but it quickly vanished when she saw the blood seeping through the bandage on his arm.

"You're bleeding again." She began to unwrap the cotton fabric from his arm and became worried when she saw the perspiration starting to form on his brow again.

"Has your fever returned?" she asked as she finished unwrapping the bandage and began to inspect his wound.

"No. My skin naturally glistens in the moonlight." He laughed, but she could tell he was in a lot of pain.

Erianna had finished with Tharynn and came to join them. Her skin emitted a ghostly hue and her eyes had a strange tint to them. "How is he?" she asked as she knelt beside them.

"I'm not sure which of you is worse off but his fever has returned and I believe his wound is infected."

Erianna tried to focus her eyes on his wound but was having trouble seeing as she spoke, "We need to get him to Archimedes. He's," she paused to catch her breath, "He's a healer in the southern region of Sylvania."

In the background, Brinn began to hear the faint thump thumping she had heard the night before. She closed her eyes for a moment and focused on the source of the sound. When she opened her eyes, they were drawn to Erianna, who looked worse than she had the past few nights when this happened.

"Erianna." Brinn reached out to her and tried to calm her but Erianna pulled away. Erianna's face began to contort with pain and Brinn heard the screaming like she had the night before. Little slivers of moonlight began to reach through the trees and into the clearing. Erianna thrashed and began to scream out loud with such anguish it sent chills down both Brinn and Gabriel's spines.

Brinn willed herself to push past the sounds in her head and focus on what was happening to Erianna. She reached out again but this time Erianna threw her back and ran into the woods.

Gabriel reached down to help Brinn. As he did, a loud screech cracked the night air.

"Erianna." Brinn scrambled to her feet and started to run in the direction she had seen Erianna go but a bright flash of light filled the air and knocked both her and Gabriel to the ground. Brinn's head hit the ground causing her to see spots for a moment. She fought to keep her eyes open but a cold draft of air filled the clearing making her feel very tired all of a sudden. The image of the dragon flashed through her mind as her eyelids slowly came to a close over her eyes.

Chapter 11

A rchimedes tidied his little hovel after another breakfast alone and was ready to begin work on a new potion when he heard a knock on the door. Unsure if he heard right or if his ears were simply playing tricks on him, he stood silent for a moment. Another pounding on the door met his ears.

"Who would be disturbing my solitude this early in the morning?" he grumbled as he climbed down his small step ladder and hobbled to the other side of the room.

Archimedes opened the peephole in the door and yelled out, "I'm not accepting visitors today, or any day, so just head right back where ya' came from."

"Please. Can you help us? We travelled all night to get here," came a voice through the thick wood door.

"I told you, the only person I want in this house is me, myself and I. Since you don't fit any of those names, you best be on your way," he growled back. He closed the peephole and began to hobble back to his table.

"My friend is hurt and needs help. We were told to seek out a healer by the name of Archimedes. Can you tell us where to find him?"

"There is no one here who can help you."

"Please," the feminine voice grunted from the other side of the door. It sounded like she was carrying something heavy.

Archimedes stopped for a moment. He had been alone in his little hovel for years. Why on earth would someone be looking for him now?

"Please," came the voice again. "He may be dying."

It sounded as if she was about to cry. "Oh merciful heaven," Archimedes grumbled under his breath as he made his way back to the door. "I can fend off dragons and all matter of winter beasts with my potions but goodness knows when a poor girl starts crying."

Archimedes huffed out an exasperated breath as he opened the door. "All right. You can come in and rest, but only for a moment, you understand?"

"Thank you," the young girl let out an elated sigh.

Archimedes looked up to see a young girl holding up a man twice her size. A grumble hitched in his throat as he looked up into her pale blue eyes. "I'll be a snow monkey's uncle."

The girl looked down at him confused at his expression. "What?" she asked.

Archimedes cleared his throat and responded with a grumble, "Nothing. Just, bring him in here."

Brinn began to half drag the prince over the small threshold.

"Careful, now. Don't hit his head on the low frame. And don't be dragging in the outdoors with you." Archimedes tried guiding them in without them destroying everything he had just tidied.

"Sit him over here. No, no. Not there, he'll break my favorite chair with his wide girth. Lay him on the floor." Frustration mixed with utter annoyance filled his voice.

She laid him down with a thud as gravity pulled him to the ground quicker than she was ready for.

Archimedes closed his eyes to keep the image of the fiasco unfolding before him out of his mind. Rubbing his small forehead, he whispered, "And today started out as such a good day."

He hobbled over to his visitors and helped settle the boy better on the floor before the fireplace. "What seems to be the problem with your friend?" he asked, lifting the boy's closed eyelids to see how coherent he was.

"It's a long story," she said in short, rapid breaths as she sat next to him on the floor.

"I don't have the patience for the long version so you better stick to the highlights," he said as he continued to examine the boy before him.

"Oh. Well," she replied trying to figure out where to start, "I shot him with an arrow two days ago because I thought he was attacking someone in the woods, which he wasn't, he was trying to help, but I didn't realize it at the time I shot him. I felt bad about shooting him unnecessarily so Erianna pulled the arrow out and we cleaned it as best we could but then someone did attack us last night and Gabriel tried to fight him. Unfortunately, he reopened his wound during the fight causing his fever to come back worse than ever. Erianna said we had to get him to you so you could heal him. That is, if you are Archimedes?"

Archimedes huffed out a breath of annoyance and shook his head. He dropped the man's large wrist and started to walk around the large man.

"What? What is it?" Concern laced Brinn's voice as she looked from Gabriel to the little man.

The little hobgoblin looked heavenward and rolled his eyes. "Was the first one not penance enough?" he muttered as he hobbled across the room.

"What's wrong with him? Will he be alright?" she asked, worried that Gabriel might be worse off than she thought.

Archimedes continued muttering to himself as he hobbled around the room and picked up different vials from around the room. "The first one didn't destroy enough of my earthly possessions? Now you have to send this one to finish the job?"

Brinn raised her voice as she became annoyed with the little goblin, "Look, I don't know who or what you are talking to but this man is very sick and he needs your help."

Archimedes growled as he responded, "Keep your skirts on, missy. Your prince has a long life ahead of him."

Brinn flushed, "He most certainly is not my prince."

"Well bless his bootstraps, one less headache he has to deal with," Archimedes scoffed as he picked up a few more vials and put them back down. He looked to the sky once more, "Is it too much to ask to live out the rest of my days in peace?" A crashing sound behind him made him cringe.

"Now what in the snow queen's name are you breaking?"

"I'm sorry. I was trying to find a cloth and some water to bring down his fever since you don't appear to be doing anything."

Archimedes grumbled. Scouring the last shelf, he finally found the purple potent he had been searching for. "Here, take this and your friend and get yourselves out of my house before you break something else." Archimedes pushed the vial into her hand and started pushing Gabriel to a sitting position.

Shocked at his abruptness, Brinn responded, "That's it? Here's a vial, now be on your way?"

"I wish I could say I've enjoyed your company but I enjoy my solitude more." Archimedes heaved trying to hoist the young man to his feet.

Brinn's last nerve snapped as she lashed out at the goblin, "You insufferable, impertinent little man. How can you possibly turn a bleeding man into the snow?"

"Very easily. Now help me get him to his feet so you can continue on to wherever you were going and leave me alone."

"No. We are not leaving until you help him." Brinn pushed Gabriel to the ground and held him there with an incredible strength that surprised Archimedes.

Curious to see what else she would do if pushed to anger, Archimedes goaded Brinn further. "Well, you are out of luck, miss priss. There is nothing I can do to help your precious prince."

"Why not?" Something sparked in her blue eyes.

A wiry smile formed on Archimedes' thin lips as he continued, "He's a springling who's been shot with an arrow laced with winter's bane. Not something especially deadly to those in this realm but if it gets in the veins of a springling, the only thing anyone can do is slow down the poison and hope their last days are comfortable."

"No." The spark of anger triggered something inside her. A seething coolness settled over her and filled her veins with an icy anger.

Archimedes smirked, "She is a doggone changer too." He braced himself for what was about to happen when another voice entered the room.

"Brinn. Stop." Erianna rushed in and grabbed hold of Brinn. "Look into my eyes and don't look away." Brinn's glacial gaze locked on Archimedes.

"Brinn, focus on me. Do not think about anything else. Just look at me and breathe." Erianna pulled Brinn's gaze toward her.

As Brinn's electrified eyes locked on Erianna's, the eerie hue that had begun to glow behind her narrowed pupils dissipated. As Brinn's eyes became normal, she looked at Erianna more fully, as if realizing she was there for the first time.

"Erianna? What happened?" she asked as she shook off the lingering dizziness in her head.

"Just the curiosity of a hobgoblin's mischievous nature getting the better of him," Erianna replied as she shot Archimedes an icy glare over Brinn's shoulder.

"You shouldn't have let her come to me alone if you were worried about her, dearie." Archimedes replied with a condescending air.

"I didn't think I would have anything to worry about, you evil old badger. I thought the man who showed some kindness to a little girl lost in the woods years ago would extend the same hospitality to someone who was injured and exhausted."

"Clearly you've forgotten how unkindly I was to you your first few days in my little home. Now, give your friend the potent I gave your sister and be on your way." Archimedes turned and began to hobble towards the hallway beyond the kitchen. As he reached the hall, a gust of wind swept through the little house and forced him back into the room, knocking him on his back in the process.

"It seems someone else insists on you helping us." Erianna smirked as she got up and began to pilfer through the goblin's cupboards to find some towels and a bowl to use for water.

Archimedes struggled to pull himself to an upright position as he responded, "You can keep your lip to yourself or you will be doing this on your own."

"I am doing everything on my own. I lived in this little hovel long enough to know where you keep your ingredients and could probably do a better job of mixing the right potion to bring him back to health than you could."

"Are you saying you don't need me now?" Archimedes scowled as he hobbled over to his kitchen to shoo her out. "Ten years you leave me alone in the middle of these frigid woods and then you send two wayward waifs in here to disturb my solitude. Not to mention the grand heroic entrance of the prodigal daughter returning home because she's gotten herself into a mess she can't get herself out of."

"I promise we will only stay as long as it takes you to help him," Erianna said as she looked at the codgering old man.

"I best set to work then. I have a big dinner planned by myself."

Archimedes took the towels and bowl away from Erianna and hobbled over to the hearth where Gabriel still lay unconscious. Erianna let out a sigh of relief as the old man began to tend to the prince. She knew she wouldn't be well received, which was why she sent Brinn in with Gabriel but she had no idea he would turn on her the way he did.

She filled another bowl with water and grabbed one of the magnifying glasses and some other tools from the goblin's table and carried them over to the huddle in front of the fireplace. Erianna handed the bowl of water and cloth to Brinn. "Here. You can wipe his face and try to bring his fever down." Brinn accepted the bowl of water and knelt beside Gabriel. Erianna walked around Gabriel and knelt beside Archimedes. She offered him a pair of scissors as a peace offering.

Archimedes accepted the scissors Erianna offered him and began to cut away the crude cloth that clung to the injured man's arm. "You have some nerve sending your younger duplicate in here to get help," Archimedes whispered as he peeled back the bloody bandages.

"I was hoping you would be a bit more accepting of her than you would me."

"Hmph," Archimedes grumbled as he removed the remaining cloth. "How did you find her?"

Erianna looked at Brinn. "Actually, she found me," she replied in a whisper.

"Hmmm. An interesting twist of fate I must say" Archimedes put one of the eyeglasses up to his eye to look at the wound more closely as he spoke.

Brinn looked up from Gabriel and asked, "What's wrong?"

"It's as I told you earlier. Winter's bane is not a friendly thing to be put into the bloodstream of a person from a warmer region."

"What will it do?" she asked.

"It is an ice poison. When it comes in contact with something, it begins to adhere to the molecules around it forming a thin layer of ice over anything it touches. In the case of it being on something that pierces the skin, like your arrow, it will attach itself to the molecules in your body and begin to slowly turn your body to ice. In most cases it can be reversed with an antidote that breaks down the ice and allows it to melt away to nothing."

"So, you just have to make the antidote and draw out the poison, right?" Brinn asked.

Archimedes looked at the fear and worry in Brinn's eyes. The same look he had seen in a scared little girl ten years earlier. His voice softened as he responded, "I will do what I can to help him."

Relief flooded through Brinn. She reached across Gabriel and touched Archimedes hand, "Thank you."

A small smile crept across Archimedes' thin lips as he looked into her sweet eyes.

Trying not to soften too much, Archimedes pulled his hand away and replied "Let's move him into my room where he can be more comfortable and I can better tend to him. The sooner I help him the sooner you can be out of my hair. Or what little hair is left." He grumbled as he began to get Gabriel to a sitting position and get him moved to another room in the house.

Chapter 12

After she made sure that Brinn was settled in her room and resting, Erianna made her way back into the kitchen and living area. She stopped in the doorway and smiled as she watched Archimedes hobble around. He collected various bottles and powders from around the room and carried them back to the large table that sat in the middle of the room. She didn't realize how much she had missed seeing that familiar sight all these years.

"Are you going to stand there gawking in the doorway all night or are you going to help an old man out?" Archimedes asked without looking up at Erianna.

Erianna smiled, "Have my ears frozen over or did I actually hear the great Archimedes ask for help?"

"I never ask for help, young snowflake. But I hate seeing people standing around doing nothing. You can make yourself useful and put a pot of tea on. Otherwise, you can just leave me to my musings."

Erianna shook her head as she crossed to the small kitchen space on the other side of the room. He always pretended to be a crotchety old man, but she knew the sweet, caring heart that resided underneath all his bristles.

"Brinn finally drifted off to sleep," Erianna said as she filled a kettle with water and set a small teapot on the counter beside her.

She began to fill a small, thin cheese cloth with various things like peppermint leaves, vanilla root and a cinnamon stick to add some spice to the homey brew. "I'm sorry I dragged her into all of this. She's been through enough the past few days to make anyone want to sleep for a week." Erianna tied up the little bag and dropped it in the pot, then crossed to the fireplace to put the kettle on the hook that hung over the warm flames.

"And you haven't been through the same ordeal, I take it?" Archimedes responded with a slightly sardonic air as he poured a few drops of a yellow liquid into the pot he was currently working over.

Erianna sighed, "You know I rarely sleep during the moon's changes."

"Hmmm, yes. I do seem to recall something that prevented you from getting much sleep as a child," Archimedes mused as he picked up a bright colored jar and measured out a teaspoon of orange powder.

Erianna shot him an icy glare, knowing he knew full well what had caused her insomnia when she was a little girl.

"Get some shortbread cookies out too, dearie. I'll be a mite hungry after finishing this potent. Besides, I never take my tea without a little something to munch on."

"How have you survived the last ten years without me to make your tea or fetch your cookies for you?" she asked as she went back to the kitchen and pulled out a small clay platter to put the cookies on.

"Oh, I've managed somehow," he replied as he looked over his glasses at the dropper in his hand to make sure he got just the right amount of the green herbal liquid.

"Clearly," Erianna replied as she searched the cupboards for the small box of cookies he had always kept hidden from her when she was little. "I'm surprised to see your house kept up and not a shambled mess without me around to keep it clean for you," her voice was muffled as she stuck her head into one of the lower cupboards.

"Part of the snow queen's enchantment, I suppose. I can't deteriorate any more than this house can as long as she keeps me in this cursed banishment." He looked up for a moment to see Erianna on hands and knees scouring the cupboard for the cookies.

"You won't find them in there, lass." He gave a small chuckle at the sight that reminded him so much of the little girl that used to fit in those cupboards herself when they played a round of hide and seek to pass the long winter nights.

Erianna bonked her head on the top of the cupboard. It was a lot smaller than it used to be. "Where have you taken to hiding them, you old rascal?" Erianna asked as she backed out of the cupboard and rubbed her head.

"Eh, it wasn't fun to hide them from myself anymore so I started keeping them on the shelf next to the herbs for the tea."

Erianna looked up at the shelf and let out a frustrated sigh. "That was kind of you to let me keep looking when they were in front of my face the whole time."

"Your eyes are a lot younger than mine, lass. You shouldn't have had that much trouble lookin' for them." He smiled as he put a pinch of a purple powder into the pot. "There, now we'll let that simmer a bit and see how it does." The hobgoblin hobbled down his small step stool and crossed to the kitchen to fetch some cups for their tea.

The kettle began to whistle and Erianna grabbed a small cloth to pull it off the fire. She crossed back to the counter to pour the steaming water into the teapot. She took the cups Archimedes gave her and placed them on the tray with the pot and cookies and carried them over to the area in front of the fire. Erianna poured some tea in each of the cups and let Archimedes get settled in his overstuffed chair by the fire before handing him a cup and a small plate of cookies. Erianna took the other cup and settled back in the larger chair across from her little friend.

Erianna inhaled and let the warm aroma waft over her and wrap her in a blanket of comfort. "Mmmmm," she sighed as she took a sip of the steamy drink. "It's been years since I've had this tea. I almost forgot how much I loved it." She smiled as she took a sip of the warm drink.

"It's about the only hot drink you liked, since your blood runs so cold all the time," Archimedes smiled as he took a sip of the relaxing drink.

Taking a bite of his cookie, he looked at Erianna, "Tell old Archimedes what in the great mage's name has been carrying on the past few days to put all of you in my home."

Erianna lowered her cup and sighed, trying to sort through the numbing mayhem that had ensued in the past few days.

"So much has happened, I don't know where to begin."

Archimedes dipped a part of his cookie into his tea and stirred it around a bit before taking another bite. "Why don't you start with how you came upon your sister."

Erianna ran her finger absentmindedly along the rim of her cup. "As I mentioned earlier, she somehow came upon me. I woke up in her garden a few days ago." She stared off as she thought back to how frightened she had been when she woke up and didn't know where she was. The girl that tried to help her. And those eyes. Her finger stilled halfway around the cup as she thought about those clear, endless eyes that had stared back at her for the first time in so many years. Frightened. Absent of memory or recognition.

Archimedes interrupted her swirling thoughts with a slight grumble and said, "Aye. You woke up in her garden. And--." He looked at her as he dipped another cookie into his tea.

Erianna brought her teacup to her lips and stared across the steaming cup at Archimedes. "You are impatient as ever," she replied as she took a sip of her tea.

"Well, when you've been alone and isolated in a hovel in the forsaken most part of the realm for ten years you get an itch to hear what's going on in the world," Archimedes huffed as he got down off his chair to get more cookies.

Erianna shook her head and smiled as she lowered her cup, "Well, as I said, I woke up in her garden the other morning. I don't know how I got there or why but when I woke up, I was lying on a bench in what she called her 'secret garden.' Guaranteed to keep all evil and unwanted things out," Erianna smiled as she remembered Brinn's description of her garden.

"I didn't even realize it was her until she looked at me," she continued." She tried to clean up some of the scratches on my face from the transformation and I overreacted and grabbed her wrist, but then she looked at me with those eyes. Those crystal clear blue eyes. I knew it had to be her, but, she didn't seem to recognize me, so I convinced myself it couldn't be her. I was terrified to think of how close I must have been to the palace if it truly was her and what would happen if the queen knew or found out I was there. I had no idea what mother would have told Brinn about me all those years after she banished me or if Brinn believed her or would have turned on me if she knew who I was." A growing agitation pushed Erianna up from her chair.

Erianna paced back and forth in the small space between the two chairs and the fireplace. Words continued to tumble out of her mouth as she recounted the story of Brinn's garden and how she imagined it to be and all the colors and things she longed to see in the other realms and finally she mentioned how her mother had banished everything from the other realms because she felt it was a threat to their realm.

"When she said her mother had banished everything from the other realms, I knew it was her." Erianna stopped in front of the fireplace. "I said her name by accident. Twice. I knew exactly who she was the moment I saw her eyes but I didn't want to believe it. It couldn't be her. If it was, she would have recognized me. Something would have triggered her memory of me. But, she didn't even know me." Erianna sank to her knees, the weight of the situation pulling her to the ground.

"She was a wee lass when you were removed from the palace, dearie. She might have been too little to remember you."

Erianna's shoulders drooped like a branch under the weight of a heavy wet snow as she whispered, "She didn't even know my name."

Archimedes wriggled himself out of his chair and he went to stand by Erianna. He pulled her head into his chest and stroked her long, blonde-white hair as she started to cry. "I'm sorry, lass. That's a hardship no person should have to endure, especially when there's been so much heartache in such a young heart."

"Why would my mother make her forget me?" Erianna cried out through the tears that had likely been held back for so many years.

"Your mother is a hard one to crack, dearie. I don't know how a mother could turn her young daughter out into the snowy white world and expect her to live on her own and face the things you had to. It doesn't make sense to me in the slightest," Archimedes choked past the lump that was forming in his own throat.

"Brinn said she banished everything from the other realms because they were a threat to her kingdom. If she banished them and banished me, that means she thought I was a threat too," Erianna sobbed into Archimedes' woolen vest.

"No, no. My dearest rose. Don't believe that. Ach, My little heart. You are not a threat to anybody. Just because you are different, that is no reason to banish you or send you away." Archimedes kissed the top of her head and began to rock her gently back and forth.

"But I am a threat, Archimedes. I lost control of my powers so many times and I could have hurt people when I wasn't myself. So many people could have been hurt or dead because of me."

"There, there, my little snowflake. I know you have had a scary time of it, especially when you don't know what you have done when you've transformed, but I know your heart and I know that a heart as good and as pure as that can't ever really do any harm to anyone, even when that person isn't completely in control of themselves."

"But, you don't understand, Archimedes." Erianna pulled herself away from Archimedes and stood up. "My transformations have become so much worse. I keep waking up in places I don't know with no memory of anything that may have happened while I was a beast." She started walking away from him.

"Easy, lass. I know you're venting a lot of emotions that should have been vented out years ago but you won't do either of us any good if you let yourself get out of control and started changing before it's time."

"Out of control? I can't remember the last time I was in was in control." She started pacing again, agitation growing within her with every step.

"I know. Just tell old Archimedes what has been going on and we will figure something out. Now, when did you start to lose control of your powers and your memories again?"

Erianna rubbed her head as Archimedes moved around her to put some more water in the kettle to put over the fire. When he had finished putting the kettle over the fire, he took Erianna's hand and led her to sit back down in her chair.

While he hobbled around the room gathering some peppermint, lavender and chamomile to make a calming tea for Erianna, she began telling him about her transformations over the past few months.

"It started getting worse three or four months ago. I would blackout periodically throughout the night or have missing parts of my memory the next morning. It was never serious. I was alone most of the time and I stayed close to the mountains like I always have to make sure I never injure anyone while I'm in my dragon form but a month ago I ended up by a village and when I woke up the entire village was--." Erianna closed her eyes and covered her face with her hands.

Archimedes put the items he had gathered into the teapot and brought it over to fill it with the hot water from the kettle.

"I don't know what happened," she cried into her hands. "There were bodies everywhere and so much blood."

Archimedes stopped short at her words and turned around. He knew she likely wasn't the cause of the destruction but he had an uneasy feeling about her being by the village and not being able to remember anything. He took a deep breath and finished filling the teapot with the water.

He set the teapot on the table next to Erianna and pulled his stool that he used when he cooked meals at the fireplace over so he could sit beside Erianna. He poured the tea into Erianna's cup and reached up to pull her hands away from her face. "Here, dear one. Drink some of this. It will help calm you down.

Erianna sniffed as she took the cup and took a small sip.

"Now, dear one. I know you think you were responsible for whatever happened in that village but I don't believe you were the cause of it."

"But, Archimedes, I have no memory of that night. I have no idea if my dragon-self got out of control or if the more carnal instincts are kicking in. This wretched curse seems to be taking a stronger hold on me than it ever has before. I don't know what I do anymore when I transform."

"I know it's frightening to not be in control of yourself and to not know what is going on, but we are going to figure it out."

"But when? My skin is becoming scalier and I have these lingering white patches that aren't going away when I transform back into a human. I'm afraid the dragon inside me is becoming a permanent part of me and I don't know if I'll be able to turn back someday."

"I know, snowflake. I know. Let me take a look at your skin and see if I can figure anything out.

Erianna pulled up her sleeve and held out her arm to Archimedes so he could examine it. He pulled out one of the eye glasses from his pocket and put it up to his eye. The larger patch on her arm looked reptilian and white, very similar to what her dragon scales looked like. He lightly brushed his fingers over it to see if it was hard like dragon scales or if it was still fleshy. Erianna winced and let out a small cry.

"I'm sorry, petal. I have to see how deep it's holding onto your skin." Archimedes touched a few more little patches that looked more like she had dried white paint on her skin. "Do these ones hurt?"

"No, the smaller ones itch mostly."

"Hmm. Lean your head down so I can look at your eyes."

Erianna bent her head down slightly. Archimedes grabbed a candle from the table and passed it in front of her eyes. Her pupils were slightly narrower than he expected but they didn't look too altered.

"What's wrong with me, Archimedes? Why is it holding on longer than it used to?"

Archimedes let out a deep sigh and braced himself for what he was about to tell her. "I'm afraid it's what you said. The curse is taking a more permanent hold. I was afraid of this, but I didn't know if it would happen or not so I never wanted to mention it when you were younger. But, I'm afraid if you don't find a way to break this curse by the moon's rise on your 21st birthday, you might never change back to a human again."

Rage and hurt surged through Erianna as she listened to Archimedes' words. "Never change back? You never told me it might get worse or that I had a timeline to find a cure or some magical way to break this curse."

Erianna stood up, nearly knocking Archimedes off his stool and began to pace again. "A curse that I wasn't even the cause of. How am I supposed to find a way to break it if I don't even know why this happened to me or how?" Erianna turned and stalked towards Archimedes.

"And you, you little evil hobgoblin. Is this all just some sick game for you to watch and enjoy because you're too bitter and stubborn to break free from this banishment so you just sit here stewing and waiting for some helpless damaged girl to come your way so you can get some enjoyment out of her pain?" Erianna dropped the teacup she had still been holding as her hand went up to head to stop a sharp pain in her head.

"Easy, lass," Archimedes warned. "I don't have room for you to be changing into a dragon in my living room."

Erianna glared at him as the pain passed. "I'm sorry to be such a burden to you after all these years. I assumed you would have been more understanding of my situation. Especially since you were the one who just told me I have all of three days to find a way to cure this wretched curse."

"I didn't know if the curse would take effect like that or not, *dearie*. Give an old man a break for being confined in this forsaken realm and not having seen you in nearly ten years, I didn't rightly know how to give you that information."

"I didn't leave because I wanted to. You were the only person who was kind enough to take me in and care for me but my powers were growing stronger and stronger every day and I didn't want to risk hurting you or have my mother find out I was here. She would have destroyed you if she knew you were harboring me here and I couldn't allow that to happen."

Another pain lanced Erianna's head. "This curse," she said in a growled whisper.

Archimedes picked up her teacup from where she had dropped it and filled it with more of the calming tea he had made earlier and handed it to her. "Here, drink some more of this. It will help with the pain and it will calm some of your overwrought nerves."

Erianna took it and began to drink it slowly as Archimedes continued. "Now, I know you are upset with me and this curse and everything about it. It has taken everything from you and it's unfair you have had to suffer through all this. I don't know why the Great Mage chose to give you this story to live but I believe he has a master plan in all of this."

"The Great Mage. What hand could he have in all this? If his hand was truly in any of this, I'd be at home with my sister living a normal life."

"You don't know that. He alone has the power to write our stories and he always has a purpose for what is written in each of our lives."

"If he alone has the power to write our stories, then he's the only one who can change mine," Erianna said mockingly as she took another sip of her tea. She stopped as she realized what she just said.

"The Great Mage. He can change my story. He can fix all of this. I can find him and have him break this curse."

"I don't think that is a good idea, lass."

"Why not? You just said he alone has the power to write or change our stories. If he can do that, he can break this curse. I have to find him." She stopped and looked at him. "And you know where he is, don't you?"

"Not necessarily."

"But you were his apprentice. You must know where he is. Please Archimedes. This could be my only chance to be normal again. If the curse is broken, my mother won't have a reason to banish me anymore and I'll be able to be with Brinn again."

"I know you want to be with your sister again. Believe me, if I could cure or break this curse for you, I would have done it years ago. But the Mage hasn't been seen in this realm since your mother's coronation and I wouldn't know where he was, even if he did still visit this realm."

"But, Archimedes--"

"No, Erianna. It's not possible. The only place he would show up at is the abandoned cathedral in the woods and that takes a special person looking for it to find it. It only reveals itself to those who are truly in need, and goodness knows I've searched those woods times enough and never found it, so I doubt if it even exists. Besides, you could never find it before the solstice moon, even if you tried."

Archimedes looked at Erianna. He sighed and walked over to her and took her hand in his. "I'm sorry snowflake. I know that isn't the news you wanted to hear. I wish there were a way to help you but it's out of my power to help you. The curse may not become permanent after the solstice moon. Who am I to say anything? I'm just a crazy old man who has been alone in this hovel for far too long. Maybe you will find a way to break it. If anyone could do it, you could."

Erianna looked down at him and smiled a sad smile. "Thank you."

"You best get some rest. You will need to take your sister back to the palace tonight."

"Tonight? But Archimedes, why?"

"Your mother is in a tight fix to find her and if she ever discovered that she has been with you or with me, she would have both our heads on a platter."

Erianna bowed her head knowingly. "What time am I to be ready?"

"I'll wake you when it is time to go."

Erianna nodded and walked toward the dirt hallway that led to the back rooms.

"Erianna, she can't remember any of this."

Erianna looked back at Archimedes and held his gaze for a moment, wishing she didn't have to do this. She closed her eyes and turned to go. "I'll take care of it."

Archimedes watched as Erianna's deflated form walked down the earthy corridor. "Great Mage, please help these sisters find each other again. Don't let their mother's punishment destroy their happiness."

Chapter 13

Brinn ran through the woods. She couldn't believe the things she had heard. She had made her way to the living and kitchen area and was about to join Erianna and Archimedes when she heard them talking about her. Archimedes had told Erianna she had to take Brinn back to the palace tonight. She had been cooped up in that icy prison for too long. The past few days had been the best days of her life. She was finally free for the first time ever. Not just the small freedom she felt when she snuck off to the hidden garden at the edge of town. She was in a completely different part of the realm experiencing life rather than just living it. She was on a grand adventure like the adventures she read about in all of her books. She, Brinnleonora was living out her own epic story. She was not going back without a fight.

She had to stop and catch her breath. She braced herself against a tree. This part of the realm was so different from the northern realm. All the trees looked the same and there was no sign of any other life anywhere.

Some of the other things she overheard Archimedes and Erianna talking about filled her mind. Archimedes had called Erianna her sister. She didn't have a sister. Nothing in her entire life had ever indicated she had ever had a sister. Why wouldn't her mother have mentioned her or said anything about her if she existed? What had kept Erianna away from their family all these years?

"Brinn."

And what cathedral in the woods was Archimedes talking about? Who was the Great Mage?

"Brinn, where are you?"

Erianna. She couldn't let her find her. Brinn took a few deep breaths and continued running. She had no idea where she was running to or which direction she was headed. The stars. She had read in one of her books about the north star. The biggest and brightest star in the sky. If she could find that star she could at least figure out what direction she was going.

"Brinn. Come back to the house. Please. I don't want you to get hurt out here."

Brinn looked back towards the direction of the sound. She wanted to go back. She was just getting to know Erianna. She didn't want to lose the closest thing to a friend she had ever had. But she couldn't go back. Not if it meant going home. She turned her head back to the trail before her just as she tripped over a tree root.

"Brinn?"

Brinn pulled at the material that snagged on a branch when she fell. She could hear Erianna coming closer. "No, no, no. Come on."

"Brinn. Are you hurt? What are you doing out here? I went to see if you wanted some tea and you were gone."

"Stop, Erianna. Don't come near me." Brinn finally ripped the material and stood up across from Erianna.

"Why? What's wrong?" Erianna asked, taking a step towards Brinn.

Brinn held up her hands. "I don't want to hurt you Erianna."

Erianna stopped, "Brinn. Calm down. We can talk about this."

"I heard plenty from you and Archimedes."

Realization settled over Erianna. "How much did you hear?"

"Enough to know you want to take me back to that god-forsaken palace and leave me there for the rest of my life."

"Brinn. Just calm down. I can explain."

"What are you going to explain? That you weren't going to take me back? I heard you tell him you would take me back tonight. He made you promise to leave me there and told you I couldn't remember anything. Why?"

Erianna felt a twinge of something changing inside her. She looked up and saw slivers of moonlight beginning to poke through the trees. "Oh no. Not now." Erianna took a deep breath and tried to hold off the transformation for a few moments. "Brinn. I will explain everything to you when we get back to Archimedes'. I promise. But we have to go now."

Brinn began to hear the pounding rhythm of the heartbeat she had heard two nights ago. She closed her eyes and focused on the sound. Brinn opened her eyes slowly and looked at Erianna. "It's your heartbeat I've been hearing."

Erianna shook off another wave of dizziness. "What?" Her breathing was becoming shallow.

Brinn's eyes widened. "And the breathing. My dream the other night. It wasn't a dream was it?"

"No. And if we don't get out of the moonlight soon your dream is going to become a very real nightmare."

Erianna reached for Brinn and as their hands touched a bright light began to shine from beneath their faces.

"What's happening?" Brinn asked?

"I don't know." Erianna responded as snow began to swirl around the two of them. She looked at Brinn and saw the necklace dangling from her neck. She looked down at her own necklace and realized her breathing was returning to normal.

"Brinn. Our necklaces are glowing. I'm not transforming."

Brinn looked at the glowing pendants each of them were wearing and looked at Erianna. The beating sound in her ears was beginning to subside.

"What does that mean?"

"I don't know. I've never been able to control a transformation like this before." Erianna looked away as snow began to whip around their faces. "But that doesn't seem to be the only thing we're doing. We have to let go of each other or this storm is going to get worse."

"No. I'm not letting go. I don't want you to transform again," Brinn yelled as gusty winds began to blow around them.

"Brinn. It's ok. I've been going through this for as long as I can remember. Just make sure I make it back to Archimedes' in the morning.

"No. We can stop it together. We just have to trust each other." Brinn grabbed Erianna's other hand and closed her eyes, willing the storm into stillness. Within moments the wind stilled and the snow fell peacefully to the ground.

Erianna looked at Brinn in amazement, "How did you--?"

"I--I don't know. I thought of keeping you safe and it just stopped."

Erianna smiled, "I guess we have a lot to learn about each other." She put her hand on Brinn's cheek and wiped away the tear that had escaped during the chaos. "Let's go back to the house. Archimedes will be wondering what happened to us."

Brinn smiled and nodded.

They linked arms and made their way back way back to the little hovel.

The shadow that had been watching them readied the arrow in his bow, and took aim.

"Stop."

The shadow stopped and lowered his weapon.

The snow queen watched as her daughters walked away together. "Follow them. But don't let them know you are watching them. I will give you further instruction when the time comes."

Tharynn complied and followed Brinn and Erianna back through the woods.

The snow queen dismissed the vision from her mirror and stormed around her massive throne room.

"The little imp. How did they find each other?" she screamed as she threw one of the jeweled boxes from one of the large tables that sat on either side of her throne.

She paced the large space, seething at the reunion of her daughters. "One thing is for certain. They cannot remain together."

A gleam shimmered in the snow queen's eyes as she walked over to the table nearest the mirror. Opening an ice blue box, she pulled out a delicate crystal. "My daughter thinks she is so happy being reunited with a long lost sister. We will see how she feels when she comes face to face with the real beast I tried to keep her from all these years."

Chapter 14

Gabriel slowly opened his eyes. His eyelids felt heavy like a wet blanket in the spring rain. As he worked to open his eyes more fully, they felt like someone had dumped a bucket of sand in them from one of the beaches in the summer realm. Not to mention someone had taken the liberty of banging on the bucket with a shovel, making his head pound like heavy raindrops on a tin roof.

His eyes finally opened enough to be useful. He blinked a few times, letting his eyes adjust to the brightness of the room. The room was a peculiar size. Roots were growing in the walls that were packed with dirt. The ceiling felt low and made him feel like he had ended up in an underground hole of some kind. As his eyes took in the rest of the room, they landed on a figure that was a brilliant white contrast to the earthy tones surrounding him. His eyes focused on the figure. She wore a beautiful flowing gown of white with threads of silver woven throughout. A long almost white braid fell down her back like a snowy ladder. She turned away from the window she had been staring out of and his eyes were met with the most crystalline eyes he had ever seen. Or had he seen them before?

"Good morning. I wasn't sure if you would be able to wake up this morning." Erianna walked towards him. She leaned down and brushed her fingers across his forehead.

Her delicate hand brought a soothing touch to Gabriel's aching head. He closed his eyes allowing the cool, soft touch to sink in.

"Your fever has subsided, which is good news. How are you feeling?" she asked as she poured a glass of water from the pitcher that stood on the small table beside the bed. A bed that seemed a lot smaller than the one he had at home. She sat beside him and helped tip his head up slightly so he could take a drink of the refreshing cup.

He laid his head back down. "I'm not sure. How should I be feeling?" he asked.

"Well, you've had an exciting few days. I don't know what trouble you are used to getting yourself into where you come from, but you've been through quite the ordeal the past few days. Do you not remember anything that has happened?" she asked, concerned that the fever may have affected his memories.

Gabriel breathed in and closed his eyes, trying to see through the fog of his mind's eye. He reached back to a few days ago to see if he could remember anything that had transpired. His brow furrowed as he concentrated, grasping at anything that came up in his mind. What had happened to him?

Erianna watched as he tried his hardest to dredge up some kind of memory of the past few days. Her hand brushed his forehead again, pushing a dark curl from his forehead, as if that lock of hair was what was blocking his memory from coming back. Her fingers trailed down his strong jaw line and traced it up to his masculine cheekbones. She stared at him taking in his features for the first time since her world collided with his three days ago.

His skin was a dark almost tan color, which was an intriguing change compared to the blanche complexions of everyone in this realm. His hair was dark as well, but had lighter streaks throughout, making it look like it had been kissed by the sun. She ran her fingers through the silky waves that topped his head and smiled. He opened his eyes as she brushed another wave from his forehead. Her heart stopped as she gazed into the royal emerald green eyes that stared back at her. Never had she seen such dark, rich colors in someone's eyes before.

His eyes widened as she stared at him and she realized her hand had come to rest along the side of his face. Embarrassed, she pulled her icy fingers away and turned to hide the slight pale pink hue that now colored her cheeks. Gabriel shot up.

"You were the one lying in the snow the other morning. You were bruised and battered and I--" Gabriel cringed as he left arm twinged from the sudden movement.

Erianna reached out to stop him. "Lay down. Don't try to think about it. Just lay down and rest." She helped ease him back onto the pillow as gently as she could.

Archimedes came rushing in as quickly as his bent legs could carry him. "What in blue blazes are you doing to the poor man? We can hear him screaming all the way down in the kitchen, which is a far jaunt through these tunnels to here, as you well enough know."

Archimedes pulled his small stool across the room and stepped up on it so he could get a better look at the young prince.

"I'm sorry, Archimedes. He forgot what happened and sat up too quickly. He put all his weight on his left arm." Fear edged Erianna's voice as she watched the pain fill the handsome face she had been admiring.

"He wasn't supposed to remember much of anything. You must have triggered his memories somehow," Archimedes growled as he began to tend to Gabriel.

"Why wasn't he supposed to remember? What did you do to him last night when you were supposed to be taking care of him?" Erianna asked as small puffs of anger began to seethe between her clenched teeth.

"Erianna, go back to the kitchen and help Brinn get some breakfast on."

"I will not leave him alone with you. What did you do to him?"

"I put a portion of an ice kiss elixir in his potent to help him sleep."

"You gave him a forgetting potion? Archimedes. You know how dangerous that can be. Why would you do that to him?"

"Hush, girl, you're disturbing the patient. Now, go tend to your sister in the kitchen, or he won't be the only one suffering from a memory loss."

Erianna's eyes narrowed at the little man. She was about to fire another indignant retort at him when Gabriel reached out his good hand and took hold of Erianna's arm.

"No, I need her to stay." Gabriel looked at her, not sure what impulse was firing through the pain to make sure she stayed with him. But something about her made him feel like he could face anything. Without her, he couldn't even imagine it. Another debilitating pain shot up his arm, taking his pleading gaze from her.

Erianna looked down at Gabriel. No one had ever needed her before. Surprise and a touch of softness filled Erianna's eyes, but when she looked at Archimedes, her look quickly changed to a look of victory over the old man's orders.

Archimedes did not miss the smirk that pulled at the corners of her lips as she knelt beside Gabriel. Archimedes gave Erianna the disapproving look of a father who had been defiantly disobeyed. A painful moan from Gabriel turned his attention back to unwrapping the bandages around Gabriel's arm so he could look at the wound.

Gabriel's wound had bled a bit during the night, causing the last bandage to cling tighter to the wound than the others. As Archimedes gently pulled at the cloth, another twinge of pain shot down Gabriel's arm, causing his entire body to seize up. His arm began to stiffen and a deep, intense pain engulfed his entire arm, causing him to cry out in pain. Erianna's eyes filled with worry as she watched the prince convulse from the wretched pain. His right hand shot out, grasping for anything that might lessen the pain. Erianna instinctively wrapped her long fingers through his and prayed some of the pain would be transferred to her through her touch.

"What is happening to him?" Erianna asked, her voice shaking like a shriveled leaf in a winter breeze.

"The bane is mastesticizing with his veins," he replied as he pulled out a small orange vial from the pouch he had brought in with him.

Erianna looked at him with a look so mixed with confusion and complete fear, her eyes almost looked like a broken reflection in a mirror

"His veins are literally turning to ice, dearie," He continued as he pulled out a long, bent needle.

The pain subsided for a moment, allowing Gabriel a chance to breathe. His eyes shot to the little old man beside him, "What do you mean my veins are turning to ice?" he asked through short, ragged breaths.

Archimedes ignored the question as he felt Gabriel's exposed arm to see how far down the ice had travelled.

Erianna watched Archimedes' nimble hands, hoping the hobgoblin's diagnosis had been overly exaggerated.

Gabriel broke the silence and asked again, "What do you mean my veins are turning to ice?" He looked to Erianna to see if she would answer.

As Erianna's eyes met his, she knew she couldn't keep what was happening to him a secret. "The arrow Brinn shot you with when she thought you were attacking me was laced with winter's bane. It's a poison that bonds with the molecules of whatever it touches and--" Erianna swallowed the lump that was beginning to form in her throat so she could continue. "As it bonds with the molecules, it will slowly begin to turn them to ice."

"Can it be stopped?" he asked, eyes pleading with her to give him even the smallest ray of hope to hold on to. Erianna's eyes flitted from Gabriel's to Archimedes. He watched as her blue eyes shimmered from the tears that were beginning to form. As she looked back at Gabriel, the look of sorrow reflecting back at him in her eyes confirmed what he feared.

Gabriel's eyes looked like the deep sea itself had been drained from them, leaving shallow pools for irises in his eyes. He turned his head to the ceiling, allowing the reality of his new situation to sink in. A small tear fell from the corner of his eye making a trail to his ear. Erianna's heart twinged at the new kind of pain that was beginning to settle into his handsome features. Her delicate hand brushed the tear away. The touch of her hand was soft and made something spark within him that he had never felt before. He allowed his face to fall more fully into her hand, drawing on the strength and reassurance of her touch.

Archimedes cleared his throat, trying to steer the situation back to less slushy ground. "Don't go melting into a puddle just yet. Let me check your arm and we will see how bad off we really are. I need to see how deeply the ice has gone and how much of your arm is still salvageable."

Erianna shot him an icy look, condemning him for using such a word. "Uh, I meant to say how much of your arm has been affected." He cleared his throat and continued, "I will have to poke around a bit with my needle and see how bad the damage is. Do you think you can handle that, rosebud?"

Gabriel breathed in a deep sigh and looked at Erianna. "Will you stay with me?" he asked.

Erianna mustered a small smile and squeezed his hand. "Of course I will."

A small smile brightened his face and he squeezed her hand in return. He turned his head back to Archimedes.

"All right, poke away."

Chapter 15

"You know, it's not your fault the boy is in the condition he is. You were trying to protect your sister."

"Some protection. I didn't even know I had a sister until last night."

"Oh, I think you knew deep down inside you that she was connected to you in some way. Why else would you have left against your mother's bidding and braved the big white world?"

Erianna peered around the corner as she watched Archimedes pour Brinn a cup of tea. Gabriel had finally fallen back into some sort of sleep, though how deep, Erianna couldn't say. She had been making her way to the kitchen when she heard them talking about him and decided to listen for a bit before making her presence known.

"I don't know," Brinn responded as she watched Archimedes twirl his shortbread cookie in his tea and decided to do the same. They didn't have drinks like this in the palace and she didn't want to look like the odd one out for not knowing the proper way to drink it. Erianna smiled as she watched. Brinn was so curious and thirsty for knowledge. What kind of life had she known all these years with their mother in the palace?

Archimedes took a small sip after biting into the softened cookie and Brinn followed suit. "Mmmmm." Brinn sighed as she took another sip of the delicious tea. "I have never had anything so wonderful in all my life. It's minty but sweet and something about it tastes like, like--"

"Home?" Archimedes inquired as he watched the young girl. "Your sister used to say the same thing when she got older." A twinkle glimmered in Archimedes' eye as he took another sip of the 'homey' beverage.

Brinn smiled at him, a twinkle glimmering back at him, as she replied, "Yes. That's exactly it." She put down her cup and looked into it as she figured out how to best ask Archimedes about her sister. She stared into the cup as if half expecting the question to magically appear in the steam.

As if reading her mind, Archimedes prompted, "You probably have a yard of questions about your mother and your sister, I reckon."

She stared harder into her tea as she began to run her finger around the edge of the cup. "I admit, all this new information is a bit of a snowstorm in my mind."

Archimedes smiled as he watched her do the same thing Erianna did when lost in thought. "Well, would you like me to start with your mother or with your sister?"

Brinn's crystal clear gaze met his as she responded with so much curiosity lurking behind her reflective irises. "Is it too much to start at the beginning?"

Archimedes' hard features became as soft as a spring snow as he looked at the sweet, curious creature before him.

"The beginning is usually a better place to start," he replied with a warm smile.

Erianna hung back, just as eager to hear the whole story as Brinn was. She didn't want to interrupt the same tale she had always longed to hear.

Archimedes cleared his throat as he began his tale, "Long ago, a young queen was born to the rulers of the winter realm. She was a beautiful baby girl with pale white skin that sat like a blanket of snow under a blonde cap of hair. She was a very special baby and the Great Mage sent a magnificent gift to the child to be proclaimed over her at the celebration of her birth."

"What was the gift?" Brinn asked as she was pulled into the story.

"Why, me, of course," the hobgoblin laughed as he took a sip of his tea before continuing. "I mean to say, the great Mage sent me to proclaim the gift over the child. He promised to give the young queen a long and prosperous rule as long as her heart remained pure as snow and unhardened by the icy bitterness and vanity of the realm."

"The queen did indeed grow in beauty and grace and became one of the most beloved children of the realm. The kingdom was full of excitement as her coronation day came and she would be crowned the next queen of Sylvania and ruler of all the winter realm. The day of her coronation came and the king and queen held a grand ball to celebrate her 21st birthday. All of the most powerful beings of the realms were in attendance and it was a sight to see indeed," Archimedes smiled as he remembered the wondrous day.

"You were there too?" Brinn asked, eyes wide with amazement and silently urging the hobgoblin to go on.

"Indeed I was, lass. The Great Mage sent me, Archimedes, to bestow his second gift on the child. I was one of the Mage's star apprentices at the time and was ready to become a wizard of my own accord." Archimedes bubbled with laughter at the sweet memories.

"Delivering the queen's coronation gift was to be my last task as an apprentice. Wouldn't you know it would be the last task I would ever perform as a free man." His eyes clouded over as he got up to get more tea.

"What happened?" Brinn asked, hanging on every word the hobgoblin shared.

"Exactly what was supposed to happen, or I suppose whatever the Mage set in motion to happen that day," he replied as he poured the tea into Brinn's cup and settled down on the bench again.

"The Mage had sent a beautifully etched floor length mirror to the queen for her 21st birthday. I had no idea what powers it possessed at the time and as I presented it to the queen, I was in just as much awe of the enchanting gift as anyone else. She couldn't resist gazing at the beautiful figure that reflected back at her and her heart became pricked with the smallest sliver of vanity that festered and turned her once warm heart to a cold, icy remnant of what had been left behind. Becoming so enthralled with her beauty she felt no one could ever be as beautiful as she. When she looked and saw the beauty that had been brought into her realm by the spring and summer counsels, she banished them from ever traversing this realm again."

"The Great Mage was distraught over her decision to feed her vanity rather than see the beauty in her kingdom so he pronounced a curse over her through me-- 'Until the beauty in your heart is reborn, you shall bear no rose but only thorn.' The queen didn't appreciate having that said to her, and that's when she banished me to this idyllic little spot, preventing me from ever becoming apprentice to the Mage or allowing me to use my magic to help others again."

Brinn's eyes clouded over, trying to process the things the hobgoblin had shared. She ran her finger around the edge of her cup as she looked up at him with questions in her eyes. "But, you helped Eria--my sister--when she came to you. How did you find her and get away with helping her without my--our-- mother knowing?"

Erianna had sunk down to a sitting position, pulling her knees into her chest, just beyond the doorway as she listened to her mother's tale unfold. She leaned her head back against the earthy wall and closed her eyes as she remembered the events that had shaped her childhood.

Archimedes sighed as he continued the arduous tale, "Your mother lost sight of all things beautiful that day her heart turned cold. A few years after her coronation, she gave birth to a little girl. A perfect bundle of snow with her ten fingers and ten toes and the sweetest smile you have ever seen that made her eyes twinkle like stars on a wintery night." Archimedes' face formed a wistful, far off dreamy look as he recollected the delicate features of the baby girl that had worked her way into his heart when she found him as a little girl. She had done wonders in softening his own hard heart after the bitterness he felt towards the snow queen and even the great Mage himself when he had been banished to this part of the realm.

"She was as perfect as perfect could be. The queen loved her as best as she could with her cold heart and took such special care of her for the first few years of the young snowflakes' life. But, around the time the girl turned four, a strange thing began to take place. Every first quarter of the moon, Erianna developed a strange habit of sleepwalking and would return to the palace all battered and bruised in the morning, but unable to remember anything that had happened to her the night before. The queen became very concerned and began to watch her daughter very closely. The night of the full moon, her little girl would walk out into the snow and look up into the moon, allowing its power to fill her and change her into a--a--" Archimedes paused to dispense the thickness that had formed in his throat as he recalled the first time he had seen the transformation for himself. The pain that overwhelmed the little girl's features brought tears to his eyes as he stood powerless to do anything to help her or stop her from changing.

Erianna's eyes closed tighter to push out the painful memories that enshrouded her childhood. Never understanding what was going on or how she could stop it from happening again and again and again. A warm, gentle hand brushed her cheek as a tear escaped her clenched eyelids. Her teary eyes opened wide and she felt a sharp intake of breath hit her lungs as she saw Gabriel kneeling before her. Her mouth opened but his finger touched her lips to prevent her from speaking. How long had he been standing there and how much had he heard? Panic filled her eyes as she wasn't sure how much of her sordid past she wanted this stranger to hear. How would he react if he found out she transformed into a beast every full moon?

He smiled when he looked back at her, causing her greatest fears to melt away in an instant. She looked back into those same, sure eyes she had gazed into earlier and wondered at the effect he seemed to have on her. He pushed a loose white lock away from her face and smiled even more as he settled in next to her.

Erianna was drawn back to the conversation when she heard Brinn ask Archimedes how he had found her as a child.

"Did mother send her to you when she found out?" Brinn asked, pain mixed with hope in her eyes.

Archimedes toyed with his drink as he let out a long, drawn out no, trying to figure out the best way to continue his tale. "No, lass. Your mother actually came to me when she discovered what had been happening to your sister and asked if I had anything that could prevent it from happening. I told her that was a power only the Great Mage himself possessed. She stormed out of here and sought help from the greatest magical beings she could find, but she refused to go to the Mage for help since he had cursed her. She was never able to grasp the thought that she had cursed herself by giving into her vanity and I'm afraid the effects on your sister were fringe effects of the curse she belied on herself."

"And me? Am I cursed as well?" Brinn asked.

"It's hard to tell, youngin'. Your mother came to me shortly after she found out she was going to have another baby and asked if I could prevent the same from happening to you. I told her the moon seemed to be the one in control of her daughter's changing so I gave her a crystal that was supposed to absorb the power of the moon and lessen its grasp over whoever wore it."

Brinn's hand went to her necklace the same time Erianna's did. "Our necklaces. They started glowing last night when we touched during the moon's rise." She looked at Archimedes. "Did you give one to Erianna as well?"

"Aye, I did. Your mother kept the one I gave her around your neck at all times after you were born. Your sister's transformations started becoming worse, causing her to take on more dragon-like instincts whenever she transformed. She didn't know how to control it at the time so she would destroy things with her icy breath or growing wings or even claw at whatever tried to stop her. Your mother was afraid that as long as Erianna was around, you would always be in danger."

"So she banished her too," Brinn said as she stared despondently into her empty cup.

"Aye. She sent her to the farthest part of the region where she couldn't harm anyone. After years of living in solitude, I never expected to see another soul in this part of the woods, except the queen when she needed something I had. But, one day, a small girl with the clearest blue eyes I have ever seen knocked on my door and asked if she could come in."

Erianna shuddered as a fresh round of tears filled her eyes. All the memories of living here with Archimedes came flooding back. He had helped her gain control of her powers and worked relentlessly on focusing her subconscious on the phases of the transformation so she could break the memory barrier and no longer be afraid of what she might do while she was a beast. He had given her the crystal as something to hold onto when she felt the moon's powers were becoming too much. And then her mother had discovered that he had been harboring her and she had to flee to the Shaelyn Mountains to live life on her own, away from anyone or anything.

Erianna felt something shift beside her and the warmth of a strong arm wrap around her. Gabriel had come to the other side of her so he could pull her in with his good arm and provide any amount of comfort and strength he could. Having never felt the touch of a mother's love, or anyone's love for that matter, Erianna's impulses told her to pull away. She couldn't let herself love anyone. Especially now with her transformations becoming worse again. She couldn't risk hurting anyone or putting anyone she cared about in harm's way. But something in the way he looked at her and held her made her feel she couldn't do this on her own anymore. She needed someone to be with her through her hardest times. For the slightest moment, Erianna let her icy veil break and allowed herself to melt into the comforting grasp of Gabriel's arm.

"Well, if this isn't a pretty picture," Archimedes said as he stood next to Gabriel and Erianna with Brinn beside him.

Erianna pushed away from Gabriel and looked at Archimedes like a little girl who had been caught with her finger in the cookie jar.

"You're as bad as your sister, you are. Listening to other people's conversations from the corners of the room without joining them like a civilized person. And you," he pointed a jagged finger at the prince, "You should be in bed. You have no right to be roaming these halls when you're supposed to be feeling poorly."

Gabriel was still warming up to the little man's sardonic humor and wasn't quite sure how to respond. "I'm feeling much better thanks to you," he replied with his most gracious smile trying to win over the old man.

"That melty, mushy sweet talk has no effect on me. You can ask both these girls. They'll tell you I'm as prickly and unloving as a grizzly bear woken up before the spring thaw."

Erianna and Brinn looked at each other and smiled knowing smiles at the little man's callous air.

"If you're out of bed, you might as well have some tea. I certainly don't want to be the one to drink it all," he said as he hobbled over to the kitchen to put some more tea on.

Gabriel looked at Erianna with a warm smile and reached out his hand to help her up. "It seems we have been instructed to join them for tea. Shall we?"

Erianna smiled back and placed her hand in his, allowing him to pull her up. "Just be careful, once he thinks he has you under his thumb, he will be relentless."

She linked her arm through his as they walked the few steps into the kitchen and took their seats for another round of tea.

Chapter 16

L aughter ensued as Archimedes recounted some of the spots Erianna had gotten herself into as a child. The cheery afternoon brightened the bleakness of the past few days and made all of them nearly forget what had brought them all together in the first place.

"So, son. What has brought you to our blighty part of the world from your realm?" Archimedes asked as he caught his breath from the last bout of laughter.

Gabriel's laughter waned and he took a sip of the peppermint tea. It had a cooler taste than the tea he was used to drinking in his realm, but he was beginning to enjoy the wintry blend. "Unfortunately, unpleasant circumstances have brought me to this realm."

Erianna sat up, eager to hear why he was in their realm. She realized she had never asked in the chaos that had ensued the past few days.

"My realm has slowly begun to lose its power over the years. The flowers that bud and bloom in our realm are barely making it past seed stages. Trees are shrinking, the grass is growing pale. It's a strange set of events to say the least and my family is convinced the answer lies somewhere in the winter realm."

"Hmm," Archimedes pondered as he took a sip of his favorite tea. "Those are strange events indeed. The spring realm is the realm of rebirth and brings about all the new life that goes out into the world every year. If that realm isn't faring well, I shudder to think what the summer realm is looking like."

"Much the same, I'm afraid. We have cousins who live in that land and last time we were together, they told us many of the rivers are disappearing and many of the animals are leaving to find better food and shelter. Though, I'm not sure where else the animals can turn to if our two realms are fading away."

Archimedes harrumphed as he took his last sip of tea and pulled himself off the bench, crossing over to the shelves that contained some of his books.

"What was the spring realm like?" Brinn asked, eager as ever to hear firsthand about the other realms.

Gabriel sighed, "It was beautiful," he breathed out, remembering the cool breezes that danced through his hair as the sun set over the valley.

"It's not as vibrant as the summer realm by any means. But everything is so fresh and new."

"And warm?" Erianna asked with a twinkle in her eyes as she leaned forward to hear more of Gabriel's tale.

Gabriel smiled, "Yes. But not balmy and hot like the summer realm." Gabriel's arm twinged, causing him to pause.

Archimedes hobbled back over the table with one of his big books, "About how long would you say the realm has been losing power?"

Gabriel rubbed his arm, "My sister and I became aware of it a year or two ago, but I think my parents and the counsel knew before that."

"Mmmm."

"Do you know what's causing it?" Erianna asked, watching Archimedes as he flipped through the worn pages of his book.

Archimedes shook his head and put the book on the table next to Brinn. "Do you know the source of your realms power?" he asked.

"Only the king and queen know, I'm afraid." Gabriel said.

Archimedes looked over his spectacled nose at the boy, "Are you tellin' me you're the prince about to be crowned 'His Royal Highness' and you don't know the source of your kingdom's power?" he asked incredulously.

Gabriel's face flushed in embarrassment. "With the power disappearing over the years, my parents didn't want to risk sharing such vital information with anyone, especially two impressionable children who might slip when talking to others."

A disgusted sound came from Archimedes as he turned back to his book. "Well, lad--and you lasses better listen well to this as one of you will be on the throne yourself someday--" he paused and looked directly at Erianna before he started into his history lesson.

"The four realms run off the same source of power, but the power for each realm is different in itself. That's so we can have the four seasons that occur in the other worlds. It seems the sun and the moon have to do a great deal with their powers. The winter realm requires so many decibels of power, the spring realm, fewer but more than the autumn realm. Summer requires the most, though winter, I suppose requires just as much, just in reverse."

Erianna interrupted with a cough. "Archimedes, as fascinating as these facts and figures are, perhaps you should begin at the beginning of how the realms received their powers so we can better understand why they are losing them."

Archimedes looked up and saw the bland expressions of his pupils. "Do you children know nothing?" he asked, irritated at being interrupted and annoyed by their ignorance.

Erianna looked around and said, "In my defense, I was banished to live on my own in the woods and surprisingly this never came up in our lessons, Archimedes," she smiled as she looked at the codgering old man.

Brinn chimed in after her, "And I was left pretty much to myself in the castle growing up. I'm afraid my mother didn't find an education necessary."

"And you, what is your excuse for being left so ignorant of the world turning about you?" Archimedes asked looking at Gabriel.

Gabriel rubbed his neck trying to come up with a better answer, "Well, I'm afraid my parents did care for our education but my sister and I were rather troublesome to educate," he finished with a sheepish grin.

"Such ignorance. Though I'm not surprised. Old Archimedes has to do everything, including educating the royal brats of each realm. Just add that to the endless duties of a banished goblin. Should I leave the door open for the offspring of the Fall and Summer realms as well?" During his rant, Archimedes had pushed the book away and crossed to the stove to get more tea, looking up and waving his finger at the sky as he seemed to be having a conversation with someone outside of the room more than to himself.

Gabriel watched, confused at the old man's actions, and Erianna smiled, remembering how often he used to do that. Some habits never changed, she mused to herself.

Archimedes came back and slammed a plate of scones and biscuits on the table followed by the steaming pot of tea. "As this lesson is going to be a longer one than I," he paused to find the right word, "anticipated, I suggest you nourish yourselves and pay attention. I don't need my students dropping like flies because they're hungry or distracted by growling insides." Archimedes readjusted himself on the bench and looked around, "Now, are we all ready?"

The three took a biscuit or scone and began buttering them in turn. They all nodded their heads in agreement.

"Centuries ago, a great Mage roamed the earth, looking to see what could be done with it. There was nothing here but the dirt of the earth beneath his feet and the expanse of the sky above his head. He thought, 'How nice it would be to see this earth as I walk upon it.' So, the Mage waved his staff and a bright, golden orb appeared in the sky, settling next to a silvery orb. They were followed by billions of little diamonds that he cast out into the great expanse of the sky. The two great orbs together, though beautiful, took away from the brilliance of the other, so the Mage shooed the moon into the darkness and kept the sun in the light. Seeing how bright the sun was by itself, the Mage sent the stars to shine with the moon so each light could be displayed and seen by those on the earth. He smiled at their beauty and continued on his walk throughout the earth."

"Next, the Mage brushed his staff along the ground as he walked and plants and grass and trees of all kinds began to sprout up and fill the earth. His feet danced as the newness of earth began to come to life and he laughed and he sang as the willow tree and wisteria came to be. And as he danced, he realized he needed music to carry on. So, he brought forth birds and foxes and bears and lions and goats and taught all of them to sing. Oh, it was a beautiful song. One like you've never heard before. The harmony and the symphony of it all. The trees and plants joined in with the rustling of their leaves and the sweet perfume of their smells. The rivers and streams began to laugh and gurgle with anticipation of what might come next. The oceans and mountains roared forth like the timpani of an orchestra. A greater sound of beauty than you could ever imagine."

"But, the Mage was not done. Though he relished in his beautiful creation and the song that they sang, he wanted someone to enjoy it and take care of it for him. So, he brought forth a man and a woman, the first king and queen of the earth. Once they were created, they joined in his song and they spent many days thereafter dancing and laughing and singing and seeing everything the Mage had made."

"Sounds breathtaking," Brinn said, imagining everything Archimedes was sharing as vividly as she possibly could.

"Indeed, it would have been at that," Archimedes beamed as he took a sip of his tea.

Erianna smiled as she took another bite of her biscuit. "But what happened to it all? What caused all the realms to separate and become as they are now?" she asked as she licked a bit of jam that had fallen to her finger.

Archimedes sighed a heavy sigh as his face clouded over at the recollection, "That, I'm sorry to say is not a happy tale." He took another sip and took a deep breath, bracing himself for where the story turned.

"As the Mage danced and sang with his new king and queen, one of the stars in the sky became jealous and wanted to be down there on the earth with them. The Mage saw the star begin to burn more brightly than the others as he tried to break free from the sky that held him. The Mage told the star that if he was so eager to take his place among the men of the earth, he could no longer be a brilliant star and cast him down to the earth to join the creatures he had created. The star wasn't content to be the only star on earth, so he climbed back up into the sky and pulled many stars down with him. His actions caused darkness to enter the earth and he vowed to stop at nothing until the beautiful earth the Mage had created was destroyed. Before the Mage could stop him, he disappeared into the ends of the earth bringing darkness and pain wherever he went. The Mage could hear the cry of trees as their songs were ended and the pain of his precious plants as they receded back into the earth whenever they were met by the evil star."

"The Mage knew his beautiful creation was no longer safe to be all together in the same place, so he came to the spot of creation and split the world into four realms, giving each a different function.

> 'As the sun sets and the moon rises, let each season do as
> it advises. Winter to spring and summer to fall, let them
> give way to one and in return, to all.'"

"The seasons creeds," Erianna sighed as she reflected on the weighty saying.

"Yes," replied Archimedes. "The very thing they were established on. But, it seems someone or something has learned to throw the balance," he replied with another heavy sigh.

Gabriel thought for a moment before asking, "Has the winter realm become colder over the past few years?"

Erianna looked up and then across to Brinn and Archimedes. "I honestly have no idea. It's just always been cold. And with my, uh, other being, I don't often notice how cold it is."

Brinn agreed. "Growing up here and never being allowed in the other realms, I don't know any different. Like Erianna said, it's just always been cold."

"Archimedes, would you say it's changed?" Gabriel asked, rubbing his arm again from the dull ache that was beginning to set in.

"Can't say that I've noticed either, but that could be the unchanging nature of this part of the realm," he replied as he got down to retrieve his pipe from the table by his favorite chair.

"Hmm. My parents were so convinced the problem lied in this realm. But if you say it hasn't changed much, I can't see how this realm would be receiving more of the power than any of the other realms."

"Archimedes, how do the realms continue to thrive every year?" Erianna asked.

Taking a puff from his pipe, Archimedes replied, "The place where the four kingdoms meet is the very place where the Mage split them up. Every solstice or equinox sun and moon fills the crystals with its power and sends out the beam of its light to bless the coming season and give way to the changes of the year. Surely you have had festivals or balls to celebrate your coming season," he said, looking around at each of the young adults before him.

Gabriel began slowly, "Now that you mention it, I believe we used to have a celebration of some sort. I seem to remember having one at the end of the winter solstice and one at the beginning of the spring equinox. We haven't had them for years though. It's no wonder I almost forgot."

"Mmm. That sounds about right. You would have been welcoming in your own season and looking forward to when your season would begin after winter's end. Come to think of it, I'd wager the snow queen stopped celebrating the solstice about when she banished me to these parts. I don't recall ever hearing of a party in town," Archimedes puffed.

"No. That would be right. We have never celebrated the solstice, at least that I remember," said Brinn. She got up and started to pace as she continued, "But we did always celebrate the equinox, which seemed odd to me. That is generally the first day of fall isn't it?"

"It is, yes." Archimedes answered.

"Yes," she continued. "Mother always made a big deal about that day and threw a huge celebration every year. I remember it because it was about the only time we had parties in the palace."

Archimedes started piecing together some of the information he was hearing. "Do you remember how the celebrations always ended?" he asked, leaning in as if the fate of the worlds rested on this very answer.

"Well, yes. We just had the celebration a few months ago. Every year we hold a big dance and invite everyone in the kingdom to come, well, mostly everyone," she said apologetically as she realized Erianna and Archimedes had never been invited to the ball.

"It's all right," Erianna replied. "I would have made an awkward dancing partner anyway," she smiled, reassuring Brinn that it was ok to carry on.

Brinn smiled, glad she hadn't made Erianna feel hurt at the slight of her, *their* mother. "Well, we would start the party as the sun began to set and dance until the moon began to rise. As it rose, the palace filled with the most brilliant light because of how the moon reflected off the ice walls in the ballroom. We would pause as the moon reached its highest point and share a toast to our kingdom."

The room fell silent as they each succumbed to their own thoughts. Gabriel disturbed the silence after a few moments by asking, "Archimedes. Isn't each equinox and solstice considered to be a double celebration of sorts? I mean, it would be the first day of one season but it would also be the herald of the season to come, right?"

"Mmm, Indeed. Each one, though a celebration of the season that is here is also the start of a journey to the season to come. I imagine in the days when the kingdoms were new the kingdoms celebrated the days together as each day was significant to the other realms as well. The changing of the seasons gives hope to the others that their celebration is yet to come," he replied.

Gabriel nodded. "So it would make sense for the snow queen to celebrate that day because it meant winter was on its way," Gabriel ventured, excitement growing within him.

"But why wouldn't she celebrate the winter solstice if that's the day winter is actually making its start every year?" Brinn asked.

"Because," Erianna started slowly, "That would mean the queen would have to say goodbye to her powers being the strongest ones for the next three seasons." An uneasy realization began to set in as she finished her thought.

Gabriel hit the table in his excitement, "The problem does lie in the winter realm, then. My parents were right. It's the snow queen that has been taking the power from the other realms over the years."

"No." Brinn shouted. "My mother may not be the kindest person in this world, but I can't believe she would ever do something so low and ill-conceived towards the other realms."

"No, Brinn. It makes sense. Why would she give up her powers for the rest of the year when she could have them at full strength the whole year round?" Erianna replied.

"But she would never do that," Brinn said, tears forming in her crystal eyes.

"Brinn, she sent me away when I was barely old enough to tie the laces on my snow boots."

"I know, but--"

"She banished Archimedes and has done many other things I'm sure we are not even aware of."

"If you only knew her--"

"Know her?" Erianna had gotten up at this point and was now standing eye to eye with her younger sister. "Brinn, she can't even bear to look at me because of who," Erianna closed her eyes and corrected herself, "because of *what* I am. What makes you think she would treat the other kingdoms with any more respect than that?" she asked, bitterness flaring in her heart.

"I've never seen her hurt anyone. So she's a bit vain and not always pleasant to be around. That doesn't make her a bad person."

"You may have never seen her physically hurt someone but I know it has happened. Brinn, our mother has splinters of ice in her heart. She can't love us the way she's supposed to. And up to date there seems no cure for it. Besides, if you ever did see anything you weren't supposed to, I'm sure she would have just kissed the memory away like she always did." Erianna felt her heart start to race and gripped the back of one of the chairs by the fireplace to prevent her emotions from getting out of control. Archimedes saw what was beginning to happen and scrambled off his bench to get some tonic to help diffuse what was coming.

Brinn stood frozen in place as the last words from Erianna landed on her ears. Her eyes hollowed and stared unbelieving at Erianna as she asked, "What do you mean kissed my memories away?"

Erianna, wishing she had never mentioned it, fought for control over the transformation that she had triggered. Her breaths were growing shallow, making her answer come out in choppy bits. "She has the ability to subdue memories with an icy kiss. I saw her do it to you when we were little. She tried to do it to me too, but I remember everything." A sharp pain seared Erianna's head as a vivid memory struck her, lighting an ethereal fire in her eyes. She snorted releasing a puff of icy smoke from her nostrils.

Archimedes pulled the green jeweled bottle from where he had hidden it years ago. "I was really hoping I would never have to use this again," he said before he turned to race across the room. In his hurry, Archimedes tripped on his long scarf, sending him hurtling to the ground.

Brinn's own emotions were beginning to spiral, causing small white flakes of snow to start falling around her. Trying to process through the things Erianna had just told her, she looked at her and asked, "What did our mother do?"

Erianna's head twitched with another piercing pain causing patches of white scales to break out across her body.

"Gabriel," Archimedes shouted as he tried to untangle himself from his scarf. "Take this and hold Erianna down as best as you can. Make sure she drinks every drop of this or we will all be in a mess of trouble."

Gabriel's eyes were transfixed on the scene taking place before him, causing him to almost miss Archimedes' words. He had seen wonderful powers in his realm, but never anything of the magnitude of these two sisters.

"Gabriel," Archimedes shouted again.

Brinn unconsciously held up her hand, forcing Erianna to face her. "Tell me. What did our mother do?"

Erianna choked under the pressure of her sister's invisible grasp. "She--killed--our-- father."

Brinn's grasp released immediately as shock filled her veins with an icy chill. Flickers of an ancient memory sparked across her eyes. Shaking her head, Brinn breathed out an unbelieving "no." Before anyone could stop her, Brinn ran from the house.

As if snapped out of a trance, Gabriel ran to Erianna's crumpled body that lay seizing on the floor. Archimedes threw the bottle to him and pulled himself up, running to help Gabriel however he could with Erianna.

Archimedes couldn't even begin to process the events that had just transpired. For once, he wished he had been able to see how this day might have ended so he could have saved them from at least part, if not all, of what happened.

Chapter 17

Brinn ran from the hovel, her head full of mixed memories she couldn't piece together in a way that made sense. The things Erianna had said couldn't be true. Her mother couldn't have done anything so horrible. But, a flicker of a distant memory pulled at her mind. One that felt like a buried nightmare that was trying to break free. Brinn paced outside the hovel while frustration and confusion gnawed at her. She couldn't think out here. She needed to go--somewhere --anywhere-- so she could bring some order to the harrowing thoughts.

She began to move towards the woods. Her thoughts moved from what Erianna had said to how she had retrieved the information from her. Shaking her head, she let out an exasperated sigh. That wasn't like her. She never used to become so angry so quickly. Something was changing in her and she didn't know how to stop it. Bringing her hand down from her forehead where she had been rubbing it subconsciously, she stared at her shaking hands, realizing just how close she had come to almost killing her new-found sister. She clenched her hands as the full reality of what she had done to Gabriel and Tharynn began to settle over her. She was out of control. Her sister was nearly killed because of her. Gabriel had more of a chance of dying than living because of her. And Tharynn. Poor Tharynn. She had somehow knocked him unconscious and could only wonder if he had come to since they had left him. If her mother knew about her powers, she was right to keep her locked up all those years, not to mention suppressing her memories, if she had any, of her powers.

A sickening thought stabbed through her spiraling thoughts. If she couldn't remember having or using her powers growing up, who's to say she hadn't done horrible things that her mother merely forced her to forget with an icy kiss? What if she had been the one to--?

No. Surely, if she had done something so horrible, her mother would have done away with her just as she had done with Erianna. Still, the thought of the possibility was too much for her. She ran through the woods, not knowing or caring where she was going. Icy tears stung her eyes as flecks of ice and snow began to peck at her face. As she ran, her scattered thoughts began to center on one thing. She had to get away from the people she cared about before she caused them more harm.

Her ragged thoughts propelled her further and further into the woods until they were stopped short by a large mass that knocked her back into the snow. Her breath caught at the impact and her eyes blurred from the puddle of tears that had been forming as she ran. Wiping her face with her snowy hand, she tried to blink away the rest of the tears so she could see what she had run into.

"It is a good thing the queen sent me to find you. You might not have ever gotten home if you keep running into things like that."

Brinn stopped at the familiar voice. It couldn't be, could it? She shook her head. Her mind must be playing tricks on her. Besides, Erianna had said he seemed to be entranced or under some kind of spell the other night when he attacked them. Even if it was him, she couldn't trust him.

She brushed the wet snow off her hands and began to bring herself to a standing position when a strong hand reached out and grabbed her hand, pulling her up with ease. Surprised, she blinked and stared into the chiseled features she had come to know so well since childhood.

"Tharynn?" she asked, uncertain if he truly was entranced.

"Is my name the only thing you remember about one of your closest friends? I would have thought you would have remembered more after all the time we spent together over the years." A sweet caring smile filled his lips as he stared down at her.

She examined his features carefully before giving him an answer. "No, I--" she paused. "It's just been such a trying few days and I'm surprised to see you here."

"I'm as real as if we were back in the palace." His smile widened as he looked down at her but clouded over with concern as he studied her. "Brinn, I was so worried about you. When your mother said you had gone missing, I--" he trailed off as he took in her features. As Brinn stared back into his familiar face, his eyes seemed to beg for an answer to the question of whether she was alright.

"Oh, Tharynn," Brinn's tears that she had been holding back began to well up inside her again.

"My dear, dear Brinn. It's alright. I'm here now. Everything is going to be ok," his strong, comforting voice drew her into his embrace. She felt his massive arms wrap around her and enfold her like a butterfly in a cocoon. A sense of home and warmth filled her as she began to melt into his embrace. As she stood there, the tears that had been welling up inside began to fall. Her tears fell slowly and softly at first but they soon became a waterfall of sobs as she poured out all the emotions and pains and experiences of the last few days.

"What happened to make you so upset these past few days?" Tharynn asked as he began to run his hand up and down her small back.

Brinn replied through shaky sobs, "I-I- c-can't tell- you."

"What? You can't tell your oldest, dearest friend your secret? You used to tell me everything" he soothed.

Brinn shuddered as his gentle baritone voice whispered into her ears. She shook her head against his chest. "No. No, I can't tell you," she replied, "It's--it's too horrible." Her body began to shake from the fresh onslaught of violent tears.

Tharynn pulled her in closer and spoke softly as he tried to calm her. "Hush now. It is going to be alright. Whatever happened is gone and behind you. You are safe now." He smiled as the tender girl began to calm in his arms. "Believe me. I won't let anything harm you or come between us ever again."

Brinn's tears finally subsided. After a few moments, she pulled away and looked up at Tharynn with tears still glistening in her eyes. "Can I ask you something?"

He looked down at her and brushed a wayward tear from her cheek. "Of course."

She stared into his face, assuring herself that she could truly trust him. "If I tell you what happened over the past few days, do you promise not to tell my mother?"

"Have I ever told your mother any of your mischief?" he asked as a playful glimmer lit up his eyes.

She studied his face for a moment before responding, "I should hope not." A small smile began to pull at her lips as she continued, "If you had, I would be sure to never have anything to do with you ever again."

"That is a harsh sentence. I had better put on my best behavior then. I wouldn't want to do anything to turn you against me." He smiled his widest fullest smile, crinkling up the corners of his eyes.

Brinn smiled back, "Well then, do you suppose we could find a place to sit so I can share the tumultuous events of these past few wearisome days?"

Tharynn looked around and spotted a log not too far from them. He pulled away and bowed elaborately as he spoke, "My lady. Might I do you the honor of escorting you to yon log that ye might rest your weary feet and unburden your weighted heart?" He smiled as he waggled his blonde eyebrows at her

Brinn laughed as she replied, "Do me the honor? My, you have gotten on your high horse since I left. I have no choice but to come back just to keep you in line."

He smiled and held out his arm to her. "Shall we?" he asked as he gestured toward the fallen long.

She curtsied as she replied, "We shall." She took his arm and walked with him to their makeshift wooden bench and waited while he dusted the snow off so she could sit.

"Now, share what has been troubling you, my pet," he said as he settled on the log beside her.

Brinn stopped straightening her skirts at the strange words. *My pet?* Tharynn had never called her that. A sudden uneasiness quickly replaced the ease and comfort she had felt just moments before. She glanced up at him, suddenly unsure if she could trust him.

She looked back down at the snowy earth and felt Tharynn shift slightly on the log next to her.

"Did you get a splinter in your dress or something?" he asked as he leaned down to see what she was looking so intently at.

Brinn quickly finished brushing out her skirt as she replied, "Oh, no. Just looking at a tear in one of the hems. It must have caught on a low branch or something while I was running through the forest last night."

A line creased Tharynn's forehead as he stared at her.

Brinn sat silent for a moment, trying to figure out a way to start the conversation without divulging too much information.

"Is something wrong?" he asked as he continued to stare at her.

"No. No. Nothing," she paused as a small smile began to form on her lips, "I just thought, well, never mind. It isn't important."

"What?" Tharynn began to eye her suspiciously as she continued.

"It's really nothing. A bit odd, but I suppose I've just become accustomed to the small little way you usually greet me when my mother wasn't around. Which is actually quite more often than I realized."

Tharynn's face grew stern as she prattled on. "What *little* way is that, my pet?" A coldness had crept into his voice that chilled a vein in the back of Brinn's neck.

Her breath caught in her throat as she stared at him. She forced a smile before she continued, "Well, you usually can't wait to steal a kiss or two when you are sure we are out of sight of my mother. And out here, we are surely far enough from her watchful gaze to warrant at least one kiss," she blushed slightly and scooted closer to him, hoping to make the part as convincing as possible.

Something flickered across his blue eyes as he gazed at her. Whether it was surprise or confusion or realization, she couldn't tell, but she was sure she had sparked something in her onlooker. She stared deep into his eyes trying to discern his next move and caught a glimpse of what looked like a small speck in his royal blue irises.

Mirror dust. Brinn let out a little gasp as she realized everything Erianna had said was true.

Brinn reached down and grabbed some snow from the ground and threw it in Tharynn's face to try to give herself a head start, but his reflexes were too quick for her. He grabbed her arm and held on tight.

"Don't you want to see your dear mother?" he sneered in a voice that sounded eerily unnatural coming from him.

She pulled at her wrist in his hand trying to break free from him. "Let go of me," she cried as she tried to pull away from him.

"Come, come dear. You'll only make it worse if you struggle." He wrenched her wrist tighter and pulled her closer to him so she would stop struggling.

"No. Tharynn, please. Let go of me. My mother is controlling you. You have to stop this." She shrieked as pain shot up her arm from where he still held her wrist.

"Your mother? Your mother simply wants you home safe and sound. Now, do try to cooperate, dear. It will be so much easier for the both of us."

Brinn struggled as Tharynn began to drag her deeper into the forest. Finally, Tharynn stopped short and turned, ready to throw her over his massive shoulder and carry her off into the woods. As he bent, Brinn impulsively grabbed his face with her free hand and pressed her lips to his. Tharynn resisted at first, but Brinn held onto him even tighter and pressed deeper into their kiss, hoping it would set her white knight free from her mother's cursed spell. As Brinn kissed him harder, a small sliver of a tear fell from his eyes and his arms began to enfold her as he kissed her back.

They pulled apart and Tharynn looked at her for a moment, confused by what had happened. "What?" he asked as he stared at her.

She looked up at him, relieved to see the sliver of mirror dust glistening on his cheek. She reached up to brush it away as she spoke, "It's ok. You were under my mother's spell but everything is going to be alright now."

Tharynn's eyes opened wide as he looked around and realized where they were. He looked back at her and asked, "Did I hurt you? Are you alright?"

"I'm more than alright now," a small blush stole across her cheeks as she smiled up at him.

A knowing smile crossed his lips as the memory of the kiss crossed his mind. "Mmm. I should say that you are." Tharynn leaned his head down to kiss her again but pulled away as a sharp pain pierced his head.

Brinn looked up at him, her eyes wide with concern at the sudden change in his demeanor. "What? What's wrong? Tharynn. Tharynn?"

Tharynn staggered back and shook his head. "Brinn--I--." Another sharp pain pierced his head, causing him to take a few more steps back. He looked at her but couldn't seem to see her.

"No. Tharynn. Don't go back to her. Please. Stay with me." Brinn crossed to him and threw her arms around his neck, trying to pull him back to her.

"Tharynn," she looked up into his eyes and saw them becoming clear again. She smiled and continued talking, "That's right. Come back to me. Please, come back to me."

Tharynn looked at her and his eyes filled with a glimmer of light as if he was truly returning to her. She smiled and stared back into his eyes, ready for another enchanting kiss when his face suddenly contorted into a painful twist of agony. His eyes opened wide again to reveal a glassy stare followed by a sharp intake of breath. Before she could discern what was wrong, he collapsed, falling limp to the wintery ground.

Shock and numbing fear pulsed through her as she collapsed beside him. "No. No. No. Tharynn, come back to me. Please." Brinn tried to look into his face to see if he was still breathing but she couldn't see through the tears that again stung her eyes. Her shaking hands were doing her no good either. She let out an exasperated sigh as a frigid breeze whipped around her.

Shivering from the cold breeze, Brinn looked up to see her mother staring down at her.

Bitter tears traced her cheeks as she looked up at her. "What did you do?"

"I did nothing that could have been prevented if you had just come along with him." Anwyne sneered as she looked down at the pathetic guard who lay sprawled out in the snow.

"Did you kill him?" Brinn stared up at her mother with menacing eyes.

"As I said, dear. If you would have just come home with him, none of this would have ever happened."

"What? You wouldn't have killed him like you killed my father?"

"Killed?" Anwyne raised an eyebrow at her daughter. "I wonder who has been filling your head with those fantastical fables."

"You know exactly who has been with me, *mother.*" Brinn spat out the word like it was something distasteful in her mouth.

Anwyne fixed her daughter with an icy stare, "You're right, my pet. I do know who you've been philandering with in the forest. I see she didn't waste much time turning you against me. Her temper seems to have rubbed off on you too, and I must say, it is not a becoming trait in a future queen of the winter realm."

"I am no queen, mother, and I never will be. Not as long as Erianna is the rightful heir to the throne."

Anwyne knelt down beside her daughter and locked her icy gaze in her own, "As long as Erianna remains an uncontrollable beast, she will never be queen over my kingdom."

She let go of Brinn's chin and stood up to go. "Come, Brinn. It's time we get you back to where you belong."

Brinn sat defeated on the forest floor next to Tharynn as her mother began to walk into the forest. The necklace beneath her chin emitted a faint glow. She looked down and remembered what had happened the night before with Erianna.

"What if she didn't turn into a beast anymore?" Her soft voice touched the winter air like a warm breath on a cold window pane.

Anwyne stopped and looked back at her daughter. "What did you say?"

Brinn grasped her necklace and stood to face her mother. "What if she didn't turn into a beast anymore?"

Anwyne's eyes widened at her daughter's words. Her questioning expression quickly iced over as she replied, "That will never happen."

Brinn looked at her. "But it did. Last night I stopped her from transforming. I don't know how but when our necklaces started glowing, I grabbed onto her hands and kept her from transforming."

Queen Anwyne's eyes filled with alarm. "That is a very interesting tale. Why don't you come home with me and tell me all about it." She reached out to Brinn.

"No. If she doesn't transform anymore, she can be queen. That is what you said."

"Brinn. Darling. Come with me and I will make sure Erianna is taken care of. I promise."

Brinn looked at her, unsure if she could trust her. "Promise?"

"Yes, my dear. I promise." Anwyne drew Brinn into a motherly embrace and placed her icy lips on Brinn's forehead.

Chapter 18

Erianna's eyes fluttered open--again. She saw Gabriel sitting in the chair beside her bed. He smiled at seeing her awake again and leaned over to brush a strand of hair from her face.

"We seem to be making a habit of this," he said. "Only, this time I'm glad we're not in the middle of the woods," his smile widened, sending a surge of warmth through Erianna's body.

She smiled in return, "I thought you would have enjoyed being caught alone in the middle of the forest with a helpless maiden."

Gabriel laughed, "Any given day that might be an enjoyable experience, but I'm afraid to admit that you and your sister have been getting the best of me. Getting beat by not just one girl, but two, can put quite the damper on a man's morale."

"My sister and I are quite a force to be reckoned with, I suppose," she replied ruefully. She pulled herself up to a sitting position and looked around the room. "Is Brinn here?"

Gabriel let out a long sigh, "Would you want me to tell you if she wasn't?"

Erianna looked at him. "Where is she?"

Gabriel cleared his throat before he answered. "She went to clear her head after your, ah, argument, and hasn't returned."

Erianna moved to get up, "I better go look for her."

As she pulled herself from the bed, her legs buckled underneath her. Gabriel reached out to catch her. "Not like that you won't." Gabriel helped ease her back into a sitting position on the bed.

"That nasty hobgoblin. I don't even want to know what he put in that potent this time."

"If it helps, I believe whatever he put in it helped bring you back. And I am glad for that."

Erianna noted the hint of concern in his voice and looked at him for a brief moment before she averted her eyes to her hands, "Why should you be glad that it brought me back?"

Gabriel looked at her, surprised by her question. "Why shouldn't I be glad? Aren't you glad that you are alive and well?"

Erianna continued to look at her hands as she replied, "Perhaps it would be best for everyone if I wasn't."

She spoke so softly Gabriel almost didn't hear her. He leaned closer and asked, "You think it would be better for the world if you weren't alive?"

"Yes."

"But why?"

Erianna kept her head down and clenched her hands as she whispered, "Because, I'm a monster."

The words sank into Gabriel's mind, "Erianna, you are not a monster."

"Yes, I am. I've ruined so many lives."

Gabriel looked at her and tried to figure out how to convince her that it couldn't be as bad as she imagined.

"I doubt that. The beautiful woman I tried to rescue a few days ago is sweet and brave and courageous and will do anything to protect those she loves."

Erianna continued to stare at her hands as she replied, "But you don't know what I've done."

"I can't imagine anything you've ever done has been horrible enough to wish you were dead."

"I'm a dragon. You have no idea what horrible things a dragon can do."

Gabriel leaned in closer and took her cold clenched hands in his warm ones, "I don't believe you could ever do anything truly horrible, even during the times you are a dragon. That is only part of you. You have amazing and beautiful powers that can be used for good, just as you shared with Brinn in the woods."

Erianna looked up for a brief moment, but quickly looked away "My magic hasn't always been controlled. I remember being scared and unsure of what my magic could do. I don't always remember where I've been or what I've done when I've been in my dragon form. I'm sure Brinn is experiencing some of the same things and I need to find her before she hurts anyone. Especially herself." Erianna tried to pull her hands away from him and stand up on the other side of the bed.

Gabriel held her hands tighter and prevented her from standing up as he replied, "Erianna. Your magic is nothing to be ashamed of. You both have beautiful magic that's like nothing I've ever seen. Making swords out of thin air. Making it snow whenever you wish. And turning into a dragon is some of the most amazing magic I have ever seen. It enhances the beautiful strength I have seen in you the past few days and shows the world how magnificent you truly are."

"You've only known me a few days. How can you know anything about me or who I really am?" Erianna asked as she continued to sit there staring at her hands enfolded in his.

Gabriel sighed, "Look. Can I show you something?"

Erianna pulled her hand out of his warm grasp and nodded.

"Just watch." Gabriel moved to a spot of dirt on the floor. As he knelt, Erianna sat up further in her bed straining to see what he was doing. She watched as he placed his good hand on the dirt. Closing his eyes, he began to sing an enchanting melody in a language Erianna had never heard before. As he sang, a warm yellow glow began to light the ground before him. Delicate strands of the golden light swirled around an object as he raised his hand up to raise it from the ground. When he finished, a beautiful red rose twirled gently to the ground.

Erianna's lips parted in amazement at the beautiful flower he had just created. He picked up the rose and carried it to her. She looked up at him with wide eyes.

He knelt beside her again and held out the rose to her. "See. This is my magic. Delicate and gentle. Not to mention the most dangerous part of the job." He twirled the stem in his hand so she could see the pokey protrusions that lined the stem. "Thorns."

Erianna breathed out a quiet sigh, "Gabriel. That is the most beautiful magic I have ever seen." She looked from the rose to his spring green eyes. "How can you be ashamed of such a beautiful gift?"

"I'm a prince. Someday I will be expected to lead and protect an entire realm. How can I protect them with flower magic?"

"But your magic gives life to the earth. You create beautiful things that fill the world with joy and happiness. Bringing life and renewal to things that were once dead, that has to be the most powerful magic there is."

Gabriel looked at her with a warmth she had never seen in anyone's eyes before, "I guess I never thought of it that way. Thank you."

Erianna smiled. A strange tingly feeling touched her heart as she looked at him.

Gabriel broke the sudden silence between them by holding out the rose to her, "My lady. May I present her Royal Highness with a rose from my kingdom."

Erianna pulled back, "Thank you, but I'm afraid our magic usually destroys things, not bring them to life."

"Take it. I guarantee you won't harm it," he winked at her sending another unusually warm feeling through her heart.

Hesitant, Erianna reached out for the rose. As she touched it, she was surprised to see that nothing happened. She looked at Gabriel with a surprised smile and drew the rose close to her. As she pressed her nose into the petals, the sweetest smell reached her nostrils and made her smile widen. Her fingers touched the soft petals and she savored the sensation of the crushed velvet feeling beneath her fingertips.

She looked back up at Gabriel who was watching her. She smiled and blushed as she played with one of the petals. "You must think me silly for fawning over it so."

Gabriel smiled, "Not at all, princess. I think you're beautiful. Like a perfect winter rose." Realizing what he said, Gabriel cleared his throat and said, "And now it is your turn to show off."

"I'm pretty sure you've seen enough of my powers. Believe me the rest of them aren't nearly as exquisite as this is."

"I don't believe that."

"You don't?"

"No. I don't. I believe your magic is just as needed as ours in the spring realm. Without winter, spring has no reason to exist. You put things to sleep for a time so they can come back to life, fuller and richer than they were before. You prepare the ground for the life to come. I believe that just like spring magic, snow magic can be used for bad, as it seems your mother has learned to do, but it is inherently good magic. Only those who use it make it good or bad."

Erianna looked at him, not quite convinced that her magic could be good or beautiful.

Gabriel leaned closer. "Haven't you ever marveled at the beauty of a snowflake?"

"What?" she asked. "There are hundreds of snowflakes in a single flurry. What could be so special about them?"

Gabriel searched for ways to convince her. He looked at her as he asked, "Can you form a snowflake right now?"

"Of course I can." Erianna flicked her wrist, causing some flakes to fall from the ceiling.

"No. No. Not a bunch of them. One, giant snowflake that is made with all the gentleness and delicacy I know you are capable of."

Erianna looked at him with confusion.

Gabriel grabbed her hand and lifted it up as if trying to help her, "Do it. Concentrate on what you are making. Don't just flippantly throw it out there. Really think about it."

Erianna looked from him to her extended hand and figured he wouldn't stop until she had done what he asked. Shaking her head, she looked to the sky and began to slowly twirl her hand in the air. As she did so, small blue dust began to swirl around and dance like little faeries in a ballet. She smiled and widened the circle of her hand, willing the blue specks to come together and form a large, beautiful snowflake. As she looked at it, she noticed for the first time the intricate webbing that went into her snowflakes. The delicate stems that formed unique patterns throughout and glistened with the sparkle of freshly fallen snow. Gabriel was right. Her magic was beautiful.

She smiled as he watched her unique display. Another idea came to mind which prompted her to bring both of her hands together as if holding an imaginary ball. She closed her eyes and threw her hands up as she threw a handful of snow into the air and smiled as a beautiful rain of sparkle and glitter filled the room.

Gabriel laughed, "See. There is beauty in your magic." He looked at her with a warm, glowing look. "Your snowflakes. My roses. They're both beautiful." Gabriel reached down and picked up some snow from the ground and sprinkled it on the rose like glitter.

"It looks like diamond drops on the petals," Erianna replied with breathless wonder.

Gabriel looked at her and saw the light of the fire catch the frosted dew drops that coated her lips. "Yes. Sweet diamonds."

Erianna looked at Gabriel and saw that he was looking at her lips. The breath left her lungs as Gabriel leaned closer to her. She felt the petals of the rose brush her hand as Gabriel lowered it and drew her face towards his.

Their lips were so close she could feel his warm breath on hers. Just as their lips were about to meet, Archimedes bolstered into the room, causing both of them to jerk back. In the sudden movement, Gabriel's hand closed around the stem of the rose on top of Erianna's hand, pricking both of their hands.

Archimedes stopped short as he looked between the two young royals. "What in high blazes are the two of you doing in here?" He saw the rose next to Erianna's hand and the dusting of snow that now covered the floor.

"You have been using your powers. You," he pointed at Erianna, "You should know better than to use your magic in the house. How many times did I have to clean up after you as a child? I'm not a snow maid, young beastie."

Erianna opened her mouth to object, but Archimedes carried on, hobbling closer to Gabriel, "And you, young pup. You should not be using your magic at all in this realm. Spring magic used in the winter realm takes its toll on springlings and in your weakened state it should have been the furthest thing from your mind. Not to mention if the snow queen ever found out, she would have your heart on an iced platter faster than you could say snowflake."

It was Gabriel's turn to respond, but his apology fell unacknowledged to the dirt ground. "Now, you almost made me forget why I came up here in the first place, you heated teenagers. Letting your emotions get the better of your judgement."

Gabriel opened his mouth again, but Erianna shook her head and signaled to Gabriel to let Archimedes continue. He harrumphed as he paced back to the other side of the bed. "Your sister has been found by your mother. It seems they have a young man with them, though I'm not sure how alive he is."

"Where are they?" Erianna asked as small scales began to form on her arm. She scratched at them trying to ignore their appearance.

Archimedes turned towards her, "I can't say for sure. They could be headed to the place where the four realms meet."." He noticed her scratching and came to examine her arm. He looked at her, "I figured the dragon juice would delay the transformation, but it doesn't seem to have stopped it like I hoped."

Erianna pulled her sleeve down to hide them, but soon reached up to scratch the patches appearing on her neck. "I have to get to Brinn before the solstice moon. Who knows what my mother will be planning." She got out of bed and walked across the room to a screened off area to change.

Archimedes called from across the room, "Erianna, need I remind you what tomorrow is?"

Erianna scratched more as she pulled the white gown off and reached for a blue and silver gown nearby.

"You said it was the solstice moon. What more needs to be said."

"It is your 21st birthday and you know what that means if you are caught anywhere near that cursed spot."

Her head was beginning to ring as she finished dressing and came out to brush her hair, which was becoming unruly as they spoke. "I have to save Brinn," she said as she puffed out icy smoke from her nostrils.

"Would you stop fussing with your hair?" Archimedes chided. "You, child, are already transforming and you're not even out in the blessed moonlight." He lifted her arm to her face as he continued, "This, love, is your fate if you step out into that moon tomorrow night."

Erianna's neck twitched as her muscles contracted under the pull of the transformation. She looked at Archimedes with an eerie glow in her eyes as she growled out, "Then I'll face my fate like a queen and become ruler of the snow dragons."

She pulled her arm from his grasp and stumbled towards the door. Looking back at Archimedes she said, "Thank you old friend, for everything you have done. I will never forget you."

Screeches could be heard throughout the tunnels as Erianna's muscles tore away into her other self.

Archimedes stood solemnly as he looked after her. He turned to Gabriel whose mind was still trying to comprehend the change that took place in this gentle girl he had found in the woods. Eyeing the rose she had dropped to the ground, Archimedes hobbled over and picked it up. Pressing it into Gabriel's hand he said, "Go after her and see that she finds a safe place to land in the morning. Perhaps there is still hope. If you can create this beautiful rose in a hard and dead ground, perhaps you can bring her back to life as well."

Gabriel looked at the little man, and replied, "I will do whatever I can to protect her."

He put a reassuring hand on the hobgoblin's shoulder and ran from the room.

Archimedes looked up to the brown ceiling above him. "They could sure use your help right about now."

Chapter 19

Queen Anwyne gazed at the girl fast asleep before her. A small fracture of a smile graced her unusually demure face as she remembered a small child sleeping beside her in this very cave years ago. A groan behind her returned her mind to the present.

"It's about time you rejoined the land of the living."

Tharynn groaned again and pulled himself up from the ground where he had been lying. "No thanks to you, my *queen*." Tharynn shook his head and looked to where the queen stood with her back to him. His gaze caught sight of a brilliant white figure lying on a slab of ice. Cautiously, he took a few steps toward the figure. As he looked down at her, a familiarity and almost warmth washed over him. He subconsciously reached out a hand to touch the frozen girl's porcelain cheek. Just as his fingers were about to brush her skin, a sudden stiffness grasped his hand, disabling him from moving further.

"Careful, my curious knight. Temptations can be fatal." Anwyne persuaded Tharynn to lower his hand with the invisible grip she still held on him.

"What is she doing here?" he asked.

"The girl is not your concern anymore." Anwyne looked between her daughter and the roguish knight that stood beside her.

Stepping toward him, she grasped his strong jaw in her long icy fingers and turned his face to hers. A small gasp escaped her as she saw a watery gaze reflected back at her. "How close did my daughter get to you before I stepped in last night?"

Tharynn's broken gaze turned back to Brinn, concern widening the cracks of the snow queen's magic in his eyes.

"Do not look at my daughter in such a way," Anwyne hissed as she wrenched his face back to hers. "You are here to do *my* bidding. Not follow some foolish whims of the heart."

Anwyne's other hand had come to rest over Tharynn's heart. "If you think I will let some stupid guards foolish feelings for my daughter ruin my plans, you have been sorely misdirected."

Tharynn's face contorted with pain as the queen's icy fingers slowly closed over his heart. "I did not come this far to lose my daughter again," she seethed as she tightened her grip on his heart.

A deep chill began to take root in Tharynn's veins as the snow queen's power laced through his body. His pale skin began to frost over as the ice magic made its way to the surface. For a brief moment, his blue eyes began to turn a milky white. Anwyne smiled a sneering smile as she pushed her powers a little further to finish him off. A small groan from the table beside them suddenly drew Anwyne's gaze from the soldier before her. Terrifying lines of anguish filled her daughter's sleeping face. Anwyne held her grip on Tharynn's heart but as she looked at her daughter, she realized the more harm she caused Tharynn, the more pain filled her daughter's face. Not wanting to cause her daughter undo harm, she released her fatal grip on the soldier's heart.

Tharynn gasped as his frigid body slumped to the floor. Anwyne walked away from the slab of ice and crossed to the other side of the room. Her icy hands gripped the table that sat beneath one of the many mirrors that hung on the walls around the icy room. She lifted her penetrating gaze to the mirror and was shocked to see a new layer of whiteness coat her eyes. As she stared at her reflection, the hairs on the back of her neck stood on end.

Anwyne opened a small silver box on the table. With a small wave of her hand, a small handful of dust rose out of the box and awaited her bidding. She moved her wrist, sending the silvery flecks into the air. Their path met their end in Tharynn's eyes, which had been returning to their endless blue hue. The flecks embedded themselves in Tharynn's eyes once more.

"Go."

Tharynn stood, grabbed his bow and arrow and bowed before he ran out of the cave. Anwyne's eyes met her frozen gaze in the mirror. A glimpse of her daughter lying on the frozen slab behind her stilled Anwyne's heart. Anwyne looked back at herself. A small tear escaped her icicle eyes and trailed down her pure white face. Anwyne blinked allowing a steely reserve to fill her eyes as she stepped back. Her hands came together in a loud crack. The mirrors that hung all around the room shattered into a sea of broken pieces on the solid floor of the cave.

Erianna set down in a clearing as the morning light began to fill the frozen sky. Gabriel slid from her silver, scaly back and stood back as a glowing light enveloped her. A swirl of snow fell to the ground as Erianna's human-self came into view. Gabriel stepped to Erianna as her slender body swayed in the pale winter light.

"I've got you," he said as he braced her slender body against his larger frame. Erianna looked up into his entrancing green eyes. Expecting to see traces of fear or shock in his eyes, Erianna was surprised to see a look of gentleness in his calming eyes.

Gabriel's good hand came up to brush her cheek. Erianna's breath hitched inside her chest as his warm fingers trailed down her face. His hand came to rest beneath her chin and lifted her face towards his. As their faces drew closer together, Erianna watched as his gaze changed from warm and inviting to concerned and questioning.

Wondering what had changed so quickly, Erianna began to pull away. As she did, Gabriel's hand came down to her neck. His thumb brushed a rough patch of white scales that still marred her skin.

Erianna jerked back as he touched the tender part of her skin that hadn't fully transformed.

Gabriel reached for her, "Erianna, I'm sorry. I didn't mean to--."

"No. Gabriel. Don't," Erianna said as she pushed his hand away and began to walk away.

"Erianna. Please. Wait."

"Wait for what? For my skin to return to normal so you can kiss me without thinking about how awful it must be to kiss a monster?"

"Erianna. No, that is not what I was thinking."

A flicker of hurt lanced her eyes as she stared back at him. "No. Of course it wasn't. Because no one in their right mind would ever even think of kissing someone like me."

"Eri, wait." Gabriel reached out to grab Erianna's arm but she pulled away before he could grab it.

"Eri?" Erianna stopped short at the name. "No one has ever called me that except my father. And he's dead."

"I'm sorry, Erianna. Please. Listen to me."

"No." Erianna's eyes clenched tight as tried to repress a painful memory that threatened to come to the surface of her mind.

"What is it?" Gabriel asked.

"Nothing." Erianna shook her head as she continued, "Nothing. I have to go." Erianna brushed past Gabriel and started walking into the white forest.

"Erianna," Gabriel grasped Erianna's hand as she walked past, "I am not going to let you go out there on your own."

Anger lit Erianna's eyes as he took her hand. "You have no right to tell me where I can and can't go."

"I'm not trying to tell you where you can and can't go. Believe me, I would never force such authority on you. I'm just concerned about you going out there by yourself."

The anger in Erianna's eyes intensified as she stared back at Gabriel. She cocked an icy brow as she responded, "What. You don't think a dragon girl can take care of herself? Believe me. The dragon side is a very real part of me that keeps anyone and anything at a far enough distance that I've never had to worry about being in any real danger." Erianna pulled her hand out of his and turned to go.

"I'm sorry you never feel you have to worry about being in danger," Gabriel looked after her as she started to leave.

Erianna stopped. "What do you mean?"

"Just that, the monster you think everyone sees on the outside may not be as dangerous as the monster you have created on the inside."

Gabriel saw Erianna's back stiffen at his words. He stepped toward her and placed a firm hand on her shoulder. "Erianna, you think people stay away from you because you transform into a dragon every full moon. The truth is, you don't give anyone a chance to get close enough to you to find out who you really are."

"You've never had to worry about people looking at you like you're some kind of freak. Or seen the terror in their eyes when they see me start to transform. All they see is a hideous, destructive beast who needs to be dealt with by killing it or sending it into the furthest regions of the realm so it can't harm anyone."

Gabriel stood closer to Erianna. He wrapped his arm around her shoulder and pulled her into his strong embrace. He leaned his head down until it rested on top of her head. His warm breath caressed her ears as he whispered, "I'm sorry for all the pain you've endured."

Erianna stood silent and stiff in his embrace for a moment. All her life she had wanted to feel the warmth of someoneone's embrace. Wanted to know what it felt like to be loved and cared for, but she had never had anyone close enough to her to feel those things. She could care for Brinn enough and hoped if she could break the curse that she would be able to hug her and show her all the sisterly love she could. But this was different. These were the arms of a man she didn't even know holding her. Why was he so drawn to her? And why was she so drawn to him? Was she so desparate for love and attention that she would fall for the first man to ever show her the slightest hint of attention?

Gabriel held onto Erianna, her body stiff and unmoving. He knew this must be foreign to her. He couldn't imagine the kind of life she had lived. Being banished by her mother, living most of her life on her own. Always running and never feeling safe around people. He would have never survived without the love of his sister and parents and the people of his kingdom. He had never seen a more beautiful woman in all his life but she was so afraid to let people in and get close to her. She had shown nothing but bravery and strength and grace since the moment he first looked into her crystal blue eyes. He didn't know why but every moment he was with her, he felt like she was a missing piece of his heart that he had always been searching for but never found, and now the pieces of their hearts were being knit back together like they had always belonged. He wished he could show her how worthy she was of being loved and fill every hurting, empty place inside her.

He placed a gentle kiss on top of her head and pulled her in closer to him. He felt her relax ever so slightly and he smiled as she eventually allowed her head rest against his warm chest and wrapped her arms around him. He relished this feeling as he felt her body continue to relax.

The blissful moment ended abruptly when Erianna suddenly pulled away.

Concerned, Gabriel looked at her and asked, "Are you alright?"

Erianna looked at him with fear etching chasms into her endless eyes. "No. I have to go."

"Erianna, what's wrong?" Gabriel reached out to grab her arm.

"No. Don't. Don't touch me. I have to go. I pray you never run into me in these woods again."

"Erian--" Gabriel's word was cut short. Erianna turned to see what had caused the abrupt silence and saw Gabriel lying face down in the snow.

"Gabriel," Erianna screamed as she ran towards him. Erianna's eyes locked onto the arrow that protruded from Gabriel's back.

"No." Erianna reached to pull the arrow out but stopped as another arrow whizzed past her and hit a tree just beyond them.

Erianna's hands trembled as she tried to gather her senses. She had to calm herself so she could listen for whoever was out there. Erianna closed her eyes and took in a deep silent breath. She sat still in the silent forest as she waited for another clue as to the whereabouts of their stalker. After a few moments, Erianna's hand shot up behind her and she listened as the soaring arrow dropped to the ground in a casing of ice.

"The queen said you would be a formidable foe," an angry voice broke the silence behind her. "Frankly, I could use a challenge."

Erianna clenched her hands and turned to see Tharynn eyeing one of his arrows with an eerie gleam of joy in his eyes.

"Clearly we didn't present enough of a challenge for you the other night," she said, as she braced her hands against the snowy earth beneath her.

Tharynn looked at her and smiled as he responded, "That little tussle? If that's the best you can do, I'm afraid it's not going to be a very fair fight for you, Your Highness." Tharynn finished his speech with a mock bow.

A chord of anger struck within Erianna. She knew he was baiting her. If he knew she was the princess, she wouldn't be surprised if he knew about her transformations as well. She had to keep her anger in check.

"Your name is Tharynn. Is that right?" Erianna eased her hands against the ground and sent a small stream of ice into the ground before her.

"Very good, princess. It seems someone has been doing their homework."

"No, I just have a very dear sister who thought highly of you at one point in time and was crushed to see you attack us the other night."

"You must be speaking of that ice girl the queen has been watching over in the fourth corner."

"You speak of her as if you don't know her." Erianna pushed the ice a little further into the ground to give it more leverage when it made its way to Tharynn. "I was under the impression that you were friends once."

Tharynn scoffed, "Friends with that spoiled brat? More like her personal valet. Always being expected to fetch this and that and walk with her everywhere she went. Just because the little whelp couldn't take care of herself."

The ice began to appear beneath Tharynn's feet. Erianna smiled slightly. "She seemed quite capable when she knocked you unconscious the other night. She also hit quite the mark with her arrow a few mornings ago. It would seem such marksmanship couldn't happen without the aid of an excellent teacher."

"I am the captain of the queen's guard."

"Yes," Erianna replied, "A better one I'm sure she could not find in all the realms. But it seems odd to me that one of such high rank would take time to show a princess how to shoot like that. Unless perhaps he had a special liking for the girl."

Tharynn stopped plying the tip of his arrow for a moment.

"Tharynn," Erianna had begun to stand slowly, all the while encouraging the ice beneath Tharynn's feet to begin its climb up his lower leg. "Tharynn, I don't believe this facade you've been wearing is really who you are. I believe you truly care for my sister and would never do anything to harm her."

Tharynn locked eyes with her for a moment and lowered his arrow.

Erianna walked slowly towards him, "That's it. Think of Brinn and what a wonderful person she is. She would be devastated if she ever found out you had harmed me." Erianna wound the ice up Tharynn's leg as she walked closer to him.

Just as Erianna was about to wind the ice tight enough to entangle him, Tharynn grabbed her and held her in his strong grasp with an arrow held to her throat.

Tharynn laughed, "Nice try, princess. I've been an iceling for far too long to be affected by a little frost." He tightened his grip around her neck.

Erianna gasped for breath. Her throat felt like it was being crushed by Tharynn's large arm. She struggled to get even the slightest breath of air to keep the oxygen going to her brain so she didn't pass out. But Tharynn's grip grew even tighter. Spots appeared before her eyes and a pressure started closing in on her head. Her eyes grew dark, but just before everything went completely black, she felt an icy blast of wind rush into her lungs.

Erianna collapsed into the snow as Tharynn's arm left her neck. She blinked as her eyes came slowly back into focus. She looked over her shoulder and almost choked at the sight behind her.

"Archimedes."

Chapter 20

"Archimedes. How did you--?" Erianna coughed.

"Easy, love. Let me take a look at your throat before you cause permanent damage." Archimedes crossed the few steps to her and bent his head to examine her throat. A faint purple hue colored her almost white skin. Archimedes lightly touched the area to make sure there were no unusual lumps.

"How did you get here?" Erianna rasped out.

"I cashed in an old gift the Great Mage gave me before I was banished."

Erianna's brows drew together in confusion and she opened her mouth to question him again.

"Ach," Archimedes clamped her mouth shut, "Will ye please refrain from straining your vocal chords."

Erianna glared at him and raised her eyebrows, waiting for his response.

He stared at her and sighed, "All right, all right. The Mage gave me a magic snow globe many years ago, long before I even knew your mother. It allowed me to see into the other worlds. I would think of who or where I would want to see and shake the globe and the images would appear. The Mage wove a special magic into the globe that would allow me to go anywhere I wanted but there was only enough magic for one trip. I've been saving it all these years for the right moment but didn't know if it would work with the snow queen's banishment so I never used it. Guess the Mage's magic is still a might more powerful than the snow queen's. It got me here anyway."

Erianna's eyes widened and her mouth dropped open.

"Don't act so shocked. Old Archimedes still has a few tricks up his sleeve now and again. I used to use it to check in on you girls on occasion."

"Arch--" Erianna let out a surprised gasp.

"Don't start talking. Your vocal chords need rest."

Erianna closed her mouth and stared after him as he went to check on Gabriel. She gently touched her throat to see how it felt before she pulled herself over to where Gabriel still laid face down in the snow. "How bad is it?" she asked with a hoarse whisper.

"Can't say until I've had a better look at it. That arrow's got to come out to be sure, but if it's too close to his heart, I could puncture it when I pull it out."

Archimedes looked up to see Erianna staring at him with wide eyed horror.

"That is to say, I'll be careful with him and try my best not to puncture his heart."

"That's kind of you to try to miss his heart," Erianna said with shocked reproof.

"You know me. Always trying to help people, not hurt them," Archimedes gave her a weak smile. "Right then, let me take a look here."

Archimedes pulled out his large magnifying glass and pulled away the material that sat limply around the arrow. After a few moments, he placed his ear over Gabriel's shoulder and listened intently. Erianna watched anxiously, wondering how long he was planning on examining him before he actually did anything.

Archimedes finally looked up and said, "It's not good, but, it's not as bad as it could be." Archimedes started rummaging in the bag he brought with him.

"Do you mind explaining your cryptic diagnosis or am I supposed to just sit here terrified that he could die any moment?"

"You better be careful how much you use your voice, dearie. You may be causing deeper damage by inflicting your vocal chords with all that jabbering."

Erianna glared at Archimedes as he inserted a dropper into a bottle and transferred a few drops to another. He stared back, "Alright, dearie. I'll explain myself, but you may not like what I have to say.

Archimedes continued transferring drops of liquid from various bottles as he spoke, "The arrow seems far enough away from his heart that we should be able to pull it out no problem. The bad news is, the arrow was tipped with bane and it looks to be already wreaking havoc on his bloodstream so the bane may already be closing in on his heart."

Erianna's eyes fluttered shut as she tried to blink away some of the tears that had been forming. A small rough hand touched hers. Archimedes was looking at her.

"He'll be alright, lass. He hasn't given up yet. And with you pullin' for him, I expect he would be a bloody fool to give up fighting now."

Erianna smiled at Archimedes and squeezed his hand. He smiled back. "You ready, lass?"

Erianna nodded. "Alright, lass, I'm going to pull it out. Pour this in the wound as soon as the arrow is out."

Erianna took the vial Archimedes handed her. Her breath froze in her throat as she watched Archimedes draw out the arrow. As the tip became visible, Erianna let out her breath and pulled the lid off the vial.

"Please, let this heal him," she whispered as she leaned over Gabriel and poured a few drops into the wound.

Archimedes pulled out a few bandages and covered the wound. "Turn him over, carefully now. Now that the arrow's out, he would probably appreciate having his face out of the snow."

Erianna nodded and helped Archimedes turn Gabriel over. Erianna brushed the snow from his face while Archimedes waved another bottle under Gabriel's nose. Erianna smiled as the emerald green of Gabriel's eyes began to appear through his dark lashes.

Gabriel looked up and saw Erianna. "We have to stop meeting like this," he smiled up at her as she brushed away more of the wet snow.

"I would have to agree. I'll have to turn in my resignation as a mage's assistant and become a royal nursemaid if you kids keep this up."

Gabriel turned his head and saw Archimedes standing just above him. "Archimedes, it's good to see you." He tried to turn and shake Archimedes' hand.

"Easy now, lad. You've been shot with another bane arrow and need your rest."

"Hmm. That would explain the uncomfortable burning in my shoulder."

"That would be the goldenrod oil from your realm. I found a small bottle hidden away in my shelves. You probably aren't used to the heat from your realm anymore."

Gabriel nodded and readjusted his shoulder. A groan from nearby drew his attention.

"What was that?" he asked.

Erianna looked behind her. "The cause of your other wound."

"We best take care of him before he comes to. Give me a hand, lass."

Tharynn's muscles felt tight as he regained consciousness later on. His arms were pulled behind him around a large tree. He yanked his arms slightly to see if he could break whatever was binding them. A rope pulled taut, preventing him from moving his hands very far.

"It seems your attacker has joined us again," he heard an old, gravelly voice say.

He saw a pair of silver shoes approach him followed by small, brown leather ones through the slits of his eyes.

"The rope is enchanted, so don't bother trying to break free," a voice as silvery as the owner's shoes remarked.

Tharynn made no response.

"Tip his head back so I can see how bad his eyes are," the rough voice spoke again.

A small hand took a handful of his hair and began to gently pull his head back. He instinctively closed his eyes, not sure what to expect from his captors.

"Closing your lids won't help me see the damage, laddie."

"Please, open your eyes. We only want to help you." That voice sounded strangely familiar, but it carried a slightly different tone than the one he was used to hearing.

A gentle, soft hand brushed his forehead and fluttered across his cheek. His chest tightened at the light, feminine touch.

"Brinn?" Tharynn's eyes opened to see the beautiful princess he had protected all of his life.

"Close, but I'm afraid I'll have to be the next best thing," she smiled at him and watched as his eyes tried to focus.

Something snapped his head forward and caused him to shake it hard. When he looked up again, the cold, mean glare he had when trying to choke Erianna had returned.

"He's fighting it on his own, which is a good sign. I need to see how deep the glass cut to see if anything's permanent. Can you hold his head to keep it from moving, lass?"

As if a trained response, Tharynn thrashed his head about to prevent them from taking hold of it. A cold, icy touch stilled his head. As hard as he tried, he couldn't break the hold the girl had on him.

"Turn him toward me. He's a bit larger than the rest of you and I need a better look at him."

His head turned towards a small, old man who reached out a child sized hand to look in his eyes. The old man pulled out some spectacles and leaned in close to Tharynn's face.

"It looks like the dust has embedded itself deep, but we'll try our best to flush it out."

The old man took a blue vial from a leather side bag that sat on the ground before him.

"Put his head back so it's facing the sky," the old man spoke to the girl holding him.

"What is that?" she asked as she turned Tharynn's head to face the branched expanse above him.

"A vial of tears. They say tears heal many a kind of ailments, but they are especially potent for pains in the eyes. Now, hold him still long enough for the liquid to get into his eyes, but let him do the rest once it's in."

Tharynn felt a cool liquid enter his eyes. He clenched his eyes shut as the salt stung his eyes. Sharp, pointed pains creased his eyes as little shards of glass scraped across them. He shook his head trying to rid himself of the pain but closed his eyes tighter, trying to keep the little specks of glass from falling from his eyes. As he clenched his eyes shut, a small sliver of tears began to fall from his eyes, pulling little flecks of the mirror dust out with it.

A strange mix of natural tears and the bottled tears filled his eyes. His eyelids blinked slowly allowing more tears and dust to fall from his eyes. He closed his eyes once more, pushing the remaining stream of tears from his eyes. His eyes opened slowly, looking like dark blue pools that resided over trickling waterfalls. He blinked a few more times and focused his eyes on an almost familiar face.

"Brinn?" he asked, trying to focus more on the face before him.

"Not Brinn. But I am her sister, Erianna," Erianna smiled as she looked at him, relieved to see a clearness in his eyes.

Tharynn blinked in confusion, "Sister?"

"Yes. I'm afraid it's a rather long story but I am her sister, for better or for worse."

Tharynn suddenly darted his eyes around him, still blurry from the remaining tears that sat in his eyes. "Brinn. Where is Brinn?" he pulled against the rope that bound him to the tree.

"We were hoping you could tell us that," Erianna replied.

Confused, Tharynn looked at Erianna. "Why? Where could she be?" he asked, panic lacing his strong voice.

Erianna looked at Archimedes before responding, "We don't know. She ran out on us last night and we couldn't find her. I'm assuming my mother sent you to find us and prevent us from finding her."

His eyes darted back and forth from Erianna to Archimedes, "Your mother?"

Erianna nodded, "The snow queen."

Tharynn looked down, a frown creasing his brow.

"Easy, love. He may not remember much of what happened while he was under your mother's curse." Archimedes tilted Tharynn's chin up a bit as he continued, "Can I look in your eyes, son? I want to make sure the dust is all gone."

Tharynn blinked and looked at Archimedes, "Dust?" He looked to Erianna again. "Did the snow queen do something to me to make me hurt Brinn?"

"We believe she implanted mirror dust in your eyes giving you the curse of shattered sight," Erianna began slowly, not sure how much to divulge to him.

Tharynn let out a frosty breath. "No wonder I've felt so strange the past few days." He shook his head. "All I remember is being sent on a quest to find the source of a harrowing screech that plagued the kingdom a few nights ago."

Erianna looked at Archimedes, knowing exactly what screech he was talking about, as Tharynn continued. "When I came back the next morning, I went to see the queen to tell her we had to ready ourselves to take on a wider search." He paused. "And, I can't seem to remember anything after that point."

"That must have been when the queen blasted you with her mirror dust," Archimedes said as he pulled Tharynn's head back to face him so he could look at his eyes.

Tharynn nodded, "Yes." He whipped his head back to Erianna, "I do remember the queen mentioning that Brinn had gone missing."

Erianna smiled as she turned his head back to an annoyed Archimedes, "Yes. She came looking for me, I'm afraid."

"If you move your head one more time, young winter lord, I will personally see to removing your eyesight permanently," Archimedes huffed as he gripped Tharynn's large chin in his small hand.

Tharynn's eyes snapped open at the little man's remark. "Archimedes' bark is bigger than his bite," Erianna said with a rueful smile, "but you best listen to him just the same."

Archimedes looked into the soldier's eyes and said, "It looks like the tears flushed most of it out." He paused as something reflected back at him. "All, except a small shard that looks to be embedded pretty deep."

"Will that harm him?" Erianna asked.

"The curse itself is broken as there isn't enough dust left to really have a hold over him, but it's something he may need to watch the rest of his life, unless it magically comes out on his own." Archimedes replied as he brushed his hands on his brown vest.

"So what does that mean, exactly?" Tharynn asked, looking at the queer little man.

"You may have an angry temper that flares up periodically for no reason, or you may have nothing happen at all. It's hard to say."

"Tharynn. Do you remember anything at all of what happened while you were cursed? Anything that might tell us where Brinn is?" Erianna asked as she waved her hand over the rope and released him from its bonds.

Tharynn rubbed his wrists and looked at her as he shook his head, "No. Unfortunately that is all a sorted mess in my mind at the moment." He looked at her more fully, taking in her delicate features. "It's incredible how much you look like her."

Erianna smiled, "I know. I thought I was looking in a mirror the first time we saw each other in her garden several days ago."

Tharynn smiled for the first time, and Erianna could see why Brinn would find him so charming. "Her secret garden. She loves that little spot of barren earth, though I never quite figured out what she saw in it."

"She has a way of seeing beauty that lies underneath."

"She does indeed," he smiled again. Suddenly his eyes grew wide and he looked up at Erianna. "I don't remember much of what happened these past few days, but I do remember something that might help us find her."

"Yes," Erianna prompted, eyes wide with anticipation.

"It's almost the solstice moon isn't it?" he asked, looking back from Erianna to Archimedes.

"Yes. Brinn told us her mother threw a grand ball every year to celebrate the harvest moon. So, are you saying she's back at the palace, lad?"

"No. Well, she might be." Tharynn looked around him. "Would you say we are close to the four corners?" he asked.

Archimedes grumbled and looked around, "Aye, I would say we are headed in the right direction. But what does that have to do with anything?"

"Sorry, my mind is still a bit jumbled. You are right in saying that the queen held a ball for the harvest moon every year. The solstice would usually go unnoticed, at least by the queen. The rest of us in the kingdom celebrated in secret. Last year, Brinn was supposed to meet me later on after her mother had left her on her own for the night. When she didn't come down, I went up to her room to make sure she was alright. Her mother had put a cloak on her and was leading her out through the back of the palace so no one would see them. I thought that was odd so I followed the queen and Brinn. They went through a mirror in the queen's chambers that let out into a clearing that met up with the other three realms. She removed Brinn's cloak and put an amulet around her neck before she brought her to the center of the clearing. A bright light followed that prevented me from seeing anything else and the next thing I remember, we were all back in the palace as if nothing had happened."

Erianna looked at Archimedes, "What does that mean?"

Archimedes ran his hand along his small chin. "I'm not sure. I've never known the queen to do that before. At least I've never been able to see or sense anything about it." Archimedes looked at Tharynn, "Do you think this is a yearly ritual or something she began last year, lad?"

"Truthfully, I have no idea. Last year was the first year I noticed anything," Tharynn replied.

"What should we do?" Erianna asked, her voice full of concern for her dear sister. She stood and began pacing back and forth, "Brinn could be anywhere, either at the palace or the fourth corner, and if we choose the wrong place, she could end up in danger with no one to help her."

Archimedes looked at her. "Calm yourself love. I think the best thing for us to do is split up and see if we can't find her and stop your mother from doing whatever sordid scheme she's got boiling under that white crown of hers."

"What do you propose?" she asked.

"Tharynn and I will go to the palace, since I'm sure he's familiar with all the ins and outs of the place. You go onto the four corners and see if your mother is already there with your sister."

Erianna's already pale face blanched, "Archimedes, you know I can't."

"You're gonna have to, snowflake. You may be Brinn's only chance."

She looked at him with wide eyes filling with fear like they had done years ago when she had been frightened as a child. Archimedes ached knowing he was asking her to do something that could cause her pain.

"Eri," he hobbled to her and took her hand in his small ones, "I love you like a daughter and you're the closest thing to family I've ever had. You know I wouldn't ask you to do this if there were any other way."

Erianna looked into his gentle eyes. She took a short breath and sighed, "I know."

Suddenly, behind them, Gabriel's body started convulsing wildly in the snow.

Erianna looked at Archimedes, "What is happening?"

Archimedes and Erianna ran over to Gabriel's flailing body. "The bane is settling deeper into his veins."

"Can't you stop it?" Erianna asked as she knelt frantically beside Gabriel's body.

"I have been doing all I can, lass. The bane is too strong for the springy herbs I've been using."

"No, no. There has to be something we can do. We have to stop this. We have to save him." Erianna cried as puffs of smoke began to appear beneath her nose.

Archimedes tried to pull Erianna away from Gabriel. "There is nothing we can do, lass. You have to get control of yourself."

Silvery patches broke out all over her body and an eerie pale glow filtered her eyes as she turned on Tharynn. "This is all your fault," she snapped. Erianna began to back Tharynn into a large tree behind him. "He was doing fine before you shot him with that second arrow."

"Erianna. Stop. If you give into your beastly instincts while you're human, you may lose whatever humanity you have left."

"Beast?" Erianna's eyes iced over as she turned to look at Archimedes. "You vile little goblin. All these years I thought you were the one person on this earth who cared for me. Now I find that your opinion of me has been the same as everyone else's. I guess I'll just become what everyone expects me to be." Erianna blew her icy breath in Archimedes face, causing him to freeze in place.

Erianna's rage grew as she stalked towards Tharynn. Tharynn turned to run but Erianna pulled him back with her magic. "Are you afraid to face a beast like me, noble knight?" Erianna heaved out as she threw Tharynn back against a tree. Erianna whipped snow around Tharynn's body and pulled icy chains taut around him.

"You think you are so strong, don't you? Coming into the depths of these deserted woods to hunt down the beast that my mother has been trying to destroy for years." Erianna raked icy crystals across his face.

Tharynn cried out as the icy daggers sliced his skin.

"You've taken the only two things that matter most to me on this forsaken earth." She slashed through his leather tunic and pierced the flesh of his chest.

Tharynn let out an agonizing cry. "You're Highness. Please. Think of what you are doing," Tharynn gasped through clenched teeth.

Erianna knelt down and bore her icy gaze into Tharynn's eyes as she clenched his face between her icy, spindly fingers. "You have pushed me beyond the point of thinking."

Erianna's other hand quickly and simultaneously clenched over Tharynn's heart.

Archimedes broke out of his frozen trance and expelled an ancient curse into the hostile air, sending all of them flying back from the clearing.

Chapter 21

A dull ringing filled Erianna's ears as she lay on the hard wintery ground of the forest. Erianna opened her eyes to see the trees sticking out sideways from the frozen ground. She groaned as she pushed herself up to a sitting position.

"What happened?" she said out loud. When no one answered, Erianna looked around and realized she was alone.

"Archimedes," she growled as she stood up. Erianna brushed the snow from her gown and began to brush it from her face and neck when she brushed something that was extremely tender and painful to the touch. Erianna winced. She gently touched the spot on her neck again and felt a rough patch of scales. As soon as she felt it, she knew something wasn't right. Kneeling in the snow, she crafted a crude looking glass out of ice and held it up to examine her neck.

"Silver scales? How strange." She looked up to see if the sun had made any progress since Archimedes' spell sent her to the middle of nowhere. The sun still rode high in the foggy sky.

Erianna looked back at the small glass. "What on earth could have triggered you?"

Suddenly, the memory of what had transpired moments before Archimedes' curse had blasted her here came flooding back into her mind. *Gabriel.*

"Gabriel." Erianna shouted as she looked around her, frantic to find him.

She set off in one direction and stopped short. How was she ever going to find her way back to him? She had no idea where Archimedes had sent her and she had no idea how to get back to him. She closed her eyes and tried to focus on where Gabriel would have been so she could figure out her bearings and figure out the best way back. As she focused, her mind focused only on the emerald green eyes that had looked into hers so many times over the last several days. There was something so warm and so deep in his eyes. They drew her in and made her feel safe and protected. And loved.

Erianna shook her head. She could never be loved by him. No matter how kind and caring he seemed to be, no one could ever truly love her. Nobody ever saw her as anything more than a monster. Besides, if she didn't find a way to break the curse by morning, her fate as a dragon would be sealed forever. Erianna sighed, "There's no point in looking for him now."

The necklace beneath her chin glowed ever so slightly. Her hand went up to touch it. She looked up at the sky to see how much time she had left and spoke into the air like she had seen Archimedes do so many times. "If there is a Mage or some greater being or power out there, please, at least let me get to my sister in time to save her so I know she'll be safe when I'm gone." Erianna took a deep breath and headed into the woods.

As Erianna ran deeper into the woods, a sharp pain pierced her head causing her to stumble forward. *What was happening to her?* She looked up to the sky for about the hundredth time since she had started running. The sun was starting its descent but it was still too high for her to be transforming. Erianna shook the pain from her head and pushed further into the forest. As she continued, a deep, sharp ache began to settle in over her muscles. Within moments, Erianna found herself falling face first into the snow.

"No, no, no, no, no." Erianna pushed herself up to a sitting position and looked at the scales that began to appear on her skin. "Augh," she let out a frustrated growl as she looked at the sky. "Why is this happeneing to me?" she cried out into the stillnesss of winter.

Erianna tried to stand but her aching body refused to support her. "I don't have time for this. I have to save my sister before it's too late," she exclaimed. Erianna got on all fours and began an agonizing crawl to the nearest tree so she could pull herself up.

She grabbed hold of the tree trunk and held on as she tried to move her legs underneath her. Erianna grunted as her feet slipped. She had never had this little control over her muscles. Even when the transformations had been exceptionally bad, she had always maintained some control over her body and its movements. As Erianna gripped the tree, she pulled herself up to an almost standing position, ignoring the intense throbbing and swelling of her muscles pushing against her.

Taking a few shaky breaths, Erianna prepared to pull herself up the rest of the way. "I am going to save my sister if it's the last thing I do," she grunted as she buried the pain deep inside her and forced herself to stand up all the way.

Breathless and shaking, Erianna smiled as she steadied herself against the tree.

"All right," she breathed out, "I can do this." She tenderly stretched one foot out in front of her. When she didn't fall, Erianna slowly inched her other foot forward. She took a few small steps and pulled herself further from the tree.

"I did it," she said excitedly.

Erianna let go of the tree as the final test to see if she could stand on her own, but, as soon as she did, her legs buckled underneath her and propelled her face first into the snow. Erianna closed her eyes as the cold snow met her face. Exhausted from the painful struggle of the past few minutes, she slowly pushed herself up and wiped the snow from her face. Her muscles raged against her skin as she turned herself the rest of the way around so she could look at her legs. Her transformation a few nights ago had been a walk in the park compared to the pain she was experiencing now. Erianna tenderly pulled herself back a few inches to the tree and let her muscles relax as much as they could once her back made contact.

She looked around at the desolate whiteness of her mother's realm. Never before had she been in a position of such utter hopelessness. She was completely alone with no way of defending herself. Everyone and everything she cared about was miles away from her and she had no idea if any of them were safe, or even alive. Erianna leaned her head back against the tree as defeat washed over her.

"Why did I have to find everyone just to lose them again?" Erianna choked out in a teary whisper.

Erianna gave into the soul-wrenching anguish that filled her as she pulled her aching knees up to her chest. Her head drooped over her arms as she whispered, "I don't understand. "What did I ever do to deserve this?"

What had she done to deserve this? Why had this happened to her? Why was she the one always left to fight her battles on her own? If she had been cursed with this as a child, why couldn't her mother have figured out a way to reverse it or break it? Or, why couldn't her mother have loved her in spite of it?

The underlying pain she had always ignored and kept buried inside pulsated through her heart. *Who was she kidding? No one could love her. Not Gabriel. Not Brinn. Not even her own mother. She was a monster. Nothing could ever change that.* That last thought was painfully evident by her inability to move or go anywhere without falling or experiencing excrutiating pain.

Erianna sat with her head bowed over her arms for what seemed like hours. Her body felt completely spent and worn out as her mind worked through every pain and every awful memory that had shaped her life. As she sat there, a cool, gentle breeze began to wrap itself around her. It pulled at the tiny wisps of hair that had worked themselves loose from her braid and swept over her like a calming sea breeze. She inhaled the cool, crisp air deeply and let the scents of pine and snow fill her with their refreshing scents.

"Erianna." A strong, gentle voice landed on Erianna's ear.

Erianna tensed at hearing her name.

"Erianna," the voice spoke again. There was something strangely familiar about that voice, but she couldn't figure out where she would have heard it before.

Erianna slowly lifted her heavy head and looked at the man who knelt before her. He appeared to be a normal man, aside from a white streak that ran through his brown hair in the front. His clothes were white like those who lived in the winter realm, but she had a feeling he wasn't from there. Something in his eyes caught her attention as he stared down at her. As she stared into his eyes, a gentleness and peace reached out to her.

"Who are you?" she asked.

The man smiled, "You know who I am."

Something tugged at Erianna's heart as she looked at the man. She studied him for a moment before she said, "You are the Mage's son, aren't you? Archimedes always told me you existed, but I never believed it."

The man looked at her without judgement or condemnation and replied, "And why is that?"

Erianna grew uncomfortable under his gaze and looked away. "Because, if you really existed, there wouldn't be so much evil in the world."

"What do you view as evil in this world?" the man asked as he sat down beside her.

Erianna looked at him, surprised by the question. She thought for a moment before responding, "I—Well, my mother might be considered evil by a lot of people. She turned a little girl out to be on her own. She kept another little girl locked up in a cold castle her whole life. I'm sure there are countless other things she has done."

"Were you truly alone?"

"I was banished from my home as a small child and have been on my own for many years."

"Yes, but you also spent some years in the home of a dear little man who cared for you and raised you for as long as he was able."

"Yes. I did spend some wonderful years with Archimedes. They were some of the best years of my life," she replied as a whimsical look entered her face. Her face fell as she continued, "And then my mother became so set on finding me and destroying me that I had to leave to protect myself and Archimedes.

"Things have been difficult for you, Erianna. I will not deny that. I was also hated by many. There was a time when my own family turned their backs on me. My closest friends ran away when I needed them most. But, through all of those hard times, I knew there was a greater purpose for my life. Much of the beauty of this world has been destroyed and taken from me and my father, but that fact pushes me to fight even harder for the beauty that remains. My purpose on this earth is to restore the beauty that has been lost."

"Like my beauty," Erianna whispered as a tear trailed down her cheek.

The man looked unwavering at Erianna as he responded, "Your beauty was never lost, Erianna." The man stood and reached out his hand to Erianna. "Come with me. I need to show you something.

Erianna looked at his outstretched hand and then looked up at the man. His compassionate eyes compelled her to trust him and put her hand in his. He gently took her hand and pulled her up. Erianna was surprised at the strength that flowed through her at his touch.

He smiled as he said, "Come. Follow me."

Chapter 22

Erianna followed the man through the large white doors of a cathedral that had appeared seemingly out of nowhere. Her breath caught as she looked at the beauty that surrounded her. Stained glass windows filled with radiant colors ran the length of the cathedral on either side and the benches were a blinding white with gold etched into the sides. A golden throne sat on a platform on the other side of the cathedral with two angelic statues standing guard on either side.

"What is this place?" she asked in breathless wonder.

"It used to be my father's," he replied as he removed his white cloak.

"Your father's? Why doesn't he use it anymore?"

"The people of this land became angry with him many years ago and shut him out of their world. He stopped visiting when the people turned against him." The man walked to the front of the cathedral and started building a fire in the fireplace that stood off to the side of the large throne.

"What a shame. Does anyone else use it for anything?" Erianna reached out to touch the golden filigree on the side of one of the benches.

"Unfortunately no one remembers that it exists. It has been many years since anyone has stepped foot in here."

"And yet you're here."

"Indeed. And so are you." He smiled at her as he put a few more logs on the fire.

She returned his smile and walked between two of the benches to look at one of the windows. The window she was closest to depicted a woman standing before an army with a spear in her hand. Another one showed a shepherd boy defeating a lion. Another showed a young queen kneeling before a king.

"What are these pictures of?" she asked as she continued to walk towards the front, stopping to look at each pane of glass as she went.

The man stood and brushed the dirt from the wood from his hands. "Those are pictures of some of the greatest kings and queens of kingdoms past."

Erianna came to stop under one window that was filled with white shards of glass. In the center stood a queen wearing a silver gown who held a scepter in one hand and a wreath in the other. A young girl wearing a blue beaded gown stood next to her with a small silver crown on her head. A white rose bloomed behind them as a white dove flew above them. Erianna reached out to touch the glass pendant that hung around the queen's neck. As she did, the picture began to swim before her and was almost instantly a blank pane of glass.

Erianna stood dumbstruck as she stared at the clear glass before her. Her reflection stared back at her in the empty pane and her attention was drawn to the patch of silvery scales on her neck. She touched the scaly spot with her hand and imagined what she would look like if she didn't have them.

"Imagining them away won't make them go away."

Erianna jumped at the man's voice behind her. "Of course not. If it did, they would have disappeared a long time ago."

"You don't like them?" he asked as he watched her reflection in the clear pane.

Erianna barely lifted her eyes, trying not to meet his gaze as she continued to look at the patchy skin. "They've deepened their hold in my life over the years and I don't care for the impression they leave on my skin."

"And why is that?"

"They tell the world what kind of monster I am on the inside."

"Who told you that you were a monster?"

Erianna's back stiffened as she looked the man's reflection in the eye, "My mother."

"Dear Erianna. You are not a monster."

"What would you know?" Erianna scoffed at her reflection and crossed her arms in front of her.

The Mage's son stepped behind her and put his hands on her shoulders and looked at her in the pane of glass. "What do you see when you look at yourself?"

"I don't like to look at myself," Erianna said as she cast her eyes to the marbled ground beneath her.

The Mage's son reached a hand around her and gently lifted her chin, forcing her to look at herself. "I didn't ask if you enjoyed looking at yourself. I asked you to tell me what you see when you look at yourself. Just look into the pane and tell me what you see."

Erianna raised her eyes to the pane and took in a deep breath as she looked at the reflection staring back at her. "I see a girl who has been hurt time and time again in her life, leaving her with deep scars that mar the beauty that might have been there."

"Is that all you see?" he gently prodded.

Erianna continued to stare at her reflection as she replied, "I see someone who was so ugly and out of control and dangerous that her mother felt she had to banish her to keep her other daughter safe. I see someone who has been afraid to face the world because she's afraid of what they would say or do if they ever knew what I truly am or what I've done. I see someone who never had a fair chance at love because of my curse, and never will because nothing can change it or make it go away before the sun rises tomorrow. I see a monster." Erianna choked out the last word as a tear fell from her eye.

"You are not a monster, Erianna. You never were and never will be," the Mage's son said as he stared back at her reflection.

"Do you know what I see?" he asked. "I see a strong, radiant woman who has fought many battles and survived. I see a diamond that fought to make it out of the dust of the earth and brilliantly reflects the light that shines around it. I see beauty that cannot be compared to anything in this world because what I see when I look at you is you. Erianna. Princess of the winter realm. Born to rule with grace and kindness and reflect the beauty of those around her."

A silvery tear ran down Erianna's cheek. "How can you see all of that in me?" she asked as she stared back at him in the window pane.

"Because, I know who you are, Erianna. I was there when the Great Mage was writing your story and I know that the Mage never makes mistakes. I know the magnificent woman who is trapped beneath a veil of fears and longs to be free. I know the confidence and strength with which you have carried yourself throughout the years. I know you have a great capacity to love and be loved and you would never harm anyone or anything you cared about. You are as beautiful and complex as a winter's rose. Tight and closed off to the world, which is still beautiful, but, given the chance to blossom and open up, you will be even more beautiful and radiant than ever. You can have that chance at love, Erianna. You don't have to keep yourself locked up and afraid of what you might do to others."

Erianna blinked as a couple more tears fell down her cheeks. "I can have a chance at love? At a normal life?" she asked as she brushed the tears away.

"You can," he replied with a compassionate smile.

Erianna turned to look at him, "Does that mean you are willing to break the curse?"

"I don't need to break the curse for you, Erianna. The power to break it is already within you. You need only believe."

Erianna's eybrows knitted together as she looked at him and replied, "But, I don't know how. I've tried all I could all these years. Nothing has ever worked."

The Mage's son smiled as he stared back at her. "You will have the power when the time is right."

He reached out his hand and placed it on the unsightly patch on her neck. A strange tingling sensation bubbled beneath the surface of his touch and slowly dissipated. Erianna looked up at him and put her hand to the place where the patch of scales had been. The scales were gone.

Erianna gasped, "They're gone."

The Mage's son laughed, "Yes, Erianna. They're gone."

"Thank you. I don't know how I could ever repay you."

"Just believe in the beautiful person you are and that will be payment enough."

"Well, thank you again," she replied as she bowed her head to him. She looked back up at him, a small glow in her eyes. "There is so much I don't know about you. So much has been chalked up to legend and I don't know what is true or what is not. Our realm has been so far removed from the Mage and his power and even from you. If given the chance, I would like to restore your presence to our realm and invite you back to bring healing and wisdom to a realm too long lost. Can you teach me about who you are and about the Great Mage?"

The Mage's son looked at her with such compassion and love as he replied, "Of course, dear one. I would be honored to be invited back into your realm. Your willingness of heart to change and believe in the power of the Mage will restore your kingdom to a beauty far greater than you've ever seen. Now, you must go to go to your sister."

Erianna's glowing eyes faltered at his words. "Go? But what about the curse? I only have until sunrise to break the curse or I will remain a dragon forever."

"Erianna. You have to trust the Mage's timing. As I told you, you have the power within you to break the curse. If you believe in the Mage and his great power, you can trust and believe he will provide a way out by morning. And even if he doesn't, he will still provide a way for you to bring beauty back to your realm, regardless of what form or shape you are in. I healed these scars that were on the outside, now you have to trust the Mage's power and allow him to heal you on the inside as well."

Erianna's eyes stared off as she thought of facing her mother and the possibility of not returning to her human form by morning. The Mage's son placed his hands on her shoulders and looked her in the eyes, "Erianna. Don't let the fear of facing your mother or anything else prevent you from fulfilling your destiny and living out your story. She has no power over you that hasn't already been defeated. You have to trust that it will all work out."

She held his gaze for a long moment before she replied, "I've never really put my trust in anyone but myself. I don't know if I can trust anyone else. Even you, and you've done so much for me in the short time I've known you."

"I know it is hard to trust someone else, especially when you don't feel you know them well, but truthfully, you know me far better than you realize. After tomorrow, we will have plenty of time to get to know one another. But right now, your sister needs you more than ever. Can you trust me enough to get you through this one last night?"

Erianna's heart cracked a little bit as she stared back at the man before her. She felt all the years of pain and hurt and abandonment move ever so slightly within her like the awakening water slowly gurgling to life beneath the frozen surface of a lake or river that was thawing out in the warm glow of the sun. She smiled as she replied, "I will trust you."

Chapter 23

Queen Anwyne paced in the small opening of the cave that sat in the fourth corner of the realm. *"Where on earth could that oaf of a guard be?"* she thought to herself as she ducked outside the cave opening and looked around the clearing. The sun was getting lower in the sky and she worried her daughter would be transformed into her beastly form before she could get her back to the cave. She stalked back into the cave and threw a crystal vase across the room-like chamber.

A groan reverberated off the icy cavernous walls. Anwyne walked down the hall to the room where her daughter he had been sleeping for the past several hours. She leaned over her youngest daughter and brushed a small lock of hair from her forehead.

Brinn flinched at the cool touch of her mother's long, spindly fingers. She focused her eyes on her mother's pale face. "Mother?"

"I'm here, pet. Everything will be alright."

Brinn tried to move her arms to feel her head but she couldn't. She looked down to see what was preventing her from moving. "What happened?"

"Hush now, pet. No need to worry yourself. You are perfectly safe with me," the queen responded as she stroked her daughter's blonde hair.

Panic filled Brinn's voice as she stared down the length of her body, unable to move anything. "No. Something is wrong. I can't move. Nothing is moving. Why can't I move my arms or legs?"

"It's alright. Let mother fix something to help calm you." Anwyne stood up and walked over to a table above Brinn's head that looked much like the one that sat beside her throne. She picked up a silver bottle and poured a pinch of ashen dust into an empty glass. She filled the glass with water and stirred it with one of the long nails on her regal hands.

Brinn tried her hardest to will her appendages to move. It felt as though her body were being weighed down by something, making it impossible to move anything. Anwyne was standing next her again and lifted her head to drink the smoky liquid.

"What is that?" Brinn asked as she weighted her head back into her mother's hand to try to avoid drinking whatever concoction her mother had made.

"It will help calm your nerves, dear one. No need to panic over nothing," she crooned as she tilted Brinn's head and put the glass to her lips.

Brinn's fear of what her mother was trying to do sparked something in her that suddenly allowed her to push herself up and away from her mother. In her attempt to sit up she knocked the glass out of her mother's hand, causing it to shatter and spill on the icy floor of the cave.

"You foolish girl," Anwyne gasped as she stepped back from the broken glass that sat at her feet. She waved her hand in the air to clean up the mess and turned to mix another potent at the table. "It appears I'll have to make something a little stronger for my precious darling girl."

Brinn fell back against the table but with a renewed resolve, she pushed herself up off the table again. Whatever invisible bond that had been holding her was weakening as Brinn continued to push past it. She finally achieved a sitting position, but her legs still felt heavy and unable to move. Careful not to disturb her mother, Brinn grabbed one leg and moved it off the table, followed by the other one. She slid herself closer to the edge and prayed her legs wouldn't collapse beneath her once she touched the ground. A quick glance at her mother assured her she was still busy with her magic and Brinn pushed herself off the table.

As soon as her feet touched the ground, she willed herself to run for the nearest doorway. Before she could take any solid steps she was a tangled mess of dress and legs on the floor of the cave.

Anwyne turned to see her sitting on the ground. "You are a feisty one, now, aren't you?"

Brinn looked at her and began to pull herself across the floor.

Queen Anwyne knelt behind Brinn and yanked her hair, pulling Brinn's head back to stare up at her. "No one escapes me, my dear," Anwyne hissed in Brinn's ears as she dragged her back to the table.

"You should have learned more from your sister while you had the chance," Anwyne sneered as she immobilized Brinn with a chain of ice.

Brinn struggled against the chains while Anwyne returned to the table to grab the glass. While Anwyne's back was turned, a steely blue circle filled Brinn's eyes as she stared at her. She angled her hands towards Anwyne and sent a blast of icy particles and snow toward her mother.

The shot fired past her mother and disintegrated against the wall. Surprise registered in Anwyne's eyes for a brief moment as she stared at the reflection of her daughter in the mirror before. "No." She turned to face her daughter.

"Apparently you've been spending far too much time with your sister." Anwyne clenched Brinn's cheeks between her icy fingers and forced her daughter to look into her eyes. "You will never make that mistake again." Anwyne pierced the pale skin of her daughter's cheeks with her protruding nails, causing Brinn to open her mouth and poured the silvery liquid into her mouth.

Erianna reached the edge of the woods just as the sun was beginning to set. The Mage's son had left her shortly before they reached the clearing saying he had some other business to attend to. She had just enough light to glance around the clearing before the sun disappeared behind the mountains. Her heart clenched inside her chest as she took in the place she had last seen her father alive. It had been almost sixteen years since she had been here but the wounds those memories dug up were just as vivid and fresh as if it had happened yesterday.

A vision of a father and his two daughters playing hide and seek around a giant rock came to life before her. Small giggles erupted from the girls as their father reached behind the rock and caught them up before they could run away from him. The laughter continued as he pretended to be a big scary monster that went chasing after them. A small smile crept up to her lips as she remembered how much fun they had as children.

Her eyes moved to a small hole in the mountain across from her as she remembered what had happened next. Her father had told them to play by themselves for a bit. She promised to keep an eye on Brinn and watched as he disappeared into the cave opening. Brinn had been growing bored and Erianna knew she loved it when she used her magic so she made her a delicate little snow doll. Brinn had giggled and clapped her hands at the pretty snow baby and wanted to go show their parents her new gift. Erianna followed her sister into the cave where her father had gone.

Their parents had been arguing with each other when they entered the cave. Erianna had never seen her parents so angry with each other. Her father was trying to pull their mother away from a slab of ice that had a strange crystal moon hanging from an icy scepter in front of it. He kept telling her they could find another way. Their mother had turned from him and sent an icy globe sailing across the room in her rage. The shattering of the globe had scared Brinn, causing her to hide under a bench along the wall. Erianna had picked up the snow doll Brinn had dropped and hid under the bench with her. She held Brinn close as their parents yelling increased. Erianna feared her parents would destroy each other or something terrible would happen if they didn't stop arguing. Suddenly, a flash of light filled the room, blinding all of them. The next thing Erianna remembered seeing was her father lying on the floor of the cave. She could still remember how still and pale he was. Brinn screamed and their mother came to pull them out from under the bench. Anwyne had pulled them away from their father before they could even see if he was alive. In the blink of an eye, she had whisked all of them home in a swirl of snow and nothing of that night was ever talked of or mentioned again.

Erianna inhaled deeply as those dark memories pierced her soul. She hadn't let herself think about those things in years and it was almost too much to let herself relive them. A cool, blue light coming from the hole she had been staring at caught her eye. She pushed the painful memories aside and ran across the clearing, quick to jump into the shadows of the mountain. As she inched closer to the opening, the hairs on the back of her neck stood on edge and she felt a cool draft pour out from the cave. Her mother was here, which meant Brinn couldn't be too far away.

Anwyne paced the length of the spacious antechamber of the cave as dusk settled in over the mountain. "Where could that boy be?" she seethed as she ducked outside the cave to look at the waning sunlight. "I need my daughter here before she changes or everything will be ruined."

Anwyne ducked back into the cave and wrung her hands as she waited for Tharynn to bring her other daughter to her. Looking for something useful to do, she walked over to the fireplace she had created in the cave years before. A bright, cerulean glow sprung to life with the flick of her wrist. Anwyne paced some more and resisted the urge to check on Brinn again. She had not been expecting the fight Brinn had put up. Anwyne had been forced to make a stronger potion than she had ever made before. She had to stop her daughter from changing into a horrible beast and she had to prevent it from ever happening again. She was already showing more signs than she had before and she didn't want to lose another daughter to the powers of the moon.

She stopped pacing and braced herself against the frozen mantle.

"Worried I wouldn't come for her?" Erianna asked behind her mother.

Anwyne froze as her daughter's voice landed on her ears. She smiled as she turned to face her eldest daughter.

"Erianna. Dear. How good it is to see you. I hardly recognize the young woman you've become."

"Or, perhaps you just don't recognize me without a tail or scales all over my body, since that is probably how you saw me last before you had me banished from the kingdom," Erianna snapped back as she held her mother's icy gaze.

"My, my. A tongue like that will get you into trouble, my dear girl," Anwyne said as she took a step towards Erianna. "It's no wonder your sister was raving like a crazed lunatic when I found her last night. She certainly didn't get those manners from me. It's clear I made the right choice in banishing you all those years ago. Your influence over her is repulsive to say the least."

Erianna clenched her hands to keep her anger at bay and ward off the queen's harsh words as she replied, "Where is Brinn?"

"She's perfectly safe now that she's away from you. And now she'll never have to worry about possibly changing again," Anwyne sneered as she ripped the moonlit chain from Erianna's neck.

Erianna flinched as the chain ripped past the skin of her neck and looked at her mother as she turned and walked towards a table that sat near the fireplace. "What do you mean?" she asked with a slight tremor in her voice.

Anwyne smiled as she held up the necklace with the moon shaped pendant and eyed the moonstone with an eerie thirst in her eyes. "I'm sure you noticed the similar pendant hanging around your sister's neck." She removed the pendant from the silver chain and laid it on the table.

"Yes. Archimedes said he gave you a moon pendant for Brinn like mine but when I first saw her, I noticed that her necklace looked quite different from mine," Erianna said as she tried to see what her mother was doing.

"Yes. Quite different indeed," Anwyne said as she pulled out Brinn's golden chain necklace from a pocket in her dress.

"What does her necklace do?" Erianna asked as she quietly inched towards her mother.

Anwyne sighed as she removed the pendant from the golden chain and laid it down gently beside the silver moon pendant. "It keeps my daughter safe."

Erianna stopped short at her mother's words, "It what?"

"It keeps Brinn from changing into a dragon, unlike you," she said as she turned to face her daughter.

"You found a way to keep Brinn from changing and you never tried to help me?" Erianna asked as tears brimmed in her eyes.

"You were too far gone, my dear. The moonstone in your pendant had already absorbed too much of the moon's power to change you back. I figured that out when I saw it wasn't preventing you from changing, it was simply making the change stronger in you. Brinn started showing signs of changing shortly after I banished you and I couldn't allow the same tragic fate to affect my other daughter so I chose to take matters into my own hands. That useless Archimedes gave me the same stone he gave me for you and I had seen how well that stone had worked on you, so I decided to try a little sun magic to see if that helped."

Realization sunk into Erianna's features as she began to put together some of the pieces. "You stole a crystal from the spring realm to make a necklace powered by the sun's magic to keep Brinn from changing." She closed her eyes as she thought of how close Gabriel had been to at least one of the precious stones that was the likely source of power for his realm.

"Yes, the spring realm and eventually the summer realm as Brinn's powers grew stronger every year. I could see signs of the dragon appearing earlier and earlier in her, so I had to continue to find stronger magic to keep her safe."

"And you bring her here every year to recharge the necklace to keep her from changing for another year. That's why the other realms are losing their magic."

"My, aren't we a smart one. You've nearly figured everything out," she said as she turned to go back to the table.

"Nearly everything. But, I still can't figure out what happened to Father."

Anwyne stopped, "Your father was a fool. I wanted to try to reverse the curse in you and so I brought you here that night to try to change the moon's power in you. I had found a rare dragon's tear crystal that would absorb the power of the moon's light and reflect just enough power into your necklace to draw out the curse and make it impossible for you to change back into a dragon ever again. I just needed some of your blood on an enchanted dagger to pierce the moonstone in your necklace. When the light hit the blood, it would have drawn out the rest of the blood and been contained in the moonstone. Your father said that magic was too risky and it could do more harm than good, especially in such a little girl. He kept telling me we could find another way, a safer way to break the curse, but in the meantime we should just love you as you were and find a way to help you control your powers. We argued and before we could reach a solution, the moon was beginning to rise. He stepped into the path of the dragon crystal and didn't have anything to absorb the powerful magic of the moon beams that were magnified by the crystal and it killed him."

Erianna sank to her knees as tears streamed down her face.

Anwyne turned and saw the glimmering tears on her daughter's cheeks. "There, there, my pet. It was your father's foolishness that put him in that position. He didn't want the dragon part of you removed. He felt we should leave you just the way you are."

Anwyne knelt beside her daughter and drew her face up to look at her. "He never saw you for the monster you are."

Erianna's eyes shot up to meet her mother's gaze, "I am not the monster here, Mother."

A white film formed over her mother's eyes as she looked at Erianna, "Oh, but you are. You have no idea how long I have searched for you, my pet. I realized that as long as the dragon within you grew, your power and strength would grow as well. I couldn't allow such a powerful beast to roam freely in my lands. I couldn't let you destroy my kingdom."

"If anyone has destroyed your precious kingdom it's you, Mother. You are the one who has allowed ice and vanity to enter your heart. You're the one who has ruled with coldness and cruelty and kept your youngest daughter locked away in a palace preventing her from ever seeing the outside world or exploring the life around her or giving her the chance to live."

"Silence, you impudent girl."

"No. I will not be silent. You kept me away for years because you were afraid I would hurt Brinn when in reality, you were afraid of losing your power. You were afraid I would become more powerful than you and I would come back and rip your kingdom away from you."

"You are brazen and insolent and have no right to speak to your mother in such a way."

"What kind of mother banishes her own child from her kingdom and hunts her like a wild beast for most her life?"

Anwyne seethed as she walked away to the other side of the room, "Your tongue has become too far insulting, my pet. You best be careful if you want to keep it a part of you."

A sharp pain seared Erianna's head as she watched her mother pick up a silver knife off the table near the pendants. She clenched her eyes shut trying to will the pain away. Anwyne separated the stones from each pendant and placed them on the hilt of of the knife. As she chanted ancient words over the knife, Erianna's head began to swim and the all too familiar aches began to break out across her body. She watched as a silver and amber glow surround the knife and fused the enchanted stones to the hilt. Anwyne cackled in glee as she looked at the menacing object.

Erianna's breathing started to become ragged and she knew she only had a few moments before her final transformation would begin. She watched as her mother eyed the enchanted knife with a disturbing look of delight in her white eyes. Erianna had never seen her mother like this. Something inside her pricked her heart with the slightest bit of sorrow for her mother. She felt sorry for the person she had become and wondered what could have happened to make her this way. Another pain lanced her head reminding her she didn't have much time to get to Brinn before the solstice moon began to rise. Erianna glanced towards an opening that looked like it led down a hall to another chamber. She mustered her strength and darted towards the opening.

"You dare leave my presence," Anwyne hissed as she shot her icy powers across the room towards Erianna.

Terror gripped Erianna as her wrists were suddenly bound in icy shackles. Her breathing became more shallow as she heard her mother's footsteps approach her from behind.

"You have crossed me for the last time," she said with an icy austereness that sent shivers down Erianna's spine. "Your monstrous form has been a blemish on my kingdom for far too long and I have spent far too many years trying to keep you away from Brinn. Do you know the amount of villages I destroyed trying to find you so

I could remove you from this earth permanently?" Anwyne asked as she ran the silver blade against the skin on Erianna's neck.

"You destroyed the villages," Erianna whispered as her breathing became even more ragged. Slivers of moonlight began to peek into the cave behind them causing patches of silver scales to break out on Erianna's body.

Anwyne smiled as she came to stand in front of her daughter, "My, my, isn't this interesting. The silver is a better color on you, I must say. The white always washed out with your snowy complexion." She touched a patch that had appeared beneath the blade on Erianna's neck, causing her to flinch.

"Please, just let me go. You can't stop the transformation now even if you tried," Erianna panted.

"Oh, I don't want to stop it pet. Silver is the final stage of the transformation meaning you are much more useful to me now than you ever were."

Anwyne removed the blade from Erianna's neck and held it up. "This is the blade I had enchanted with moon dust to remove the dragon's blood within you so many years ago. But, now that I have the stones from both of your necklaces, it can do so much more."

Sparks of sheer terror coursed through Erianna's veins as she struggled helplessly against the icy chains. Her eyes changed color and she let out a harrowing screech as the moon's rays streamed into the cave.

Anwyne glared at the light shining in from outside. She reached for Erianna's hand before and sliced her silvery skin with the moonlit dagger.

Chapter 24

Gabriel thrashed back and forth on the cold forest floor. Images of Erianna falling prey to an evil monster plagued his mind. His head wrenched to the side as he saw Erianna stand before a shadowy figure, fear lacing her ethereal eyes. His head wrenched to the other side as the shadow walked towards Erianna. "No. Erianna. Watch out," he cried out into the still winter air.

Perspiration drenched his brown hair and made his face look like a dewy meadow in an early morning spring. The fever Archimedes had dispelled a couple days earlier had returned and it seemed intent on taking a deeper hold. His muscular body shook with chills as the bane settled further into his arm and chest.

His tortured dreams continued as he watched Erianna's delicate form tighten and stiffen against the encroaching shadow. A sharp chill ran down his spine as long, spindly fingers reached out and touched Erianna's cheek. He wanted to reach out and stop the menacing force from hurting Erianna, but his muscles felt heavy and unable to move despite his urgent bidding.

"Gabriel." A strong but gentle voice called to him from beyond his dreams. Gabriel turned his head to try to see who was calling to him. His attention was drawn back to Erianna as she clenched her head in terrible pain. What had that vile shadow done to her?

His features contorted as he tried to reach out to her again and ease her pain.

"Gabriel." The voice called again. He couldn't leave his rose. His beautiful rose was in danger and he wouldn't leave her. But the voice kept drawing him away from her.

"Gabriel. Look at me, Gabriel." His head pulled toward the voice but his eyes remained on Erianna.

"She will be alright, Gabriel. Trust in me."

Gabriel felt a hand touch his forehead as a foggy white cloud filled his mind. Visions of Erianna faded away as a calmness filled the depths of his soul. The sound of water trickled beside him, reminding him of a clear, crystal pond fed by a rippling stream in the spring realm. Soft, supple grass tickled his fingertips and filled his nose with the fresh, new scent he loved so well as a child. His eyes opened to a brilliant, blue sky etched with the contrasting green pines. A golden warmth graced his skin. He closed his eyes and drank in the beautiful sunlight.

A soft voice called to him again, landing on his ear like a whisper of the wind. Gabriel opened his eyes and looked around him to see if he could see where the voice was coming from. "Gabriel."

"Yes. Who is it? Who is there?"

"My name is Dadain. I have come to help you."

"Where is Erianna? What have you done with her?" Gabriel asked, searching the meadow.

"She is in grave danger. You must go to her."

Gabriel looked around, "But I can't. I don't know where she has gone or how to get to her."

"Trust in me, Gabriel. I will lead you where you need to go."

"But how can I save her once I reach her? My arm. It's—it's of no use to me now."

"Remind her of the beauty within."

"The beauty within? How will that save her?"

"Remind her of the beauty within." The words continued to echo in Gabriel's mind as a vision of the rose filled his memory.

Slowly the rose faded into the darkness that had settled into the spring meadow of his mind. As Gabriel's eyes opened, they came to focus on the bare branches above him.

"Erianna." Gabriel shot up and pulled out the rose he had stuffed into his pouch in Archimedes' hovel. He then saw a sword leaning against a tree nearby him. He smiled. Whether it was Archimedes who had left it or the voice from his dream, he was glad they seemed to be two steps ahead of whatever was going to happen. Gabriel grabbed the sword and looked around. The sword glowed as it pointed the direction Erianna had been swept away to. Gabriel smiled and set off into the wintery woods.

The dusk light settled on the palace courtyard as Archimedes and Tharynn approached its massive walls. The blast from Archimedes' enchantment had sent them somewhere near the queen's palace. To avoid any welcoming committee's the queen may have set out for them, Tharynn led Archimedes around to the side of the courtyard where the stables resided. He led Archimedes in through a gap in the walls and ducked into one of the empty stalls. Peering out around the stall, he saw Terrence brushing down one of the large horses they used in their search parties.

Tharynn looked around to make sure no one was with him before whispering to get his attention. "How does the cock fly when the moon is high?"

Terrence, accustomed to the code he and Tharynn had developed, slowed his brushing and replied without turning around, "The hens are in the coop and all is silent."

Tharynn whispered back, "And the bee?"

"Out looking for her wildflower, sire."

"Excellent." Tharynn stood and walked out of the stall, "And how is the young fox?"

Terrence turned, "Better now you're here, sire." The two men smiled and gave each other a brotherly hug, grasping the other's forearm and pulling each other in with a pat on the other's back.

"How are things here?" Tharynn asked as his massive hands came to rest on the boy's shoulders.

Terrence looked away, "I'm afraid things have gone a bit haywire since your departure, sire." He pulled away and went back to brushing the brown and white horse.

Tharynn rested his hand on the horse's hind side. "How so, Terrence?"

"The men became restless after your sudden departure and have been fighting like cats and dogs over who will take over the command. They've even been planning to hold a tournament after the solstice to determine who would be the best person to lead."

Tharynn looked beyond the horse and nodded.

Terrence continued, "The queen has been nasty mean since you left. I'm afraid a few of the servants have received the worst of it, getting ice slashed through 'em or frosted over, or some such nonsense when they weren't quick enough to do the queen's bidding."

Tharynn looked to Terrence, "Are any of them--?"

Terrence's light blue eyes met Tharynn's deep blue, "No. Thank goodness, no. The healer has been to see most of them and says they should recover."

"Good. At least no permanent harm has come to anyone."

Terrence looked at Tharynn a moment longer and then quickly turned his eyes away before asking, "Sire. There are rumors floatin' about as to why you left so sudden like. And why the princess has gone missin' and what could have caused the queen to fly off like she did."

Tharynn patted the horse's side and replied, "Ah, I can imagine. The people of this kingdom were always rather keen on a good story to spread around."

Terence glanced at him while he ran the circular brush through his hands, "Why did you leave so quick, if I may be so bold to ask?"

Tharynn looked at him, "Boldness is a good character trait. Just be careful how you use it with the queen."

Terrence looked at him fully now, "Is that what you did?"

"Let's just say the queen sent me on an unpleasant errand that I remember very little of," Tharynn grimaced as he remembered the look on Brinn's face when he had attacked them in the woods. And how still and cold she had looked the last time he had seen her.

"You said the queen was out of the palace, correct?" Tharynn asked, changing the subject.

"Yes, sire. She left late last night and hasn't returned. And there is still no sign of the princess I'm afraid."

"They must be at the mountain at the edge of the kingdom then," Archimedes groveled as he stepped out from the stall where he was still hiding.

Terrence jumped back a bit, whether from surprise at the little man's stature, or the surprise of seeing another person come out from the stall, Tharynn wasn't sure. But, the reaction brought a small smile to his face nonetheless.

"Terrence, this is Archimedes. He is a mage's apprentice long lost to us," he smiled at Archimedes as he continued, "And this is Terrence. A young man with excellent characteristics who has been a help in these stables since he was a young lad of five."

"Enough with the niceties and good graces. We have a couple of princesses in need of our help and we aren't going to help them much by standing around here catching up on the local gossip."

Tharynn smiled, "Of course, you are right, good sir." He turned to Terrence, "Is the secret entrance into the palace still hidden? We need to get into the queen's chambers and I don't want to risk running into the other guards."

Terrence nodded, "Yes, sire. No one knows about it 'cept you and me as far as I know. And the princess, of course," he added with a smile.

"Excellent. Can you make sure no one knows we have been here? I don't want any further rumors to start if the queen's business is as murky as I believe it to be. The last thing we need is a mutinous kingdom on our hands."

Terrence nodded and said, "Rath De' ort, Captain."

Tharynn grasped the young man's forearm, "God's grace be with you too, Terrence. By that grace, we will have the princesses back home before the solstice. Coming Archimedes?"

Terrence smiled and returned the captain's grip, "Aye, sire." Terrence's crooked smile faltered as he realized what the captain had said, "Sire. You said princesses, not princess."

Tharynn turned back to him as he stood in the doorway, "You are right on the nose, Terrence. You will see on the morrow." He smiled and pulled his hood up over his face before ducking into the rising night air, Archimedes hobbling behind him.

Chapter 25

G abriel stopped at a tree near the edge of a large clearing to catch his breath. His lungs burned from the cold air that had been filling them as he ran. His left arm was heavy from the ice that was now in his veins, but he felt considerably better overall than he had a few hours ago. Gabriel peered around the trunk of the tree to see if he could figure out where he was at. The shadow of what seemed to be a large mountain rose up across the clearing, looking ominous and foreboding in the silvery moon's light.

"Oh, Lord. If I have to climb that mountain tonight to get to Erianna, I'm going to need some supernatural strength," Gabriel sighed. He leaned his head back against the tree and pulled his left arm into himself trying to relieve some of the pressure the deadweight created. Gabriel closed his eyes for a moment allowing his breathing to become more normal before continuing on. As he did, a soft, gentle breeze wisped around his face carrying with it the familiar sweet scent of the cherry blossom and apple blossom trees that would be blooming in his realm. The corners of Gabriel's mouth turned up in a contented smile as he took in the delightful remembrance of home.

Home. Gabriel's eyes opened as he realized he had only ever smelled that scent in his own realm. So strange he should be smelling it here in the barren winter land. He hadn't smelled anything like it since he had crossed the border a couple of weeks ago. Gabriel followed the scent like someone following the scent of their favorite homemade meal or a favorite baked pie. The sweet aroma drew Gabriel from the cover of the trees and towards the edge of the clearing. As Gabriel looked up, he saw the moon shining through the partially bare branches of what looked like a larger copy of the other trees that littered the winter realm—dead, barren, and stripped of beauty.

Gabriel's hand reached out to touch the rough, brown bark. His heart twinged as his fingers came in contact with the etched outer casing of the tree, as if something called out to him from within the tree to be set free from its barren prison and be allowed to live again. Gabriel ran his fingers along the bark sensing the pain and darkness that enshrouded this magnificent tree. As his fingers continued to run across the course grooves of the tree, something warm tingled in the tips of his phalanges. His fingers stopped for a moment to take in the new sensation before continuing on. Closing his eyes, he allowed the new sense to pull his hand around the edge of the tree, until it stopped on a piece of bark that was completely different from what he had been feeling.

Gabriel opened his eyes to look up at the seemingly different tree connected to the dying one. Surprise registered in his eyes as he saw the shadowed fullness of the tree branches above him. A gentle breeze circled his arm and wound its way up to his shoulder and then down his back and around both of his legs. He took in a deep breath of the spring air and exhaled slowly, allowing the spring breeze to fill his lungs and his entire body. His body relaxed as it took in the welcoming breath, and Gabriel smiled, feeling as if he had just taken his first real breath since entering the winter realm. He was so close to being home.

As Gabriel took in another refreshing breath, he sensed that something was wrong with the realm he held so dear. A coldness emanated from the spring tree, giving its life force a shallow feeling, like a stream that had once flowed with strength and boldness but now only produced a trickling stream of water. What had happened to his realm?

A heavy sense of longing and helplessness filled him as he gazed up at the tree. His realm was dying and he couldn't figure out how to bring life back into his land. His hand came to rest on the place where the tree split between the realms. Leaning his head against the tree, he whispered into the still night, "Help me find a way to heal my realm." *And help me find Erianna,* he added in his mind.

Looking up, he saw the moon rising high in the sky, half hidden by the blossoming branches of the spring realm and shining brighter than normal through the scraggly branches of the winter realm. The moon. Archimedes had mentioned something about the solstice moon being the most powerful moon in the annum and how the winter moon gave way to the spring sun. If the solstice was tonight, perhaps the morning sun would be the answer he needed. He just needed to find Erianna and figure out a way to harness the power of the sun and send it out into his realm. All by morning.

Tharynn and Archimedes finally found their way into the queen's quarters. Her room had given way to a chamber of mirrors. They had accessed the chamber through an icy staircase they had found behind the large full length mirror in her room. After examining the seeming hundreds of mirrors below, Tharynn found the one that had the runic tree of life etched into the top and whose roots wound around the edges of the mirror with symbols from the other realms etched throughout. When they tried to open up the mirror's gate into the fourth corner, Tharynn remembered the queen using a special crystal to get through. Archimedes pulled a moon shaped amulet and a sun shaped amulet from his bag and placed them in the hollowed out spaces above the tree carving. A bright, ethereal light beamed from within the mirror inviting Archimedes and Tharynn to step through.

When they stepped out on the other side, they found themselves in a small, dark cave. A blue light danced on the walls of a tunnel just beyond them. "If Brinn or Erianna are here, I'm guessing they would be down that way." Tharynn said as he pulled an arrow out of his quiver.

Archimedes grumbled and replied, "Glad to know I'm travelling with someone who has a brain under all that long blonde hair of yours."

Tharynn glared back at him, though Archimedes couldn't see it in the dim light of the cave. Tharynn placed the tip between where his fingers rested on the grip and returned his hand to the nocking point in the middle of the string where he would draw his arrow back if needed.

They made their way through the narrow tunnel, Tharynn having to turn sideways several times to squeeze through, and soon found the opening where the flickering blue light had been coming from. The opening let out into what appeared to be a much larger room than the one they had just come from. In the middle of the cavernous expanse, Tharynn saw a young girl laid out on a slab of ice. A sense of familiarity came over Tharynn giving him the feeling he had been here before, and not too long ago either. Tharynn glanced around the room to make sure no one else was there before stepping out of the rocky doorway. He crossed slowly to the icy slab, Archimedes taking a few short steps behind him. His heart lurched as he realized that the lifeless form was Brinn's. Tharynn dropped his bow and arrow and took a step towards her but was stopped by Archimedes' halting, "Wait."

Urgency and panic filled Tharynn's eyes and voice as he replied without taking his eyes from her pale body, "Why?"

Archimedes stepped toward the ring of blue torches that encircled the tablet. He waved his small hand between two of the torches to ensure the safety of passing between. Sensing no magic, he nodded to Tharynn saying, "Go to your princess. It's safe."

Tharynn took the few remaining large steps that separated him from his precious Brinn and he quickly knelt beside her. Her body was so still and so cold. Tharynn's eyes were rimmed with tears and it became difficult for him to breathe or swallow as a thickness formed his throat. He took her small, delicate hand in his large, rough one and placed a gentle kiss on the back of her knuckles. His heart twinged as he took in her pale, slender features. It was normal for people in the winter realm to have paler skin, but when a person's skin turned white, it usually meant they were dead or close to it.

"Oh, please don't die," Tharynn groaned out with such deep agony, it gave Archimedes a pang of remorse in his heart.

Archimedes hobbled over to Tharynn and placed a small, comforting hand on Tharynn's side. Tharynn looked to him and rasped out, "Can you help her?"

Archimedes returned his gaze and replied, "I'm going to do the best I can."

Gabriel caught a glimpse of a cerulean glow coming from a cave entrance on the side of the looming mountain. Leaving the cover of the massive four realms tree, Gabriel scudded across the expansive clearing towards the mountain's base, hoping no one saw his moving shadow in the bright moonlight. He drew out his sword as he reached the mountain and began inching along the rocky façade towards the entrance.

Just as he reached the entrance, a sudden chill caught his outstretched arm and wrapped around the fingers that held the sword. He shuddered at the icy air that reached out to him.

He sheathed his sword and reached his fingers across the cave's entrance to see if the cold air was coming from there. As he did, another arm of frosty air reached out to him from just beyond the cave's entrance.

Gabriel darted across the entrance. Unsure of what was inside, he turned to face the entrance and took a few steps back. His back came in contact with a cold, solid mass behind him. Reaching behind him, he felt the smooth texture of a slick sheet of ice. Turning to take a look at what he had run into, Gabriel's breath caught as he gazed up at what looked like a giant wall of ice that ran vertical to the mountain just behind it. The winter moon moved behind a cloud, casting a single beam of light through the opalescent ice and illuminated a small shadow hunched over just beyond the icy veil. Something was trapped inside the ice.

Archimedes hovered over Brinn trying everything in his power to find a pulse or the slightest beating of her heart to give him a sign of life within. Tharynn rubbed his rough fingers over the gentle skin of her hand and stared at her, willing some of his own life into her. The middle of his thumb caught on a small callous where her thumb would have constantly rubbed the string of her bow after many hours of practicing. A small smile lifted his tight lips as he remembered the persistence with which she had begged him to teach her how to shoot. He would catch sight of her practicing late at night behind the barn and would watch as she sometimes threw her bow to the ground in frustration and would walk away for a few moments. But when her jaw became anchored with the determination to keep trying, she was unstoppable, and she would finally get her target. Anguish washed over him as he wished he had been there to protect her from this.

Archimedes rubbed some herbs together from his pouch and brushed them across her forehead, hoping the smell would awaken her senses.

"Will she come back to us?" Tharynn asked, his voice raw and husky from the tears he had been holding back.

"The herbs should help, if she is still able to be helped." Archimedes sighed as he wiped the remaining herbs from his hands. "And pray. The Great Mage is always desirous to hear from his children, whatever the circumstances."

Tharynn nodded and followed Archimedes' lead in bowing his head over the ice maiden.

Gabriel focused his eyes on the dark shadow and hoped the moon would help just a little bit so he could see who, or what, it was. As if in response to his thoughts, a small sliver of light cut through the clouds and filled the ice casing just enough to let Gabriel see in. He glanced up and smiled. When his eyes adjusted to the new light, he saw the silhouette of a girl slumped over on the ground. Without needing to see her face or other features, he knew it was Erianna.

"Erianna. Thank goodness." Relief spread through him as he began searching the wall for some door or entrance into the icy prison.

"It's no use," came a cold and listless voice from within the ice.

Gabriel looked to Erianna as worry creased his eyebrows. "I'm going to find a way to break you out of there, don't worry."

"Don't." She took a slow, shallow breath before continuing, "I can't leave."

Her voice was so stale and placid, like her spirit had frozen over. Gabriel's heart ached to hear the lifeless tone with which she said her words. "What happened to you? Has the queen trapped you in there?"

If it was possible, her shoulders sagged even lower towards the ground. "I am locked up like the monster I am."

"No. Erianna, you are anything but a monster. Please, let me help you."

"You can't."

Gabriel was about to respond when a horrid thought registered in his mind. *Monster --dragon--*. He looked up at the moonlit sky and looked back at Erianna. She should have transformed into a dragon long before now. An unnerving uneasiness settled over him.

"Erianna, why didn't you transform?"

She looked at him with glowing eyes from within the ice. "I did."

Her head lifted up to the moon as she took another shaky and shallow breath. A loud thump thump sounded behind Gabriel. A cold breath bristled the hairs at the nape of his neck. He looked at Erianna as his hand closed around the handle of his sword.

Chapter 26

Tharynn watched Brinn intently as Archimedes continued to pray over her. The minutes they had spent trying to bring some spark of life back to her had seemed to drag on for hours, and now that he sat there watching and waiting for the smallest breath to release from her frosted lips, time seemed to come to a complete stop. If only he had told her how much he cared for her all these years.

Archimedes stopped praying and looked up at Brinn. Seeing no change in her still features, he sighed. "We should see if Erianna is here."

Tharynn's eyes blinked for the first time in minutes. "I don't know if I can leave her."

Archimedes came to Tharynn and placed his hand on his arm. "She would have wanted us to make sure her sister was safe."

Tharynn swallowed back the thickness that still coated his throat and nodded. "You're right."

Archimedes pulled gently on his arm, "Come, lad. Let's see what other terrors await us."

Tharynn stood slowly and looked down once more at his beloved princess. Brushing a small blonde wisp from her face, his eyes drank in the rounded eyelids that hid her mystifying blue eyes and the soft, feather like lashes that graced the top of her cheeks.

His finger traced her high cheek bone that still shimmered with the silvery flecks of moonlight and met her jaw as it descended toward her porcelain chin. His eyes drifted to her delicate lips that looked like they were covered in an icy dew. His thumb brushed her lips as his body leaned over.

He allowed his head to come within inches of hers as he whispered, "I will come back for you." Bowing his head over hers, he closed his eyes and covered her lips with his in a tender kiss. As he pulled his lips from hers, her body filled with a long, full breath.

Tharynn stared down at her, holding his breath and hoping he hadn't just imagined what he had just heard. As he stared, her eyelashes fluttered and eventually opened, revealing her crystalline eyes below. Tharynn took in a sharp breath of relief as she continued to wake up. As Brinn's eyes focused, a slow gentle smile spread across her face.

Archimedes coughed as he remarked with mocked gruffness, "Ach, should have known your kiss would resuscitate her."

"Do love stories make you ill, you old crow?" Brinn laughed softly as she looked at Archimedes.

"Only the sappy ones," he patted her hand and smiled. "Glad you're still with us, snowflake."

Brinn smiled back at him. "Me too, dear friend."

Archimedes sniffed and wiped his face with his sleeve, "Well, we best see if Erianna needs our help."

"Are you well enough to move?" Tharynn asked, concern mixing with admiration in his deep eyes as he looked at her.

"I might need another kiss to help with the weakness," she smiled slyly up at him.

He smiled back, "You vixen." He leaned closer to her and kissed her perfect lips again.

"Now I can move mountains," she said as her hand came up to touch his cheek. As she did, a shiny sliver fell from his eye and landed on her thumb. She wiped it away and looked at him with a questioning look.

He chuckled, "It seems you saved me from the last sliver of your mother's mirror dust."

Archimedes guffawed, "All right you turtle doves. Enough with the mishy mashy 'Love conquers all,' bit. We have two more royals that need just as much saving as you two did."

Gabriel turned to face the monster that sat behind him. Looking up, he saw the silvery white neck of a dragon. The dragon snorted, raining a mist of icy water down on Gabriel's head. His back pressed against the icy wall behind him. The dragon sat with its long elegant tail wrapped around itself. The light, opalescent wings nestled into the dragon's back and its neck curved upward toward the sky like a white tower. The narrow shape of the dragon's head gave it a feminine touch. In fact, the overall presence of the dragon seemed poised with grace and struck a chord more in the tune of awe in Gabriel rather than fear. Just as it had the night before when Erianna had transformed into her dragon self.

Anwyne slid from her seat just below the dragon's neck. "Ah, so you're the warmling who has been traipsing through my forests. Didn't your parents warn you that this realm was forbidden to those with sunnier dispositions?"

Gabriel stared at her. She stood tall and confident, the collar of snow spindles that stood out behind her neck adding to the dimension of her height. Her dress was long and white and elegant but washed out against her pure white skin. Aside from the evil glare and sniveling curl to her lips, he could see a fair resemblance to her daughters. No wonder they were both so beautiful.

"Has the winter wind frozen your fleshy tongue to the inside of your mouth?" she asked with an icy edge in her tone that sent chills down Gabriel's back.

Gabriel swallowed, "By no means, Your Majesty. I have rather enjoyed my journey through your lands."

Anwyne looked him over and saw his left arm hanging stiffly at his side. She smiled her vile smile, "And clearly will leave with an eternal remembrance of your stay here."

"Your daughter is indeed an excellent marksman," he replied with a slight bow.

Anwyne cackled, "My daughter? My daughter knows nothing of such things."

"Your daughter knows far more than you give her credit for, your Majesty. She is stronger and braver than you ever wagered, I'm sure. Both daughters are," he replied with as much coolness and calm as he could muster.

Anwyne scoffed, "What do you know of strength and bravery, *prince*. Your job in your realm requires delicacy and beauty. It is no wonder you were a soft target for the maidens of the north." Anwyne turned and walked back toward the dragon.

"On the contrary, your Majesty. We face many evils and hardships in our realm that many know nothing about. But unlike the poor maidens of the north, we have the love and support of our family and kingdom to help us through. It pains my heart to see how the two maidens I have encountered have had to become so strong and brave at such an early age. My sister is indeed strong and brave and I am confident she could fend off any evil that attacked her, but your daughters, they had no choice but to harden their hearts and steel themselves against the icy winds that blow in this world."

"Enough," Anwyne hissed.

"Just because something pierced your heart beyond repair years ago, you decided you couldn't have anything beautiful in your kingdom. So, you sentenced your daughters to the same cruel fate, banishing one and hiding away the other, but still the same fate of loneliness. That's an icy cold prison to let yourself live in."

Anwyne turned on Gabriel and quickly closed the gap between them, "How dare you speak to me that way."

Anwyne's hand shook as she reached for Gabriel. Her piercing eyes penetrated his and locked his gaze on her. Her voice was low and raspy as she spoke. "Everything I did, I did for my daughters. And no one will ever tell me differently."

Anwyne's icy fingers laced around Gabriel's heart and began to close around it. Gabriel's chest tightened causing him to wince, but Anwyne stopped when his face registered less pain than her victims usually did. She pulled away and saw small white veins in his chest surrounding his heart. A malevolent smile spread across her face as she let go of Gabriel's heart.

"It seems someone has already touched your warm heart with ice's death. How unfortunate for you. You'll forgive me if I leave you in your misery. I have much work to accomplish before morning." Anwyne closed her hand as she turned and walked back to the dragon, pulling herself up onto it.

Gabriel slumped to the ground and gripped his chest with his good hand. The pain he thought had dulled or gone numb now flared up and pierced him with the intensity of a spear going straight through his heart.

"It's a shame you won't be around to see the last dawning light on your realm before I absorb the sun's remaining light," Anwyne shouted from on top of the dragon, "I only hope the rest of your family dies more nobly than you when I put an end to their realm."

Chapter 27

Brinn, Archimedes, and Tharynn made it to the cave's entrance just as the queen pulled herself onto the dragon. Brinn let out a quiet, "Oh, no," as she watched the queen take control of the dragon.

"What's wrong?" Tharynn asked.

"My mother has control of my sister."

"Your sister? Erianna?"

Brinn looked at Tharynn with a questioning glance. "Yes," she replied slowly, "How do you know about Erianna?"

"They met in the woods before she came out here looking for you, lass." Archimedes replied as he hobbled to the front of the group.

"Yes. We had some unfortunate misunderstandings while I was still under your mother's curse," Tharynn added.

"I suppose you will fill me in later," she said, quirking one eyebrow up at Tharynn.

"Yes, that's a story we can go over after we save your sister, which might be a bit more complicated than I anticipated," Archimedes said as he stared at something in front of the silvery dragon.

"What do you mean?" Brinn asked.

Archimedes nodded toward the ice casing to the right of the cave. Brinn looked where he nodded and gasped.

"Erianna. But how can that be?"

"Your mother is very powerful. It seems she has trapped Erianna in an ice casing," Tharynn replied.

"No, the dragon is Erianna. Or, at least, it was," Brinn shook her head, "I mean *she* was."

"I thought Erianna was the girl I met in the woods, which would make her the same girl that's now trapped in the ice, if I'm not mistaken."

"Erianna has been turning into a dragon since she was a little girl which is why my mother sent her away and erased my memories of her. That dragon is the same one she transformed into a few nights ago. But, the human Erianna is trapped in the ice. I don't understand how both can exist apart from each other."

Archimedes shook his head, "It seems your mother has finally figured out how to cast an encasing spell."

Brinn looked at Archimedes and asked, "What is an encasing spell?"

"It's a spell that was forged for people, like your sister, who can transform into something else, whether by choice or by external means. The inventor's hope was to separate the animal part from the human and let the human live a normal life again. Unfortunately, the inventor discovered that when separated from the other, the human can only survive as long as the animal survives. Other inventors and mages and apprentices have come along and tried for centuries to figure out how to keep the human alive while destroying the animal, but they all have failed in some tragic way or another. The encasement spell was the closest to successfully separating the two beings, preserving the one while the other lives a mostly free and normal life. But, each life is still dependent on the other. If one dies, the other will also die."

Brinn's face filled with worry. "What if the encasement is broken? Will Erianna's human-self die?"

"Not necessarily. If a human willingly reunites with their animal self, I believe they have a chance at surviving."

Brinn's eyes brightened a little. "So if we can break the encasement and Erianna regains control of her dragon self, she will be back to her normal transforming self?"

Archimedes' face looked grim as he responded, "In most cases, I believe it would work, but Erianna's is a special case. Her transformation is connected to the curse enacted on your mother all those years ago."

Brinn looked at Archimedes with confusion dimming her bright blue eyes, "What do you mean?"

"When the curse was put on your mother, it affected both you and your sister. Erianna was born under a solstice moon 21 years ago, and as that powerful moon streamed into your sister's cradle that night, it sealed her fate to be tied to it for the rest of her life. When she began transforming, your mother begged the Mage to remove his curse and spare her child. The Mage knew changing the child back wouldn't change your mother's heart, but he showed compassion for the child and decreed that if the child found someone who loved every part of her, dragon and all, by her 21st birthday, she could be changed back into a human. I had always hoped that part of the curse wouldn't be true, but watching your sister these last few days, I knew the curse was becoming stronger. I'm afraid if the curse isn't broken by morning, she will be a dragon forever."

Brinn's mind turned as it absorbed the information Archimedes had just shared. She stared at him and asked, "You said if someone loved her, dragon and all, the curse could be broken?"

"Aye, lass, I think that's the only thing that could break such a powerful curse."

"I love her Archimedes. I love every part of her."

Arhcimedes smiled, "I know you do, lass. I do to."

Brinn got excited as she replied, "Then that should be enough to break it, shouldn't it?"

Archimedes rubbed the back of his neck and sighed, "I am not sure, lass. Curses are funny things. You don't always know what will break the curse and what won't."

Brinn looked at Archimedes with pleading eyes, "Please, Archimedes. I have to do something."

Archimedes looked at her and tears filled his eyes as he saw the earnestness in her eyes, "All right, dearie. We will figure something out," he assured her as he patted her hand. "We've got to."

Gabriel caught sight of Archimedes and Brinn as Queen Anwyne made her way back to Erianna's dragon. Archimedes met his eyes and nodded. Gabriel nodded back. Clenching his teeth, Gabriel bit back the pain that pierced his chest and pushed himself up. His chest was beginning to feel the same tight numbness his arm had felt when the bane had begun taking control of it. He glanced back at Erianna and saw her frail body writhe under her mother's direction of her dragon. The pain he saw in her pushed him to pull himself up all the way and fight for her no matter the cost. After standing up fully, he drew his sword and glanced back to Archimedes. When Archimedes gave him another nod, Gabriel called out to Queen Anwyne, drawing her attention to him.

Queen Anwyne smiled, "You have more gumption than I gave you credit for, prince. If it is a fight you want, I'll give you a fight."

Queen Anwyne pulled back on the dragon's head and prompted the dragon to prepare to shoot icy darts from its mouth. Just as it was about to let go, Tharynn ran around the backside of the dragon and called out to it, drawing its head towards him. The icy spears launched through the air and struck some trees behind him as he tucked himself behind a large boulder.

Anwyne saw Tharynn dart behind the boulder as her dragon misfired and called out, "You have some gall coming back to face me." Anwyne stroked the neck of the dragon and whispered something to it as Archimedes and Brinn ran to where Gabriel had stumbled back into the ice. Gabriel's arm that held the sword dropped and Brinn rushed to support him before he fell.

"Gabriel. Are you hurt? You don't look good," Brinn looked at the almost pale features that lined Gabriel's face.

"I am well enough to fight," he replied as he almost pitched forward. Brinn and Archimedes braced themselves against him to keep him upright.

"Your mind may be well enough, but your body is far from it, I'm afraid." Archimedes nodded at Brinn, "Help me get him to the cave, lass."

"No." Gabriel pulled against them. "I have to save Erianna." He looked back at her over his shoulder and wanted to reach out to her, but Archimedes and Brinn started pulling him toward the cave.

"You can barely stand let alone wield a sword. How do you expect to fight against the queen and a dragon who may not play nice with you under her control?"

"I will do whatever it takes," Gabriel responded as his chest clenched at another pain, sending him to his knees and bringing Brinn down with him.

"Not in the condition you are in, son," Archimedes took a look at his chest, "That bane is spreading towards your heart. If you don't stop and let me take care of you, you will be of no use to the princess now or anytime in the future."

"But, I love her, Archimedes, I have to save her," Gabriel replied between bouts of pain. Archimedes looked at Brinn. Her face filled with a small smile of relief at hearing the words Gabriel had just spoken.

Archimedes cleared his throat, "Well, we better get you to a point where you can stand so you can save your bonnie lass."

Archimedes and Brinn helped Gabriel back to the cave. "Lay him down here," Archimedes said as they lowered him down until he was sitting up against the rocky wall of the cave just inside the entrance.

"Brinn, this next part is up to you and may be the trickiest part of all."

Brinn nodded, "I'm ready. Tell me what to do."

Archimedes pulled an oblong crystal from his bag and put it in Brinn's hands. "This is a dragon's tear. A very powerful crystal. It is the only thing sharp enough to pierce the ice that has your sister trapped. Thrust it dead on into the ice, or you will merely crack it and may cause greater problems than we have time to address."

Brinn's crystal blue eyes were wide as Archimedes continued, "Once the ice is broken, the dragon side of Erianna will likely falter a bit. From what I've been seeing of your mother, it looks like the dagger she's been holding is what's controlling your sister. If you can get that dagger to Erianna, she can control the dragon and reunite it with her body. She won't have a lot of time once she is exposed, so you'll have to hurry." Archimedes' small jaw clenched as he closed Brinn's hands over the crystal, "She will know what to do."

A slight twinge of panic crossed through her clear eyes. Archimedes looked at her, "You will do alright, lass. I'm confident in you." He smiled and gave her hands a reassuring squeeze. Brinn nodded and smiled back.

She went to the edge of the cave and waited until she saw Tharynn call out to the beast again and divert its attention from the cave's entrance. When all was clear, Brinn ran back to the ice casing. Looking back at the dragon to make sure it was still distracted, she raised the crystal above her head and whispered, "We are going to make things right, Erianna, I promise."

Brinn plunged the crystal into the ice. When the crystal made contact with the ice, a loud sharp crack resounded throughout the realm and sent Brinn falling backwards into the snow. Queen Anwyne's head whipped toward the casing and her white eyes flashed as she saw what Brinn had just done.

"No," she hissed under her breath. Looking back to Tharynn she shouted, "Now I know how you regained your sight so quickly, you palace dog. You will pay for turning my only daughter against me."

Chapter 28

The ice casing cracked all the way up the middle and shattered sending icy shards flying all over the clearing. Brinn looked up just as some pieces were about to hit her and rolled out of the way while covering her head with her arms. Tharynn looked to her to make sure she hadn't been harmed just as Anwyne prompted the dragon to spew its icy blast directly into him. Brinn's heart beat fast as she sensed Tharynn watching her and she turned just as the dragon reared its head back and dispelled its icy frost across the clearing.

"No." Brinn shouted above the shattering noises of ice hitting the ground. She stared in the direction where Tharynn had been standing but remembered Erianna needed her help. Brinn waited as long as she could for the fog of the blast to dissipate so she could catch even the smallest glimpse of Tharynn, but seeing nothing, she made her way to where Erianna would have been. When she got back to where the casing had been, Brinn's eyes searched the icy rubble but she couldn't see Erianna. Suddenly, behind her, the dragon reared out of control and came crashing to the ground. Brinn turned her urgent gaze back to the shattered casing and finally caught sight of a fallen form amidst the rubble.

"Erianna." Brinn ran towards her and spotted a moonstone. She bent to pick it up and hurried to her sister's side.

Erianna moaned as Brinn knelt beside her, "Erianna. Erianna. Can you hear me? Are you alright?" Brinn turned Erianna's body over so she could look at her face. Her hands trembled as reached out to see if her sister was alright.

Erianna moaned again and slowly opened her eyes. "Brinn," she whispered with a slight smile.

Brinn let out a small squeal and threw her arms around her sister, "Oh, Erianna. I'm so glad you are alright. I was so worried."

Brinn's overpowering embrace almost knocked Erianna backwards as she tried to sit up, but she caught herself and gladly returned her sister's embrace. Erianna pulled back and looked at Brinn's sweet face. Doing as she had done days ago, she wiped the tears from Brinn's cheeks and smiled, "I'm glad you are alright as well," she paused when she saw the marks of red on her sister's cheeks.

"What happened to you?" Erianna asked as she brushed her thumb over one of the marks.

Brinn pulled back, "It's nothing. Really."

A sharp pain shot through Erianna causing her fold into herself. Brinn pulled Erianna closer and cradled her as she looked toward the dragon. It was getting up and still seemed to be under the control of the snow queen.

She looked back to Erianna, "The dragon. Archimedes said if you are willing to reunite with it, you won't die."

Erianna took a shallow breath and looked up at Brinn, "He's right. And I am willing. You have to get the dagger."

Brinn nodded and started to get up. Erianna reached out to her, grabbing hold of her shoulder. "When you get the dagger, you need to slice the dragon's flesh and put this stone back on its hilt," Erianna said through ragged breaths as she held out the crystal Brinn had dropped when she knelt beside Erianna.

Brinn looked at the moonstone and looked back at Erianna. "Won't slicing the dragon's flesh hurt you?"

"Our mother intended to destroy me with it in order to keep you from changing. She sliced my hand right before I transformed and took one of the dragon tears that fell from my eyes when she threw me out into the snow. That is how she separated me and trapped my human-self in the ice." Erianna took a shuddery breath before she continued. "I need the dragon's blood to reunite it with my body. Now go. I know you can do it."

The ground shook as the dragon stumbled and fell to the ground again. Brinn helped Erianna lay back on the ground and took the moonstone. She ran to the place she thought she had seen her mother fall. She searched for the dagger in the cloud of snow and dust the dragon had created when it fell. A glint of moonlight shone through the foggy mist and glinted off the silvery blade. She reached for it and took a few steps toward the dragon. Brinn raised the dagger ready to slice the dragon's flesh.

"I'd be careful with that dagger, dear. It's a lot sharper than it looks."

Brinn stopped at the sound of her mother's voice behind her. "Sharp enough to destroy your daughter?"

"I lost her years ago when the moon's light took her from me. The blood on that dagger would have saved you from ever turning into the same monster that she was."

Brinn lowered the dagger as she turned to face her mother. "So it's true. I'm a changer too." A gusty wind began to sweep through the clearing, picking up snow and bits of dust with it.

"You showed tendencies as a child but I found a way to protect you from becoming like her."

"But you didn't save her. I would much rather live with a sister who is a little different than live with a mother who did everything she could to destroy her."

"I did everything in my power to keep you safe," Anwyne shouted as the billowing storm Brinn was creating started to strengthen.

"I guess everything wasn't enough," Brinn yelled as she once again raised the dagger to slice the flesh of the dragon. The dragon let out a blood chilling screech as the blade bit into its flesh. Brinn ducked as a shower of snow and ice rained out over the clearing. When she made sure the blade had the blood on it, she ran to find Erianna.

"Everything may not have been enough for you, my pet, but before you try to destroy everything, make sure you are holding all the right pieces."

Brinn stopped short as a sharp pain pierced the depths of her heart. She fell to the ground and gripped her chest as she looked around at her mother. Anwyne stilled the snow flurries that were still blowing through the clearing. Brinn gasped when she saw her mother's hand clenched over Tharynn's heart.

"Make your choice carefully, dear. You can only save one."

Brinn heard Erianna gasp for breath behind her. She looked back at her mother holding her hand over Tharynn's heart. Tharynn caught her glance and held her gaze. Brinn read the look in his eyes and knew what he wanted her to do.

Tears filled her eyes as she turned away from Tharynn. The pain of a thousand heart aches filled her chest as she picked up the dagger and walked towards Erianna. Tharynn's cries of anguish filled her ears as she knelt and put the dagger in Erianna's hand.

Erianna looked up at her and tried to push the dagger back into her hands. "No, Brinn. You can still save him."

"He would hate me if I chose him over you. Just do it before it's too late for both of you."

Erianna watched Brinn's face crumple into a waterfall of anguishing tears as she turned to watch Tharynn's final moments. A soft, "I love you," fell on Brinn's ears as Erianna plunged the dagger into her heart.

Brinn turned as Erianna's hand fell limply to the snow and released the dagger. Erianna lay cold and still on the hard ground.

Brinn looked up at the sky and saw that the glowing moonlight was beginning to dim.

The moon. What if Erianna didn't have enough moonlight to transform? Archimedes had said if she wasn't human by the time the sun reached the sky, she would be a dragon forever. But what would happen if she wasn't even her dragon-self by the time the sun rose?

Brinn's panicked eyes looked down at Erianna. "No. Please. She has to change. She'll die if she doesn't." Tears streamed down Brinn's cheeks as she touched Erianna's pale face. She leaned her head over her sister and whispered, "I love you."

A snowy veil enveloped Erianna and Brinn stared as the delicate snow began to lift her sister off the ground. The snow wrapped itself around the beast behind her and began to draw Erianna's two halves together. As both were completely shrouded in the snowy magic, a bright light shone out over the entire clearing.

The transformation finished and Erianna stood against the backdrop of the mountain. Her scales glinted in the dim pale light of morning's beginning and the opal webbing of her wings looked like a rainbow that rose over a waterfall mist in the spring realm. Gabriel had pulled himself up to stand in the cave entrance as Erianna transformed and he smiled. She was even beautiful as a dragon. Archimedes finally pulled Gabriel back into the cave and began to once again apply the green herby paste to his chest where the bane was getting worse.

Brinn looked up at Erianna and smiled at seeing her dragon form once again reunited with her human form. As she gazed at her, an uneasy feeling filled her bones as she remembered she hadn't seen their mother since Erianna's transformation had begun. What had happened to her? Brinn glanced around the clearing as the remaining snow fell to the ground. Instead of seeing her mother, Brinn's eyes came to rest on a tall, masculine figure standing on the other side of the clearing. Her heart leapt with joy at seeing her beloved knight standing perfect and whole on the other side of the clearing. He bowed his head to her and rewarded her with his dashing smile. Brinn beamed back at him and was about to run to him when Erianna let out a painful screech behind her.

Brinn looked behind her and saw an icy arrow lodged in Erianna's front leg. Brinn looked around frantically for the source of the arrow. Her eyes landed on her mother standing up in the middle of clearing. She watched as Anwyne raised both of her hands and summoned the deepest recesses of her icy powers to direct them at Erianna.

Brinn's eyes filled with a steely gaze as she stepped out in front of her mother. Lifting her hands she turned her mother's powers back on her. A beam of light pierced through Brinn and reached back to Erianna. The force of the overwhelming light knocked Anwyne back onto the snowy earth.

As the sun's light pinkened the sky, Anwyne regained her footing and was about to blast the light before her when a sharp piercing pain entered her heart. Anwyne's knees collapsed beneath her and she fell back into the arms of Tharynn who had come up behind her. Knowing the arrow had not come from his quiver, Tharynn looked up and saw a middle aged man who wore a brilliant white doublet with gold embroidery woven throughout. His brown hair was interrupted by a bright white streak in the front. The man looked at Anwyne and Tharynn could see a look of pain cross his face as he moved his hand down slightly.

Anwyne gasped for breath as the arrow lodged itself in the shard of glass that had embedded itself in her heart all those years ago. Tharynn stared in amazement as he realized the correlation between the queen's pain and the movement of the man's hand. The man looked at him and nodded as if telling him to step back. Tharynn helped the queen to her knees and stepped away from her.

As Anwyne looked up at the robed mage, her eyes began to sting as the icy veil that had covered them slowly cracked and shattered. She gasped for breath again as the arrow lodged deeper in her heart. The mage continued to look at her as tears began to fall from her eyes, drawing the white of her eyes away with them. A tender warmth mixed with sadness filled the mage's eyes as the crystalline blue that reflected in her daughter's eyes became visible in her eyes once again. If Tharynn could read his thoughts, he would imagine the mage saying, "I'm sorry it had to come to this to make you finally see."

The mage turned slightly and gestured behind him. Queen Anwyne's tear filled eyes looked to where he gestured and she saw the figures of both her daughters walking towards her. A sob caught in her chest as she looked at her beautiful girls for the first time.

Gasping for air, she looked down at the arrow that now protruded from her chest. She closed her eyes and let the pain consume her body. She hadn't felt pain in years. The bane that tipped the arrow had gone directly to her heart and just moments after she had felt the fresh pain of a fleshy heart, the bane began to creep throughout and turn her heart to ice once again. The mage pulled away and Anwyne fell forward. As her face met the earth, she took in the scent of the freshly fallen snow and felt the cool wetness on her face as she took one of her final breaths.

As she fell, Brinn saw her and ran to her side. She pulled her mother into her as Erianna came to stand behind her.

Their mother looked up at both of them and smiled. "You are both so beautiful."

Brinn smiled down at her mother as she let the words she had always longed to hear wash over her as her mother continued, "I'm sorry I never said it to either of you or saw how beautiful and exquisite both of you are. Especially you, my dearest Erianna."

Erianna stood in place, refusing to look at her mother. How could she be saying these words now? Something inside her made her almost wish her mother had just died without trying to make amends for all the years of pain and hurt her mother had caused her.

"I know you probably don't want to hear those words from me, especially now, but I'm sorry I wasn't able to see the beauty in your transformation."

Erianna continued to look down, trying to push down the unpleasant emotions her mother's words were stirring up in her.

"Can you forgive me?" Queen Anwyne asked as a sharp breath cut through her, cutting off her words.

Erianna's eyes sparked with emotion as she looked at her mother. Forgive her? She could never--

Suddenly, Erianna felt the presence of the Mage's son behind her. She turned and her eyes were met with the most compelling gaze she had ever beheld. He seemed to be telling her, "You can forgive her."

Something pricked Erianna's heart as she held his strange gaze. Turning back to her mother, she saw a broken woman whose hard heart had cost her the love of her daughters and was now paying for her coldness with her life. Compassion and sorrow filled Erianna as she knelt beside her dying mother.

Taking her mother's hand in hers she whispered, "I forgive you."

A peaceful glow filled her mother's face as she took a shallow breath. Anwyne looked at both of her girls and breathed out a nearly silent, "I love you."

Another sharp breath filled Anwyne as the icy fingers of her fate closed around her heart. Slowly, her heart came to a stop and a final wintery breath expelled itself from her lungs.

Chapter 29

Erianna wrapped her arm around Brinn's shoulder while her other hand laced itself through the cold, lifeless fingers of her mother. She sat staring at her mother's still body as Brinn cried beside her. The fact that she had never really known her mother kept Erianna's emotions at a distance, but she felt compassion for her dear sister. Even if their mother hadn't been the best mother, Brinn had still grown up with her as a very real part of her life.

Erianna pulled Brinn's head to her shoulder and let her cry as they sat in the snowy clearing. The mage's son came up behind them and touch Erianna's shoulder. She looked toward him and let him speak.

"The spring prince will need your help."

"Where is he?" she asked.

The mage nodded towards the massive tree that towered over the four corners of the realms.

"Will you stay with my sister?" Erianna asked as she stared at the mage with pleading eyes.

"Of course." The mage knelt beside Brinn and let Erianna get up. As she began to walk toward the four realms tree, she saw Tharynn standing just beyond them watching the entire scene that had taken place. Stopping beside him, Erianna looked at him and placed her hand on his shoulder.

"Brinn needs your support more than ever."

Tharynn blinked and looked at Erianna. She smiled and nodded her head back to Brinn. Tharynn took her hand and gave it a reassuring squeeze before crossing to kneel beside Brinn.

A strange coldness filled Erianna and drew her attention back to the oversized tree that filled the edge of the clearing. As she looked, she saw a larger figure bent over a smaller one making their way toward the border that separated the spring realm from the winter realm. Erianna picked up the folds of her skirt and ran towards them.

Archimedes was just pulling Gabriel across the border as she reached them. Erianna pulled Gabriel's stiff arm around her and helped him stagger the last few steps into the spring realm.

"Lay him down here, lass," Archimedes directed as they lowered Gabriel to the pale green grass before the tree.

"Erianna," Gabriel called out in a weak voice.

"I'm here," Erianna knelt beside him and took his hand in hers.

He looked up at her. The sky had lightened considerably since he last saw her and the rising sun shone around her, giving her a pleasant glow. Her soft, blonde hair fell around her shoulders in gentle curls, crowned with a small silver circlet. Long, white sleeves split and hung from her exposed shoulders, making her look like an angel with delicate wings. He reached up and touched her neck.

"The scales are gone," he said.

Erianna wrapped her hand around his. "It looks like you are stuck with just another average, ordinary princess," she said as she leaned her head into his hand and placed a gentle kiss on his palm.

Gabriel smiled, "And here I was hoping I would be the only prince who married the dragon instead of slaying it." His face contorted with pain as his chest tightened.

Erianna moved her hand from his left hand and placed it over his chest, "Married? I didn't know the prince was seeking a bride."

"He wasn't. He just happened to stumble upon the most beautiful girl in the woods one day and knew his heart would never be the same without her."

Gabriel's body seized as the bane took control of his heart. Erianna wrapped her hand through his and held on tighter, trying to soothe the anguishing pain that filled him. His body calmed for a moment, giving him an opportunity to look up at her and say with shallow breaths, "The rose."

Erianna looked at him and asked, "What?"

He pointed towards the pouch on his side. She reached inside and pulled out the red rose he had made in Archimedes' hovel.

Gabriel closed his hand around hers and pushed the rose toward her heart. "So you'll always remember--" A deep chill settled over Gabriel's body causing his entire body to shake violently. Erianna watched in horror as a white frost began to form on his skin, giving him an alarming ghostly hue. The deadly frost spread from his heart and already white arm across his chest and to his other arm, down his legs and up to his face, drawing every last feature into its icy grip like white quicksand. The frost's final victory draped his emerald forest eyes in a milky white film that reminded Erianna of her mother's eyes.

Erianna's heart numbed as one final, misty breath released over his frosted lips. A stabbing pain filled Erianna's heart as she looked down at Gabriel's frozen features. A sob like no other welled up deep inside her and poured out over her silver cheeks, falling like rain onto Gabriel's body. Her trembling hands touched his face and brought his head closer to hers as she wept over the loss of her precious prince.

Archimedes watched as the dear child he had been so careful to care for and protect felt the pain of a thousand deaths wash over her. He looked up as he whispered, "Why did you have to take him from her? She doesn't deserve this." He pulled an embroidered handkerchief from his pocket and wiped his eyes.

Brinn and Tharynn had come up behind him and looked at Gabriel and Erianna. Realizing what had happened, Brinn's eyes filled with tears once again and her heart broke for her sister who had lost so much in such a short time. She leaned into Tharynn and let his strong arms wrap around her and pull her in close.

Erianna's head pulled back slightly to look at her Gabriel. "You weren't supposed to die. You were supposed to come to our realm and save the spring realm. And now it's too late."

She looked down at the dark red rose that had fallen to his chest. A slight smile touched her lips as she picked it up. Erianna took in a sharp breath. One of the thorns pricked her and left a bright red spot glistening against her pale skin. As she looked at it, a drop of blood fell from her finger and landed over Gabriel's heart.

Erianna looked back to Gabriel's face and she felt a strange peace wash over her as if she knew everything was going to be alright. Looking at his lips, she smiled as if an idea were dawning on her and drawing her lips towards his. She obeyed the notion within her and bowed her head over his, allowing her cool lips to meet his frosted ones.

As they kissed, a swirl of snowflakes filled the air and mixed with the warm glow of the sun that was beginning to reach through the blossomed branches of the tree above them. Delicate pink petals fell from the tree and began to circle around them, whisking the contrasting snowflakes into a warm gentle breeze with them. Red and gold flecks swirled over Gabriel's heart and formed the shape of a rose in the air before planting themselves within him.

Erianna pulled away and smiled as a golden glow began to fill Gabriel's heart and disperse over him, melting away the frost that had drawn the life from him. Slowly, the sun kissed color of his skin returned and the white drained from his features, restoring the vibrant spring features to their original hues. At last the white dissipated from his eyes and his emerald green eyes stared back at her with a golden glow shining underneath.

Gabriel smiled and pulled Erianna into another kiss that caused those who had been looking on to cheer. Pulling away, they looked to where Brinn and Tharynn and Archimedes stood. Brinn ran over to them and threw her arms around them.

"I can't believe it," she squealed. "We've been living such an adventure. Not that I would want to repeat these circumstances, but this has been better than any of the stories I've read in the castle."

Gabriel and Erianna smiled at each other over Brinn and pulled her in tighter, returning her enthusiastic embrace. Erianna glanced at Archimedes and her smile widened.

"Come old friend, you won't deny me a hug after all that we've been through," she held out her hand to him.

Archimedes tried to scoff, "Ach, One itsy bitsy hug and that is all." They pulled him in and gave him a bigger embrace than he would ever admit to liking.

Gabriel noticed a magely looking man standing not far from them. He pulled himself from the happy huddle and strode to the majestic man. He bowed as he said, "Your Majesty."

"Gabriel," the mage nodded and acknowledged Gabriel.

"I am afraid your visit to the spring realm has been ill timed, my Lord."

The mage smiled, "Nothing I do is ill-timed, Gabriel. And you may rest assured that I do not come to judge the spring realm for its loss of color. I come to bring healing to what has been hurt and life to what has died."

Gabriel smiled and nodded, "Then it seems the timing of your visit is perfectly timed, as you said."

The mage laughed, "Indeed, my son."

Gabriel's attention turned back to the small group not far from them, prompting the mage to continue, "Please, do not let me keep you from your friends. You have all been through quite an ordeal and deserve a time of celebration."

Gabriel looked at him and smiled, "Thank you, my Lord. I hope you will join me on my journey back to my parent's castle. I know they would relish seeing you again."

The mage nodded, "I thank you for the invitation, but I have some other matters to see to at present. But, you may tell your parents I will visit in due time."

Gabriel nodded and bowed, "I will relay your promise. Safe travels, my Lord."

"Safe travels, Gabriel."

Gabriel returned to Erianna and their small group. Erianna looked up at him. "Do you know the Mage's son?" she asked, wrapping her arms around him.

"Yes. Quite well. He is a great and mighty King who oversees all of these realms as well as the worlds that exist beyond our four realms. He has often visited our spring realm. I did not realize you knew him as well. It was my understanding he hasn't been in these parts for many years."

"I met him when Archimedes' enchantment sent me to the other side of the realm, though I admit I knew him before that. I just needed to be reminded of who he was." Erianna replied, looking after him. "He was with us when my mother died."

"He is a man that exists in many places. I am sorry to hear about your mother," Gabriel replied as he looked at her.

Erianna looked back up at him, "She died with her sight restored and a forgiven heart."

"That is wonderful news. Though I am sorry she couldn't live longer to enjoy her freedom and get to know her daughters," he replied as he pulled Erianna closer into him.

"If she had lived, I don't know if I ever would have been able to forgive her," she sighed as she laid her head against Gabriel's warm chest.

"I believe you would have. You have a warmth and kindness in you which your mother did not."

She pulled away slightly and replied, "Warmth and kindness. I'm not sure how much of that can exist within the heart of a winter royal. We are born with coldness in our hearts."

Gabriel looked down at her and caressed her shimmering cheek with his warm hand, "Believe it or not, everyone is born with some sort of coldness or darkness in their hearts. You have to choose to let beauty be reborn within. No one's heart is ever too barren or too cold to be restored to its former glory."

"Former glory. That sounds like a lot to live up to," she said as she looked at him with a twinkle in her eyes.

Gabriel let out a soft laugh at her response. As he looked at her, something inside him made him want to be sure he could spend every moment of every day looking into her beautiful face.

"Erianna."

She smiled and looked up at him as she melted beneath his intense gaze. "Yes," she replied with a breathless whisper.

"Erianna, I don't ever want to be apart from you again. I know it seems impossible and even unlikely that I would have come to care for you so immensely since we met less than a week ago. But, the moment I saw you, I knew I wanted to spend the rest of my life with you."

Erianna gazed up at him, a pale pink hue coloring her cheeks as she asked, "Are you saying what I think you are saying?"

"I hope so," Gabriel swallowed before he continued, "I love you, Erianna. I love you with every spring fiber of my body and I would love nothing more than to have you by my side as my wife."

Erianna's breath caught in her throat as she stared at her prince. Her realistic side began to cut through the haze of her mind and threatened to ruin this breathtaking moment. "How can we be together when we are from two completely different realms?"

"We will think of something, I am sure." Gabriel leaned his head closer to hers, his lips begging to be kissed by hers again.

"But, how can we rule two kingdoms?"

Gabriel smiled as he said, "How could we not?" Gabriel's lips closed over Erianna's in a warm and tender kiss. Erianna's heart fluttered as she wrapped her hand around his head and pulled him in closer for a deeper kiss. Her body tingled as his arms wrapped more fully around her and held her close.

As they kissed, the rose that she still held began to transform beneath her touch. A swirl of blue mixed with gold encircled the gentle flower and allowed a pure white to emerge at the base of the petals. The dark red that had been there before now graced the tips of the petals and the sweetest smell of winter and spring filled the air.

When they pulled away at last, Brinn gasped as she saw the flower transformed. "Your magic is beautiful together."

They looked at the rose and smiled. Gabriel's forehead rested on Erianna's and he looked longingly into her eyes as he asked, "Will you marry me?"

Erianna smiled back at him as she replied, "I can think of nothing I would love more."

His smile widened, "I love you, my winter rose."

"I love you too," she replied.

He smiled and pulled her face close to his, kissing her again and filling her with all the wonder and magic of a spring reborn after a long winter's dream.

Chapter 30

Erianna sat and stared at her reflection in the icy mirror. Her hand reached up to the spot on her neck where the white scales had marred her skin only weeks before.

"I don't think they're going to come back if that's what you're worried about."

Erianna's eyes jumped to the reflection of her sister standing behind her.

"When did you sneak in?" Erianna asked as she reached for one of the jars sitting on the dressing table.

"Oh, just long enough to see you reminiscing about your scaly past," Brinn teased as she flounced onto the bed behind Erianna.

Erianna darted an icy glance at her impish sister, "Shouldn't you be getting ready?" she asked as she picked up another jar and looked at it.

"I couldn't resist checking on you before the coronation. And besides, I brought you something." Brinn bounced off the feather white bed and stood behind Erianna. "Now, close your eyes."

Erianna gave Brinn a questioning stare in the mirror.

"Come on. Please. Just close your eyes for a second. I want it to be a surprise." Brinn clasped her hands together and pooched out her bottom lip in a pout.

Erianna rolled her eyes. "All right. But don't think you can always get away with whatever you want just by giving me that sad pathetic look."

Brinn laughed and slid something out of the pocket on her dressing gown, "Oh, you'd be surprised at how much it gets me."

Erianna felt something cool and hard rest around her neck. She reached up to touch it.

"Ah-ah. No cheating. You can see it in a minute."

Erianna scowled with her eyes still closed and lowered her hand.

"There. Now you can open your eyes."

Erianna opened her eyes to see a beautiful diamond necklace hanging around her neck.

"Brinn. It's beautiful. Where did you get it?" Erianna asked as her fingers gently touched the beautiful gems.

Brinn's eyes darted away from Erianna's. "I got it from Mother's room. I hope you don't mind. It was one of her favorites and she wore it all the time. I think she would have wanted you to wear it today."

Erianna's hand reached up and squeezed her sister's delicate hand that had come to rest on her shoulder. "It's beautiful. Thank you."

Brinn's smile sparkled as she leaned down and gave her sister a hug. "You're beautiful," Brinn smiled wider as they stared at their reflections. "You're going to be an amazing queen. I know Mother would be proud of you."

Erianna smiled and squeezed her sister's side. "She would be proud of you too. We're going to do great together."

Brinn kissed her sister on the cheek. "Well, I better get ready." She turned and started to go but turned back when she reached the door. "Oh, and you don't need to use any of those face creams or cosmetics. You are beautiful just the way you are."

Brinn rode with Erianna to the coronation. Erianna had chosen to hold it at the cathedral in the woods as a symbol of restoring that part of the kingdom's history. Tharynn helped Brinn out of the snow white carriage and stepped aside for Gabriel to help Erianna down. Gabriel's breath caught in his throat as Erianna stuck a silvery shoe out of the carriage. Her gown was pure white with shimmering crystals woven throughout. Her hair had been draped up in curls and braids and had little snowflakes placed delicately between the weaves. A white rose could be seen by her right ear. When his eyes met her Icelandic blue eyes, his heart stopped.

Erianna stood in the carriage door for what seemed like an eternity. Brinn shoved Gabriel and Gabriel shook his head and cleared his throat as he reached out his hand to the beautiful young snow queen to be.

"My humblest apologies, my queen. Your enchanting beauty took my breath away and caused me to lose all awareness of my senses for a moment." He smiled and bowed his head and brushed her knuckles with a warm kiss."

Erianna blushed and averted her eyes. "You don't think it's too much?" she asked.

Gabriel straightened and locked his emerald gaze on her. "Nothing about you could ever be too much."

Erianna relished the warm feeling that surged through her as she gazed into his eyes. "Thank you. You are too kind."

Tharynn cleared his throat and stepped forward. "I beg your pardon, your Majesty. But the ceremony is about to start. We better head into the cathedral."

Erianna and Gabriel broke their gaze. "Of course. You're right. Thank you Tharynn." Gabriel offered Erianna his arm and escorted her to the front of the cathedral where Archimedes stood waiting. Tharynn bent down and told Archimedes they were there and proceeded inside to alert the mage's son that they were ready.

"It's about time you showed up. Just because you're about to be crowned queen. it doesn't give ya' the right to take your

time and make everyone on God's snowy earth wait for ya'."
Archimedes turned and saw the beautiful little girl he'd taken care
of transformed into an elegant, radiant young woman.

"Ach, that sight right there is worth the wait. You look beautiful,
lass."

Erianna smiled and bent down to give the little man a hug.
"You codgering old man. You're the closest thing I ever had to a
father. Thank you for everything."

Archimedes returned the hug and held onto his little girl for a
long moment. "You were worth every blessed minute, my special
girl."

After a long moment, Archimedes sniffed and pulled away.
"You best be careful. Don't want to get your fancy dress all wet
and soggy now, do we?" Erianna smiled and wiped away a few of
his tears with her gloved hand and stood up. Archimedes brushed
his sleeve under his nose and wiped away the rest of the wet on
his face.

Tharynn came back out and asked, "Are we ready?"

Erianna wiped away the rest of her own tears and smiled. "As
ready as I'll ever be."

Gabriel pulled out the ceremonial cloak and wrapped it around
Erianna. It was a plush crimson velvet lined with the softest white
wool. Next, Erianna knelt as Brinn placed a crown of hyssop and
holly berries on her head. As she stood, she looked around at the
small group of people that had become the dearest people in the
world to her in such a short time. She was truly blessed to have
such a special family. Especially one she never dreamed she'd have.

Brinn started tearing up as she looked at her. "You look like a
queen," she half smiled, half cried.

"Oh. Don't you start that. You'll start all of us crying and then
what kind of mess would we be in. Come here." Erianna hugged
Brinn.

Tharynn cleared his throat again. "I'm sorry your Majesty, but
we really should begin."

Brinn pulled away and wiped her eyes. "Oh Tharynn. Can't two sisters have a moment?" She looked at Erianna, "I'm not so sure making him your chief advisor was the greatest idea."

Erianna laughed. "Well, I'm not going to have authority to make anyone anything if we don't get started so I'm afraid he's right this time."

Brinn smiled and rolled her eyes. "I know. I know. Just as long as it doesn't go to his head." They all laughed. "All right. I'll see you in there. You're going to do great." Brinn squeezed Erianna's hand and finally allowed Tharynn to pull her away and escort her inside the cathedral.

Gabriel looked at Erianna one last time before going in. He reached up his hand and cupped her face drawing her close to him. Tenderly and gently he kissed her lips and filled her with warmth from her hair down to her toes. After he kissed her, he looked into her eyes and whispered, "Last one before you're queen."

Erianna smiled and replied, "As long as it's not the last one forever."

"Poisoned arrows couldn't stop me." He smiled and held her hand over his heart. "I'll see you inside." He kissed the palm of her hand and went inside.

"It looks like it's just you and me. Are you ready, snowflake?"

"I'm ready."

Archimedes held out his little hand and led Erianna inside. When they entered, Erianna saw that the cathedral was full with everyone from the kingdom. Archimedes stepped aside and left Erianna at the back of the cathedral by herself. She looked around and took a shaky breath as the eyes of the kingdom were on her. She wasn't sure if she could actually do this. She had been absent from the kingdom for most of her life and now they expected her to lead them as their queen? Her eyes darted around and landed on Gabriel, Brinn and Tharynn standing at the front. Then they flitted to Archimedes who stood holding her crown. Finally, her eyes landed on the mage's son who stood waiting for her in the center of the windows that opened up into the forest at the front of the cathedral. He smiled at her and made a motion to take in a small breath. Erianna took a breath and smiled at the mage's son. She could do this.

When the mage's son saw that she was ready, he nodded to the musicians that stood to the right of the platform up front. They started playing the melody of an ancient song that filled the cathedral with the sweetest of sounds. A couple of the musicians began to add their voices to the song and the words of the song carried throughout the cathedral like a bird winging through the stillness of a wintry dawn. The words talked of white dove flying through the air and spreading its wings of hope over their land, filling it with blessings and peace and endless days of blue skies. As the song proceeded, Erianna kept her gaze on the mage's son and walked down the aisle.

When Erianna reached the front, she entered a spiral made of pine needles and cones and rose petals and made her way to the center of the spiral. Once in the center she bowed before the mage's son and listened as he began to say a prayer over her. After he prayed over her, he knelt and removed the crimson cloak that hung around her. The mage's son turned the cloak over and replaced it around her shoulders with the white fleece side facing out. He then reached out his hand to her and pulled her up to a standing position. The lilting melody continued as he pulled her out of the spiral and turned her to face the rest of the cathedral. He carefully removed the crown of hyssop and holly from her head and pronounced words of blessings over her as he handed the crown to her sister. He then took the silver circlet from the pillow Archimedes held and asked Erianna a series of questions as he held the delicate crown over her head as a way of declaring Erianna's vows to protect and uphold the laws of the kingdom and to rule with grace and mercy as long as she lived. Erianna affirmed her vows and bowed her head as the mage's son placed the crown on her head.

"People of Silvania. I give to you your new queen. All hail Her Majesty, Daughter of the King Most High and Ruler of the winter realms, Queen Erianna."

The people broke out in rapturous cheers and filled the cathedral with shouts of joy and applause.

Something had been restored to the winter realm that day and the people of Silvania realized their land had been lost for a long time under the rule of the heartless snow queen. The Mage and his power and love had been long ago banished from their realm by the queen whose once beautiful heart had been pricked by the subtle poison of vanity and cast their land into darkness and isolation.

It would take many months to restore all that had been lost in their land, but the people looked to the new queen with hope and faith that she would lead them back to the ancient ways of kings and queens that ruled long before their time. With the help of the Mage's son and the prince from the spring realm, Erianna and Brinn worked hard to restore the people's views of their mother and remind the people that they had been just as lost as she had been and no one was excused from the barren pestilence that had resided in their land during their mothers reign.

The beauty of the winter realm was being restored one heart at a time and with the help and guidance of the Mage's son and the new queen and the princes, the beauty would be restored to a glory far greater than the realm had ever seen.

The End